The Once and Future Witch

Blacksun

Dedicated to Pete Pathfinder Davis,
founding Archpriest of
the Aquarian Tabernacle Church,
whose vision, wisdom, and hard work
has benefitted Pagans everywhere.

This is a work of fiction. All characters, places, events, and whatnot are not real. Besides, you shouldn't take what I say seriously. It's mostly about politicians, and you KNOW you can't take what they say seriously!

ACKNOWLEDGMENTS

I could fill the rest of these pages expressing my gratitude to the many people who have figured, in one way or another, in the making of this story and this publication. But my wife, Jean is at the very top of my list. She has lovingly endured my thousands of hours of inattention and not once complained. Furthermore, she has been my best cheerleader, my most helpful critic, and the person who has comforted my moods. She is my friend, my love, my goddess.

❧ 1 ☙

The new Circle Plaza in DC was magnificent. The view from her limo was limited, but she'd asked the driver to slow down so she could savor the moment. Normally, she wouldn't be up this early, but she'd been far too excited to sleep much the night before and the first light of dawn at four that morning was enough excuse to rise and prepare for the rest of the day. Seven concentric rings of seating, broken only at the four directional points, encircled the nineteen-hundred foot field. Though she couldn't see much of the turf from the road, she knew that it was set with a stage with a clear canopy over the platform that could be lowered to a warren of tunneled roads under the entire complex. In just six more hours she would be shuttled along one of those access routes and up the elevator to that stage. It was for both security and dramatic effect that she was to be placed on the stage in that manner and she was sure that both would be accomplished as planned.

Senator Starr Draper would be the first to be sworn in as President in the huge area that had cost several hundred millions of the taxpayers' dollars. Today was Saturday, June 20, 2076 and she would become the first Wiccan President of the United States of America at noon sharp. And she would, as one of her first official acts as Madam President, lead the solstice observance for the entire nation the next day at this same spot.

It was a service and honor that she had performed seven years earlier at the old Circle of the Winds in Massachusetts. At that time it wasn't televised outside of the local area though it still attracted a good deal of attention because of its proximity to the legendary town of Salem. She remembered it also because she had been approached afterwards by a half-dozen powerful members of the Earth Party and been asked to enter her name for the upcoming race for Senator from Massachusetts.

She'd been flattered, of course, but she was more surprised than anything else. Her term as representative to the state assembly had only begun the year before and she was still learning the state's political ropes. At first she'd declined, saying she hadn't any intention of going into the national arena. But then the group's spokesman said the one thing that would counter any arguments she might have had.

"We are asking this of you at the behest of Lady McGuire," he'd said. "She has had a vision that you will go to the capitol and lead the party in a sweep of the nation's legislative bodies in the coming years. She said to tell you that it would be a waste of your energies to fight what she has seen as your destiny."

It was because of Lady McGuire that Starr had begun her political career in the first place. She'd met the legendary seer a few years earlier, and it seemed at the time like a once-in-a-lifetime experience for Starr. The woman was in her early nineties, still healthy, and a majestic beauty. It was rumored that she still took lovers at Beltane and both of the solstices. Their meeting had taken nearly a year to arrange but even then it wasn't certain that Starr would be able to actually come into the presence of the most powerful seer in the western hemisphere. Lady McGuire had the distressing habit of turning away some who had appointments and not bothering to explain why to anyone.

Her visions and predictions were almost always correct and valuable, even though sometimes disturbing. She never asked for money or material considerations of any kind from anyone but it would have been unseemly to walk away after receiving her counsel and not leave something in appreciation. Not that she'd ever need it, of course. Her dealings in the stock market early in life had made her one of the wealthiest women in the world. Now, it all was in the hands of so-called experts whose only mandate from her was not to lose it all in the first hundred years. She lived simply for one of such great means, but she held sway with politicians and people of power the world over and in some ways her word was better than the laws or policies that governments were always trying to impose. If Lady McGuire said it, everyone would immediately consider it as so and they would act accordingly. It had been that way for over fifty years and would probably continue to be true for another fifty at the least. Starr knew better than to oppose the word of the woman.

It was at that first meeting that Starr had been told that she would, "be wise to enter the state's political arena." The elderly woman had smiled when Starr had replied that she had been contemplating such a move only the week before. "You *will* do this, my dear, because it is the right action for you to take at this time. And don't be surprised if you are encouraged to go to greater heights in the future. The gods have made you for great deeds and we all must bow to their wisdom." Starr had tried asking the woman to explain her words more before having to leave, but she had merely brushed the air and turned away, saying, "Everything else will be as it should and you need not worry about trivial matters. Go now and do what you see must be done."

So at the word of the Lady McGuire, Starr had gone into politics on the state level and been elected to the Massachusetts House of Representatives. And, again at Lady McGuire's directive after the solstice circle, she'd entered her name and was elected as the Senator from Massachusetts to the US Congress.

Five years later, when she was to begin campaigning for her second term, she had received another message from Lady McGuire, this time summoning her again to her home. Though unexpected, one did not ignore such a request, especially from the person who had practically pushed her into her senate seat. So, on a beautiful late summer day, Starr Draper walked up the wide steps of the Lady's residence. The door was opened just before she was about to ring and a secretary greeted her and took her coat. Then Starr was led to the kitchen where Lady McGuire was making cookies. The senator was bemused to see the old woman occupied with such a task but didn't let it show. She was much more interested in why she had been summoned.

The seer held out a long wooden spatula with a big chocolate chip cookie balanced on it. "Would you like a fresh cookie, my dear?" As Starr reached for it the woman said, "Be careful: they're still quite hot. I don't want it said that I tortured you to accept our proposal." Starr paused and lifted an eyebrow in question at the woman's words. This evidently pleased the woman greatly as she lifted her head and laughed heartily.

"I just love how people react sometimes to what is so obvious," she said. Then she cocked her head and studied Starr for a moment. "Haven't you figured out why I've asked you here? Surely you must have *some* idea of how the winds have been blowing these past few years, don't you?" She cocked her head again and smiled encouragingly, finally saying, "My goodness, do my words always have to be a surprise to everyone?" She glanced to her left, where a small statue of a white-bearded mage sat on a shelf. "Merlin, was Arthur also so blind?" Then she laughed some more and flipped her paddle, sending the cookie flying toward Starr, who just barely caught it in time. As she took a small bite (indeed, the thing *was* very hot!), Lady McGuire asked her assistant to take the tray of cooling cookies out to the "gentlemen waiting for us."

By now Starr had learned to control her expressions, a talent all politicians must acquire. But it wasn't her face that the Lady McGuire studied; the woman's senses were attuned to a different kind of read. As usual for her, the seer came right to the point once she'd made her appraisal. "I truly wish you had better sight, my dear. It would make my part in all this considerably easier. History will probably accuse me of manipulating you and everybody else to suit my twisted sense of humor." She gave an exaggerated sigh and came around the counter island to take Starr's arm. "Let me lean on you, dear. I've had a busy day and I'm not as young as I used to be. I saw this century come into being and I'll see the next as well, but today I'm feeling older than usual." She chuckled softly and then seemed to change the subject. "Did you know that when I was a youngster, they still thought Wiccans were evil devil worshippers?"

"Yes, it's amazing how anybody could believe such things of us. I don't think I'll ever understand that sort of prejudice."

"Oh, don't be too surprised; that stuff has been going on since we first dropped out of the tree while trying to catch a falling banana. And believe me when I tell you that it won't stop. Even now, with so much of the country Wiccan, there is plenty of hate and fear to go around. You know, of course, that prejudice is only the outward face of fear."

"Yes, I know that too. Thank the gods that Wiccans don't act that way."

The older woman stopped abruptly and turned to stare at Starr. "Great Nike tennie-runners girl, I never expected *you* to say such an insane thing." She looked up toward the sky and said, "And *this* is the priestess you want?" She pulled free of Starr's arm and quickly headed down in the other direction, belying her earlier remark about feeling old. "You stay right there, girl; I'll be back in a moment." Starr watched the woman rush around the corner, dumbfounded at how she might have offended or disappointed the great seer.

Seconds later, the woman returned. Moving quickly, she grabbed Starr's hand and jabbed a pin into the base of her thumb. "Hold still, girl. I want to be sure I haven't made a big mistake before I let loose the dogs of war." Then she squeezed the wound until a sizable blob of blood appeared. She then took a square of toilet paper and pressed it to the growing spot of red. "Don't worry," she said as she pulled away the tissue, "that pin was sterilized before I stabbed you. Even if you aren't who you're supposed to be, I don't want to start the next great plague." She turned her back on Starr and hunched over the stained paper. She mumbled something and there was a bright flash and a wisp of smoke. Lady McGuire shook her hand and touched her fingertips to her lips. Turning back to Starr, she glared from under her brow.

"This better not be some kind of joke from the gods. I took down my altar to Coyote a long time ago just because he used to pull stunts like this. I've never thought of Herne as being quirky, but then it wouldn't be the first time I've misjudged." Looking at the palm of her hand where some soot from the tissue had been deposited, she said almost to herself, "Damndest, *dumbest* thing I've seen in a long time." Then she looked back up and pointed her finger at Starr.

"Listen to me, Senator Starr Draper: if you think we Witches are any better than anyone else, you are completely off your broomstick. We're just as prone to prejudice and stupidity as anybody... of *any* belief. Case in point: the dumbass statement you just made. Now, if you're going to be President of the United States, we *all* are going to expect you to stop spouting such drivel, do you understand?"

✥ 2 ✥

Starr starred at the older woman and her jaw fell open. She couldn't have heard right! Had Lady McGuire just said she was to become President? Of the United States?

"Ahg... ghaaw... olle... duh!" It seemed her tongue wouldn't work. And she was worried that her lungs weren't either. She felt weak and dizzy.

Then Lady McGuire beamed and stood up straighter. "Now *that's* the smartest thing you've said all day!" She turned and gruffly motioned Starr to follow her down the hall. Dumbly, the senator followed, still unsuccessful at making her mouth form words. They came to a large room that had been sectioned off into four distinct areas. On the wall to Starr's left was a mural of a glorious sunrise that took up the entire wall. A small table sat in the middle of this wall and had the usual items one would expect for an altar to the Element of Air. The next wall was painted in vivid hues of red, orange, and yellow with some black lumps and small spots of brilliant blue-white sparks. It took a moment before Starr realized it was a painting of a lava flow, possibly in Hawaii somewhere. Again, a table and symbols of the Fire Element stood in the middle of this wall.

Next, in the west, there was a large fountain, with several jets rising and falling in time with soothing music. A large oval pool lay beyond the open patio doors in back of the fountain and she saw there was somebody in the water. As she watched, the swimmer turned and Starr saw the face of a pretty woman that brightened with joy as she spied Lady McGuire. Long arms reached out of the water and the woman quickly made her way to the side of the pool. As she rose out of the water, Starr guessed that the woman was probably in her early thirties. Her body was athletic and toned to nearly perfect proportions. And, of course, she was sky-clad.

"That's my great-*great*-granddaughter, Lisandra. Isn't she gorgeous? Believe it or not, I once had a body like that. I used to be able to make even the old goats stand up straighter on circle. That was when seventy was considered *really* old. Now days, of course, they seem like randy young pups to me, but times change." She moved Starr towards the north wall, where there was an open sun patio and a large table under the shade of a palm tree. Two men in suits occupied the table with open looks of admiration on their faces at the living goddess walking toward Lady McGuire. With a gentle shove, Starr was propelled forward. "You go along to Trenton and his friend while I try to get this daughter of Aphrodite to wear some clothes before joining us."

Starr knew Trenton Hartford, of course – he was the head of the Earth Party. She had seen the other man before but didn't know his name. As she walked up to them, both stood to greet her, reluctantly surrendering the luscious sight of Lady McGuire's water nymph relative. Hartford held up his right hand with the fingers splayed, and as Starr touched her fingertips to his, he spoke. "Merry meet, Senator Draper. I'd like to introduce you to one of the most brilliant political minds of the century, Allen Barnstead. Allen's behind every long and short-ranged political move planned for the next three hundred years. He's our secret weapon against the opposition."

Starr touched fingertips with the man, who accepted Hartford's words without comment and then she took a seat at the table. Lady McGuire's cookies sat in the center and Starr quickly took one so she could wait for her hostess and not be required to hold a conversation with either of the two gentlemen before she'd learned more about what was going on. Chewing slowly, she studied the man she'd been introduced to. Allen Barnstead was shorter than she was but seemed to be comfortable in his skin. He had the aura of a man who needed nothing to support him or anything to prove. It wasn't physical strength or political power, but it was solid and reliable. The senator was surprised to hear Hartford's description of him as some kind of political genius. She thought herself familiar with the party's strategists and Barnstead wasn't one of them. Both Hartford and Barnstead seemed content to wait for Starr to finish her cookie. She drew out her nibbling as long as she could while waiting for Lady McGuire. Just as she was about to reach for another one, the Lady walked up to their table and sat gracefully. She looked at the senator while talking to the two men.

"I'm afraid I spilled the beans to the good senator, boys. Sorry about that. I'm sure she's wondering about my sanity by now, aren't you, my dear?"

"Actually, I'm wondering why I've been made part of this plot of yours, Lady McGuire, whatever it is. About your sanity I have little worry, so I'm curious about what role I'm to play in this and why."

The old woman smiled, picked a cookie off the tray and said to the older man, "Allen, care to fill her in?"

"Of course, Maggie. Senator Draper, we have been very watchful of you during your term in Washington and you have surpassed our hopes and," he glanced over to Lady McGuire, "predictions. Forgive us for not letting you in on all of our plans until now. It was important to see exactly how you handled your political station. Suffice it to say that we are all very pleased. Now, as to..."

Starr held up a finger and arched her eyebrow. "Excuse me, Mr. Barnstead, but that is the second 'we.' Exactly *who* is 'we?' As I'm sure everyone here knows well, in politics there is always some private agenda tunneling around under any public plan. I won't consider any plan from you or even from Lady McGuire here until I have a better map of those tunnels and the part 'we' plays in all this. So please, let's not begin in the middle; begin at the beginning and tell me the whole story."

The fellow looked at Lady McGuire, who just smiled and said, "See, Allen? I told you she was in command of her power. *That's* why she's the right one." She turned toward Starr. "My dear, you're quite correct. The 'we' in question are the people at this table and only a few others. And there are plenty of hidden goals in what we are trying to do. You would have been told before, as Allen has said, but we had to be sure of what you were made of. I think you just convinced Allen that my judgment was spot on."

9

The man leaned toward Starr and said in a stage whisper, "Grandma Maggie's *always* 'spot on,' and she never misses an opportunity to rub it in. It's disgusting sometimes." He said the last with obvious admiration, but put a frown on for show. Then he leaned back and began again.

"Yes... well as I was saying, Senator."

"Please, if we're going to hatch plans to take over the world and divvy up Mars land titles, let it just be Starr."

⤚ 3 ⤙

Lady McGuire took over the conversation. "Very well; Starr it is. And you will please address me as Maggie from here on, eh? You are quite correct that we should all be on a first name basis for this. Anyway, let us begin at the beginning, as you so insisted." She pretended to arrange herself with notes and a pair of reading glasses. "In the beginning, there was the Void. And God said, 'Somebody turn on the lights.'"

Everyone broke out laughing; Starr recovering quickly enough to hold up a finger again, saying, "I think we can skip that part, thank you. Why not get to the juicy stuff."

Lady McGuire pretended to be confused for a second. "Oh, very well, we'll skip that. But it really was a good story. Well, Starr, the 'juicy stuff' is actually a little nasty. In fact, it is the 'juicy stuff' that made me react to you the way I did in the hallway when you made that completely foolish statement.

"The short version of 'the juicy stuff' requires a little background, and it goes like this, my dear: Even before the turn of the century, in fact nearly fifty years before that, our faith has had a tremendous growth. Did you know that my mother was Roman Catholic before she converted to Wicca?"

"Yes, I'd heard that. But I didn't know if it was true or not."

"Oh yes, quite true. She told me that her parents almost bodily threw her out of the house when they found out she was investigating Wicca. She was only sixteen and fearless about everything but she wasn't ready to be tossed, so she pretended to

11

recant and be a nice Catholic girl for a while longer. Anyway, back then... we're talking better than a hundred years ago, mind you... back then you had to know somebody that knew somebody before you could even lay your hands on reading material. And almost every witch in the country was under cover. They used to say they were 'in the broom closet.' So my mother had it rough, to be sure.

"Later on, she met my father and to hear them tell it, it was a love story that beat Romeo and Juliet. I came along and both of them raised me in the Craft. Zoom past the part about all my trials and tribulations." There was a snort from Allen, but Starr wasn't going to be distracted. "And now I'm treated like some Witch Queen and everybody comes to me with all their troubles, thinking I'll somehow magically fix them.

"Some troubles, my dear, aren't easily fixed. Since 2021, when the Freedom of Spirit Bill was enacted, Wicca has seen an even more impressive explosive growth, as I'm sure you know. Even before that, in fact for just over sixty years, we've moved from a country that swore up and down it was completely Christian to one that is truly multi-faith. And in that time the Pagan faiths have more or less come to accept one name, much like the Protestant faiths of old. Now, no matter what tradition you may follow, you're considered Wiccan. The label, of course, doesn't matter, but it is confusing for any who want to go back and study our history.

"In that sixty-some years, a great deal has changed. Nearly all the public swimming pools are clothes optional and the handshake has been replaced with the five-points-of fellowship finger touch. Even if that's what the tabloids think is important, it's only a small part of it. There are many other social-political changes that have come about and become so universal, especially here in the States, most of our society has no idea life could be anything different. Take our recycling as an example. Did you know that at one time, there weren't any laws that said you had to recycle? It's true. And the Renewable Resource Reserve hadn't even been thought of when I was a child! They were using *trees* to make paper, for the love of the goddess. Hemp growing, the cash crop that nearly all of the so-called founders of this country were all involved in, was *illegal*. They were all worried that everyone was going to get high and the economy was going to go to hell in a hand basket. Ridiculous, but true.

"But, along came the Wiccans. Actually, back then most people lumped us all together under the term 'Pagan,' but that's irrelevant. In the twentieth century, most Christians were a little upset about us, but they didn't go nuts about it. Except for a few who loved to holler and jump around about how we were all in league with their minor deity called Satan, the Prince of Darkness. Well, as usual, the noisy ones got the attention, so they also got their hands into a lot of the politics of the time. For a time, in fact for several years there, they got the political movers and shakers to believing they were so powerful that they could dictate who was going to be elected and who wasn't.

"In a way, it's sort of like how they treat me these days. Everyone thinks I'm infallible. They believe I don't make mistakes and all my predictions come true. They're wrong, of course, but part of the reason some of my predictions come true is because people believe they're going to and then *they* make them come true. I've traded on that sometimes and this is, at least in part, one of those times."

Starr leaned forward to interrupt. "I think anyone who has watched carefully would realize that you have missed a few times. But face it, Lady McGuire..."

"Just Maggie, remember?"

"Let's face it, Maggie; you *have* been right on some very important things. Your announcement about Mt. Rainier erupting saved thousands, maybe millions of lives. And finding the child of that mining boss propelled you into the national spotlight. Don't discount how valuable you are to all of us, please."

"Fine, but I'm *not* infallible. That's all I'm saying."

Hartford picked up the dialogue. "The Earth Party was, as you know, an outgrowth of what was a struggling Green Party that began back in the twentieth century but never really got a foothold in national politics. The Christian fundamentalist faction that was trying to run things back around the turn of the century began to lose power when the second President Bush made the backing of the Fundy Christians either a joke or a curse, depending on your point of view. From that point on, fewer and fewer people wanted to be involved in anything connected to the Fundies. It didn't take long for their faith organizations to begin to feel the pinch. More and more crazy stuff was sticking to their label and they became bad news to almost everyone except the crazies. The general public got tired of them and most decided that politics and religion should never be cooked together in the same kitchen."

"And so we eliminated religion from politics," Allen piped in, obviously being sarcastic.

"Not likely; maybe not even possible," Lady McGuire said. "Look at our party: we are almost exclusively a party of Wiccans, no matter which tradition under that term you identify with. Right now, we hold better than 65% of the electorate. That's quite a margin. But it can be thrown away. And for the last twenty some years, there have been currents in the political tide within our own party that make it look like we are about to do just that."

Starr looked at the faces of each of her companions at the table. It was obvious that they all believed what they were telling her. But she wasn't aware of any signs her party was losing power. Right now, better than 50% of both the House and Senate was from the Earth Party, as was the president himself. Four Supreme Court justices were nearly always favorable to the same ideals as those supported by her party. And they were the youngest of the justices. She couldn't see any of the factions within her party or even from outside of it that might be a threat to its healthy command of political power and she said as much to the others.

Allen took the lead in making a reply to her. "Believe me when I tell you... and please don't take offense, Senator... that a great deal of the power in Washington is disguised well enough that you would probably not be aware of it. It's been my job to look closely at how things function and strategize how to keep these powers in check or at least so they don't end up blowing up in our faces."

"And Allen's done a remarkable job, too," her hostess said. "His psychic talents are quite unusual and the Earth Party has used them well."

Trenton added, "He can tell not just what a person is thinking at the moment, but what they thought about hours, even days ago! He's our 'spy in a time machine.' Thank the gods he works for us."

Lady McGuire took the conversational ball at that point. "Tell me, Starr, what is it that makes you a Wiccan?"

The Senator was a little surprised by the question so she took several seconds before answering. "I'd say it's something in the way I see the magic and the gods in everything. For me, at least, it's completely internal. By myself, I'm not psychic to any degree; I certainly don't have your powers. But my heart tells me that I am part of it all, that I have that divine spark within me that gives me a personal stake in the conditions around me. How I use that spark, what I create, is my worship to the gods."

"Well said. Now: how would you decide if another was a Wiccan or not?"

"How? I suppose I'd ask them what they felt and then see what they did with their lives."

"What if you didn't have time to observe them that closely or for a long enough period of time to make a sound judgment?"

"Hmmm. Well, I guess I'd take their word for it until and unless they proved otherwise to me. But I really don't feel qualified to say what is or isn't Wiccan."

"Oh? So whom do you believe *is* qualified?"

This time, she didn't have a good answer. Her silence lasted for nearly a minute but they patiently waited her out. Finally, she looked up and said, "I don't know. I think that perhaps *nobody* is."

"Even if they had my power of inner sight or Allen's talent for mind reading?"

"No... definitely not. Besides, does it really matter? I mean, we're all children of the gods, right"

The older woman sat back and beamed at her. "*That's* my girl."

Then Trenton leaned in and spoke quietly to her. "But wouldn't it be nice if you knew who your friends were?"

Allen also leaned over and said, "I'm not the only one who can read your mind, you know."

She turned to face him with a steady, challenging look. "Then read *this*, buddy."

He quickly sat back in his chair, shock registering on his face a moment, but then he laughed uproariously. When he finally was able to speak again, he said to her. "Oh my, Senator, what big *teeth* you have! Did your mother teach you that one?"

"No, my magic teacher did. And I hope you can't get it up for a year." Then the rest of them, including Starr, laughed.

Lady McGuire pushed on. "To continue, then: When I was touring Europe back in '51, a gentleman approached our group and asked to speak with me privately. I could tell he was quite agitated, so I broke away from the rest of my group to sit at a local outdoor café with him. The fellow was born in The European Union but had taken UN citizenship and was speculating in Martian and Lunar trading ventures. You'll recall that back then such commercial startups were very risky. But this man was destined to make a killing in those markets.

"Anyway, I soon learned the source of his agitation. He said he was Wiccan, some tradition that purportedly was a *true* Gardnarian line, he said, whatever that meant. But he was convinced that the Wicca of that day was mostly a great 'perversion' as he termed it and he wanted to enlist my help in backing a movement to rid ourselves of these 'impure' spiritual forms."

"That sounds a lot like the line one of the representatives was using months ago at the strategy conference. He was from California if I remember rightly." Turning to Trenton, Starr asked, "Do you remember that luncheon? I believe it was on Thursday where the man was denouncing the Party for allowing in everyone who wanted to be a part of us. I thought at the time what a stupid bunch of ideas."

"Oh yes, I remember it very well. You might have considered him a whack job, but there were several in that crowd who thought the same way as he." He turned to Allen. "Tell her."

Allen smiled grimly. "Trent's right, there were plenty of folks who agreed with Mr. Holly. And what he was saying at that luncheon is just the tip of the iceberg. There have been similar speeches at hundreds of luncheons or other sorts of meetings for many years now."

"At least twenty years that we know of, Starr." Lady McGuire shifted in her chair, looking unhappy. Then she seemed to gather herself and spoke again. "That fellow in Paris, the one who was so adamant about the 'purity' of the Earth Party? Well, that man was Eric Stamper... *the* Eric Stamper."

Starr, along with everybody else on the planet who had ever read an article on the Net, knew that name. Eric G. Stamper controlled more than 80% of all interplanetary commerce. To say he was rich was like saying the Pacific Ocean was wet. To say he was influential would have been a completely inadequate description of the power he wielded. But, other than the usual large donations to campaigns, Starr wasn't aware of any kind of 'morality' issues Stamper's companies might be involved with. Politics generated plenty of strange alliances. Most of them focused on money issues. Since the Free Spirit Bill, there had been several 'morals issues' enacted. But the number dwindled every year and many of the new and some of the old ones were being thrown out in the federal courts. The current temper of the nation as well as the courts was less concerned with what a person professed and more about their actions.

"Are you saying Stamper is behind this 'spiritual purity' notion?"

Allen answered her. "He's behind it to the tune of several billion dollars over the last few years. He's been building a power base in Washington that will be unstoppable if it remains unchecked."

Trenton locked eyes with Starr. His energy was serious but calm and she knew even before he spoke that he was going to tell her the point of her visit today. "That's where you come into the picture, Senator. Maggie knew where this was headed before it was a blip on the radar for the rest of us."

Lady McGuire added, "This situation could spell our doom more thoroughly than any other threat we've faced in the last two hundred years, Starr. I don't mean to make it sound so dramatic, but we four are quite likely the only ones who can change the energies sufficiently to dodge this bullet. If the Wiccan fundamentalists gain much more political power, it will trigger a reaction in this country that will make the Burning Times look like a mere campfire. The Christians and the Muslims, and possibly even the Jews will unite against us and it could get bloody. As I said earlier, there's always going to be prejudice and hate; all that's needed to bring it out in full bloom is a handy target."

"That's why," Allen said, "*you* must become our next President. Stamper's forces will likely take over the House this election and I believe he's thinking about trying to promote one of his people into the White House this term as well. We've got to make a preemptive strike in that area before he does."

They were all looking at her. She looked at each one and knew that the next words out of her could change what they thought of her, but she had to be honest with them. "I don't know what you believe I can do, but I'm afraid I have to decline this. I don't *want* to become President."

Lady McGuire reached over and put her hand on top of Starr's. "We know that, dear. And that's exactly why we want you. Stamper *wants* power so much he'll take it wherever he gets the opportunity. When that happens, it'll look just like the twenties, when the Christian Fundamentalists were ousted from every political position people found them in. Only it will be the Wiccans who will undergo a purge this time. And it won't be pretty. We're long overdue for an economic crunch in this country and when it hits, everyone will be feeling the pressure. Think about the lesson Hitler taught the world: He used the Jews as a focal point for hate and cruelty and that energy was what built the Third Reich, making Germany prosper more than it ever had in history. If we are going to survive, we can't allow Stamper's form of idiocy to get into power. It will be the trigger for a series of events that many believe... right now... to be impossible. But we can become the same kind of animals as what the Third Reich produced; the beast lives inside each of us. And, though he doesn't have the slightest clue, Stamper himself will start the second Burning Times. In his efforts to 'purify' our faith, he'll kindle the flame that will grow to burn us all."

She looked into the old woman's eyes and it was as if she could see the future there. She saw forests burning, strip mines poisoning and ruining the land, and millions of people fighting in streets, fields, and even within their own homes. The sheer terror of what might be was overwhelming. She was shocked and moved, but she still couldn't understand why *she* should be chosen for the task ahead. The vision she'd seen through Lady McGuire's eyes made her blood run cold, but she felt that she was not the right one to change such a tide of energy.

"You must be mistaken about me. I'm not who or what you apparently think I am. I'm really just a very ordinary person, I'm afraid."

"Exactly. If you were anything else, if you were some super special wonder-witch, you never could do what you will need to do, my dear." The woman was patting her hand as if trying to calm a child's fears.

Maybe that was what these were: childish fears. "And... and *exactly* what is it that I will need to do? How in the world can you expect to put a plain, ordinary witch in charge of the most powerful nation on this planet and expect her to keep this vision of yours from coming about? Why me? I'm just barely able to get anything through the Senate. How in the name of the Goddess do you expect me to run the country?"

Trenton answered. "The country runs pretty well without any help from the president. The truth is, Senator, Congress and the bureaucrats do most of the job. But the president makes a *big* difference in directing of the energies of the country."

"Fine, but why me? Why not somebody more qualified and more experienced in manipulating energy? Why not Lady McGuire here?" She nodded toward her hostess but stayed looking at the person who was supposedly the leader of her political party.

It seemed that whenever Starr asked an important question, Lady McGuire would change the subject with another question. And she did it once again. "Do you remember who Sam Walton was, my dear?"

By now, Starr was getting tired of the Lady's tactics. She tried not to show her temper, but it was getting increasingly more difficult. "No, but I kind of find the name familiar. Who was he?"

"Well, in a way, he was a great philosopher. He created what was to become the largest retailing company in the world for a while. It all started with a small retail shop in Arkansas around the middle of the twentieth century. He started Wal-Mart, which even today has a big footprint in retail sales. He said something one time to the effect that plain, ordinary people could do *anything* if they were given the opportunity, the motive, and the support to do it. He operated his company on that idea and built it into an empire. Even when he'd become richer than God, Mr. Sam continued to walk around in jeans and a golf shirt and talk to his employees, inspiring them to do what everyone said was the impossible. And they did. He wasn't greedy but Wal-Mart took in billions of dollars here and in other countries every month. His company's *net* earnings surpassed many countries' gross national product. And it was all done through the energies of plain, ordinary people."

"Okay, but I'll bet they were not led by plain, ordinary people. I'll bet they recruited top-notch executives to run it. Am I right?"

"Oh, yes. After Sam Walton died they did just that and killed the goose, I'm afraid. While he was alive, most of the important spots were filled from within the ranks of the people who had grown with the company. But eventually, the leadership of the company allowed it to deteriorate at the base and fall prey to old age, just as we all do. But Sam Walton's ideas weren't wrong. They're just as true today as they were a hundred years ago."

"All right, so convince me that *this* plain, ordinary person can make a difference in what obviously has been in play for decades."

And they did. They talked for hours, eating dinner under the palm tree, and discussing politics and energy work until the small hours. Lady McGuire offered to put them up when they were all yawning more than they were talking.

Overnight, Starr had apparently worked on the problem in her subconscious and come to a decision. When she descended the stairs the next morning and found Lady McGuire reading the morning news on her PerCom, she said with the utmost calm, "Fine, I'm in. Either you found a way to invade my dreams or my own brain has mulled it over and you've won the argument. Now tell me how in the name of

Hera I'm going to win the election?" And so they all sat down again over coffee and sweet rolls and worked out the details.

That had been a little more than a year ago and Starr Draper was now to do what she still thought of as the impossible. She was on the way to her inauguration and she still had moments of complete terror where she wanted to bolt out of the car and run away.

She'd never wanted the damn job.

"Which is why you'll be perfect for it, my dear."

In the time between the election and the inauguration of a president, there are ten thousand things that require a decision from the president-elect. Actually, there are about a million things, but if the president-elect is smart, she'll make a few early decisions about her staff that will greatly reduce the number of items that require her personal attention. Primary in this process is the Chief of Staff. This person often is the filter between the president and the rest of the world. He or she is the keeper-of-the-gate for the Oval Office and holds a great deal of power in the political circles of Washington. Often it is the Chief of Staff that determines which bill gets the nod from the president and which doesn't.

Because it's possible for the Chief of Staff to make the president look incredibly stupid or dictatorial simply by making the wrong decisions about the power mechanizations of the thousands of politicos and influence peddlers, the president's choice of the right person is crucial. The Chief of Staff makes hundreds of decisions every hour with the authority of the president's office and if that person is not in tune with the president, if they are not on the same page with the priorities and agendas of the Commander in Chief, then almost everything that the president plans will likely fail. President-elect Draper's choice might have been a surprise to some political pundits, but she had no doubt who it should be from the moment she had entered the race. Helios D'Amico was the second son of an immigrant to America and was first in his class at Harvard Law. Other than a small government education grant, he had paid for his college education by being a program strategist for Sony Games. Their meeting, Starr and Helios, was one of those happy coincidences that later seemed more like fate. It was at a Full Moon circle she attended while on an assignment for her e-news company. A friend of hers was part of the group that hosted a community circle each month and Starr had accepted her invitation to join in while she was in Boston. Helios was there as well and they had hit it off from the start.

Though neither one of them had any psychic talent to speak of by themselves, together they seemed to make a connection that was very close to mind reading for each other. For some, such a relationship might prove to spark a romance. For others, it could be a living hell. But for Starr and Helios, it was a synergy that made a wonderful change in each of them. Starr had the benefit of Helios' marvelous legal and strategic mind and he had access to her nearly photographic memory and eye for details. Their meeting marked the beginning of Starr's political career. She had toyed with the idea before but felt she lacked the abilities needed to be effective. Helios filled in the gaps and he too had hoped to enter governmental service in some way but had doubts about his ability to sway people with words. They found that as long as they were within about two kilometers of each other, their communication was nearly complete. It took some getting used to but they quickly learned to use their unique situation in a wide variety of ways. When Starr first had an audience with Lady McGuire, she and Helios had known each other less than a year. But by the time she had made her bid for the Senate, they had become an invincible team.

The same had held true during the presidential race. Few people knew about their joined status, even after she had named him as Chief of Staff. His own accomplishments in the public sector had made it seem sensible for him to be her choice. It was no secret they teamed up on causes and political movements over the years, so little was said to question her choice. Only Allen, Trenton, and Lady McGuire knew of their unusual psychic symbiosis.

They couldn't really call what they had a total mind reading; it wasn't as if they knew the actual thoughts of the other. It was more like their own minds were operating along parallel lines with the addition of the other person's knowledge and skills. Each had discovered that they were aware of the other's proximity even before they could be sensed in any other way. Being able to parallel process information in this way, they found their own native abilities were greatly enhanced. Not only could they arrive at a decision more quickly, they would invariably arrive at the *same* conclusion. If she had to utilize anyone else in the Chief of Staff position, Starr would probably have been terrified. As it was, she was still unsure of being put in the position of President. Maybe she'd grow more used to it as time went on. But today, only hours before she was to be sworn in, she was close to a panic attack.

As her limousine turned the corner onto Pennsylvania Avenue she saw the Capitol building that, more than any other piece of architecture in the world, symbolized a complex mix of dreams and ideals that had driven some to impossibly great accomplishments and others to unimaginable stupidity. Her breakfast today with President Picossa would be his last official act as President. In a way, she envied him; his tour of duty was now over and he could live the rest of his life with the prestige and power afforded all past presidents without the harrowing pressures that she knew she would have to face in just a few hours. Helios would also be getting together with the current Chief of Staff. But he had sat with her two months earlier when the president and his wife had hosted them for a private luncheon. Of course the president had helped campaign for her and they were on much more familiar terms than just political colleagues, but the first half of the luncheon was for the media, so the president and the president-elect had appeared without any other officials to get in the picture. It wasn't until they had shooed away the reporters and cameras and actually sat down to a meal before Helios had joined them. Though it might have been considered strange that he had been part of the meeting, President Picossa understood the reasons Starr had requested he be included. The president had included his current Chief of Staff in their meeting as well in the hope that he could help D'Amico in some way. The current Chief of Staff was young, probably only in his forty's, but had proven a capable CoS for the outgoing President since his appointment a year and a half before. His name was Douglas Eisenhower and was a distant relative of a president who had come into power just after the only atomic bomb to be exploded in war had been used against Japan by the United States. He was, as the media had said many times in describing him, as good looking as a chic-flick vid star. Perhaps the most unusual point about him, however, was the fact that he was a Pentecostal Christian. And President Picossa was a devout Roman Catholic who had ridden into the White House as the Earth Party's candidate. Though ironic in the extreme to those who analyzed politics in DC, none of it seemed to matter to anyone except those political pundits. Starr wasn't the only one who had become more or less blind to a person's professed faith identity; most of the country was just as unimpressed by what label a person used and more concerned with how they interacted with their world. What might have once been considered an odd combination of ideologies was now hardly a blip on the collective consciousness. The luncheon had proven to be helpful to Starr and Helios in several ways and she had enjoyed the humor of the First Lady immensely.

The breakfast meeting she was about to have with President Picossa would in all probability be slightly more somber, more like a wake she imagined. There was something almost sad about a president going quietly into the night. After eight years of holding the most powerful office in a country that still could be considered the leader of the world, slipping out the south door to board Marine One for the last time without every reporter in the world watching would certainly have to feel strange. She wondered what he would be thinking about for the hour and a half trip to his home in California.

Her limo and the accompanying cars of the Secret Service people pulled into the security tunnel that led to the underground garage of the White House and Starr was escorted by no less than ten alert, grim-faced people with audio and optical implants to the personal dining room of the president of the United States. Though this wasn't used for public state functions, it was nevertheless quite large and boasted a table that would easily accommodate thirty. She knew that the president and his wife would often sit at the cozy six-person table in the corner of the private kitchen that overlooked the south lawn to take their coffee. Starr expected it offered a much more pleasing atmosphere than this room. But some protocols had to be followed even for a private meeting, so it was the so-called 'private' dining room where the two of them met.

Starr's VP running mate, the somewhat elderly Thomas James Hunt was having a similar breakfast meeting with the outgoing VP over at Blair House. Starr had known Hunt only distantly while in the Senate; they didn't have a close relationship. But she'd felt compelled to choose him because of his expertise in international relations and his sound understanding of world trade. With China controlling much of the economy, knowing how money moved around the planet was crucial for understanding the power fluctuations of the world political situation. Starr could use TJ's help and he had appeared early on in the campaign as the one who would be her best choice. His bid in the primaries looked strong at the beginning but he had decided to pull out after a bad showing in the New England states. And he'd enthusiastically thrown in with Starr's campaign, where he was welcomed with open arms by nearly everyone. Also, his sizable campaign money chest was added to hers, which was most welcomed because she wasn't the best at raising funds.

When their breakfast had been served and the staff had left them alone, President Picossa gave his CoS a slight nod. Eisenhower stood and asked if he and Helios could be excused to hold their conversations in another room. The president agreed and he and Starr were then alone, the First Lady having left earlier after only a glass of orange juice.

Starr smiled at the president and said, "I don't have to be psychic to know you arranged for us to be left alone here like this, Mr. President. Are you now going to pass on the keys to the closets containing all the skeletons?"

"Hardly; I might need them to keep the hounds at bay after I leave here today. But I will tell you that if you're smart, you'll not look too closely under some of the rugs."

She gave a polite chuckle. She knew the president was only partly joking. "So, what do we talk about now, sir?"

To her surprise, he reached into his jacket and pulled out a gold cigarette case. Holding it up between them, he asked, "Do you mind?"

She had no idea the president smoked. Of course, it was against all the rules for him to smoke anywhere inside any enclosed

26

space, but how could she refuse the man one small vice? "Of course not, Mr. President. I have no problem with it. Tried them once but never caught the habit. Couldn't get past the coughing."

"Ahem, yes… well, you get used to it. Of course, as my daddy used to say, 'You can get used to hanging if you hang long enough.' I never wanted to test that theory, but then maybe I'm doing just that with these." He took out a matching gold lighter and put flame to cigarette tip. Taking a deep drag, he sat back with a look of pleasure. "In old times, they used to serve brandy with these, I believe. Now days, the doctors say I shouldn't have either one. What do they know, eh? I'm ninety-seven and can still chop wood and haul water if I need to."

One of the things she loved about him was when he put on his homespun persona and relaxed. Both he and the First Lady were solid Midwestern farming stock and very practical people at the core. "I believe, Mr. President that the tradition was brandy and *cigars*, but I'm sure the difference is of no consequence."

They sat in silence a while as he took a few more draws on the pencil slim tube of tobacco. Then he stubbed it out on his plate and wrapped the remains in a napkin that he put in his jacket pocket. "Can't have the evidence around for the help to write a tell-all book on, can we?" When he looked back at her again, Starr knew he was going to get into whatever was the real reason he'd made it so they were alone.

"Starr," he said, then coughed and looked at her almost shyly. "I'm going to call you Starr and you can call me Robert or Bob. Here, we're just two people dumb enough to take this job. So let's drop the formalities, okay?" She smiled and nodded, then gestured for him to continue. "Yes, well… oh, hell, I'll just say it. How well do you know TJ?"

Of all the things she may have thought the president might discuss, the VP-elect wasn't one of them. But she trusted the president, even if she didn't know where this was going. "About as well as I know you, sir. Meaning I haven't any real knowledge other than public record. But the party gurus recommended him and I can't say he's not come through on the campaign. Personally, I find him a little… I don't know… a little formal? I guess I'd characterize it that way. But he's never been anything but helpful. I don't know if I'd say we're friends, but I believe we have a respect for one another. Can I ask why you're asking?"

"You can, but I'll answer you only after I get an answer to my next question. What connection does TJ have with Stamper?"

Starr carefully set down her glass of wine and considered how she would answer the president. Until now, Stamper's name hadn't come up in any conversations dealing directly with politics except within the walls of Maggie's home. Allen and Trenton and she had met there only a few times since the campaign had begun. To Starr, who had been focused more on the campaign than on Stamper's activities, the president's question sounded an alarm bell. She wanted to learn what he might know about Stamper but she didn't want to tip her hand and destroy one of the reasons she had run one of the most grueling races any politician can face. After only a momentary pause, she replied with a disarming smile. "None that I know of, Bob. Please don't tell me that TJ has done something financially that's against the rules?"

"Hah! Him? He's a Puritan when it comes to political ethics. But only on the public side. And who the hell knows anything more? The man's never married and I have no idea what he's like on the inside. He's a Wally, you know."

Just as there were people with natural psychic skills, so were there some who could not be read even by the most gifted of psychics. They were called a Wally because it was like running up against a wall for any who tried to go into their thoughts. The term had made the name Wallace rather unpopular for the last fifty years and was considered somewhat derogatory. She picked her words carefully. "As, I believe are several politicians we could mention. In our business, it might be considered a bonus, don't you think?" The president also had been called a Wally. She had no direct knowledge whether that was true or not because she couldn't read anyone that way herself. Her reply didn't actually come out and say he too was a Wally, but she knew he would understand the subtext correctly. She didn't know how he would take her remark, but in less than three hours, she would be the one behind the desk in the oval office and he wouldn't. So she thought it was high time to stop playing games.

"What's going on, Bob? Let's not waste taxpayer dollars here. If I need to know something, just come out with it."

"Okay, I'm sorry. I know I've got a reputation as a Wally too. And I am. And, as you pointed out, it can be an advantage in our game. *But that doesn't mean I'm not psychic.*"

Political training aside, Starr caught her breath as she realized that the president hadn't spoken his last sentence with his mouth. She was amazed not only by the fact that he'd projected his thoughts to her, but also because it had come through as distinct words, just as if she had heard him say them. She was used to the kind of communication she and Helios had, a sort of parallel thought processing. But to have individual words come through, as in a complete series of words, processed as if they had come through the auditory channels and into her language processors in the brain, this was completely unexpected. She had, of course, heard of this ability, but it was very unusual.

Contrary to popular belief by those who didn't know much about psychic phenomena, mental telepathy, as it was commonly called, wasn't really like verbal communication. Psychics often likened most telepathy to 'shared meaning.' Our words are really not the meaning in some respects. They are just sound-symbols that point to the meaning of what we wish to communicate. But verbal words are sometimes confusing because they can often mean one thing to one person and quite another to the next. Therefore, in some ways, telepathic communication was considered superior because it bypassed the 'translation' of words and dealt directly with meanings. For a person to communicate in words by mental means only was very, *very* rare. People who were able to project their thoughts into another person were usually trained to project meaning instead of words. So even if a child could do what the president had just done, they were usually taught what was considered to be a better means of utilizing their skills.

Starr had to laugh at her own naivety. She had never thought of a Wally as anything but psychically inactive. Now that she considered it, it did make sense that they could just have amazingly superior mental shields. She realized that the president had purposely tricked her and was now enjoying himself by watching her process the experience. It had taken her only an extra second to respond, but it was obvious that he'd accomplished what he knew would be a shock to her.

He grinned like a boy with his first deck of tarot cards and said, "What's the matter, Starr? You think you witches are the only ones who have psychic skills? I may be just a good old Catholic boy, but I can still give a lot of you Wiccans a good run for the money. Poor Barnstead hates it when I do that. He hasn't been able to crawl around inside my head and yet I'm able to get past his best shielding and lay eggs in his language cortex. It really burns him when I do that, heh heh. But I'm making a point here, young lady. There's a lot that you and Mr. Sunshine, your Chief of Staff, won't be able to guard against unless you crawl into a cave high up in the Andes Mountains. And one of those things is Thomas Hunt. Allen can't read him, Maggie can't see him, and most of us can't trust him."

"Then why in the world did the Party recommend him? I'm dependent on Allen and Trent's help in these matters, for goddess' sake. Why would they give a pass on TJ if they couldn't trust him?"

"Take it from an old political war horse, Senator... excuse me, I guess I should get used to calling you Madam President."

"I thought we agreed on Bob and Starr."

"Ah, right... so we did. Well, take it from me: not everything a psychic thinks is necessarily right. Sometimes I believe this Party relies way too much on what they call magic and far too little on what I call political experience. I may not be all that good a seer, but one thing I do know is that TJ Hunt and Eric Stamper have some, shall we say, similar tastes and are closer than most people believe."

"Similar tastes? Are you saying they're secret lovers or something?"

"Oh, no. They're both hetero. And they're both confirmed bachelors. Now, let's not be naive, how do rich men usually satisfy their sexual desires?"

"With the prettiest women who are willing. But I doubt that either one of them have any trouble attracting their share of women. There are a million women in DC alone who would happily bed down with the very rich and powerful just for the thrill of it."

"Quite true, but also consider the fact that any time one of us goes to bed for a quick bounce, half of the press corps will do anything to get the juicy details the next day. Sex may not be a bad word anymore, but it still sells e-mags. One of the things that the professional ladies here in DC have learned is that they can sell more than their lusty bodies; they can market their silence for a high price. And when high prices don't mean a hell of a lot because you're rich, then silence usually means even more.

"TJ Hunt and Eric Stamper share similar tastes in their women. And they apparently don't mind even sharing the same room with each other. Maybe they trade off or something, but I really don't care. My concern is that they are more than close; they have emotional ties as well. I know about McGuire's and Trenton's worries about a fundamentalist movement within the Wiccans. I brought my information to Trenton when TJ's name started to be sent around as a possible VP choice for you. Know-it-all Trenton decided that I was being a prude or something. Told me that men needed to get laid and Wiccans had a different view of sex than Catholics. That's true, but it doesn't change what sex does to your mind. I have no idea what it does to women, but there's a reason guys say they're 'eff'd up' when they talk about going off their rocker or something. Sex to a guy has a tendency to make you lose your ability to think straight. That doesn't change because of the religion you practice."

Starr knew the president wasn't just concerned with two men who might make fools of themselves with women. But she wasn't clear what exactly he was worried about. "I too am alarmed if they're doing as you say. What do you mean though? Is Tom one of Stamper's people? Am I being set up?"

"I don't know; that's the short answer. TJ has seemingly a spotless record with the Party. But the fact that he's a Wally isn't just what worries me. I've wondered about his political rise for a while now. If you look back at some of the stuff he's been messed up with, it's amazing he's come through so squeaky clean. Most people who have dealings with him seem a little brainwashed about him. A lot of them say the same things about him. I mean *exactly* the same things, word for word. Even Trenton told me the exact same words about him that I'd heard from two other people in the Party not more than a week earlier. I know sometimes we learn to say some things the same way because of advertising or strong public relations blurbs, but I worry that this might be more insidious."

Starr was thoughtful about the president's words and held off comment for a long moment. She thought about possible explanations for what she too now recognized as a pattern of how TJ Hunt seemingly impressed people. She finally asked the president, "Do you think it possible Hunt can mentally influence people without being open to other psychics?"

He nodded slowly and steepled his fingers. "I know that modern Mentation Theory says that's not possible, but that's exactly what I fear."

"So you believe TJ Hunt is a Trojan horse that has been passed by both Barnstead and Lady McGuire. And you think he can mentally influence others without ever giving any kind of signal to some of the world's best readers, is that about right?"

He pointed his finger and thumb like a gun and 'fired' at her, saying, "Bingo."

"Let's suppose you're right and we've now put the fox inside the henhouse… or at least damn close to the White House. What do you propose we do?"

"That, Madam President, is *your* decision. I'm just passing on the concerns of an old political hack. I've talked both to Trenton and Allen and they've told me I'm wrong. Maybe I am. It's up to you now. But if I'm right, if your VP is one of these Wiccan fundamentalists and is hiding it well, you'd better watch the fine print in any piece of legislation that passes. I'd have a team of legal-eagles combing the wording of everything that is voted into law. Not just the stuff that lands on your desk either, but the regulatory stuff that happens as well. I'd find money to keep these lawyers busy 24-7 and make sure they're kept shielded."

Every president had a bevy of legal advisors who were engaged in keeping the oval office free from scandal and legal intrigue. But Starr didn't know any who had set up a team of them to do what the president proposed. How she could do that without some hint of it leaking and causing a huge conspiracy rumor would be difficult. But Picossa had awakened a fear in her that, the more she thought about it, seemed quite possibly a real threat. In fact, she now wondered why she had accepted Hunt as her running mate in the first place. When Trenton had come to her with the idea, he'd brought along Senator Hunt with him. That in itself was odd. Usually, the candidate would be proposed and vetted before actually being approached. When Hunt had shaken hands (he was 'old fashioned' that way according to him) with her, she'd made up her mind about him that moment. Every other candidate seemed grossly inferior from that day on. It made her wonder if the president wasn't on to something.

Wherever Helios had gone with the president's CoS, it wasn't far. She was just about to call him when a soft bell sounded. They both turned to the door and the president said, "Open for entry." The door unlocked and the light over it turned from red to green. Eisenhower entered with D'Amico right behind him. Helios looked straight at Starr with concern written all over his face. She gave a slight nod of her head but said nothing. He immediately knew that they would talk later but she didn't want to say anything about what was worrying her at the moment. He gave a mental acknowledgment as the president's CoS said out loud, "Please excuse the interruption, sir. Mr. D'Amico said the president-elect was going to be late if we didn't wind things up in the next few minutes."

The president looked over at Starr and grinned. "It would seem you have begun your training as of now, Madam President. Trust me, your Chief of Staff will run you like an old time train. You won't be able to sneeze if it isn't on the schedule." He rose and reached across the table, touching fingertips with her. "My very best wishes to you, Madam President. If you need me, I will of course be at your command. Just try not to make it during fishing season, mmm?"

"Of course, Bob. Thank you for everything. And give the First Lady my thanks as well. You both have helped this country in a million ways. Go catch a boatload of trout." She turned and left with Helios. The ever-present Secret Service people assigned to her were waiting just outside and they fell in around the president-Elect in perfect unison with the P-E's step. She heard one of them say into an invisible throat mike, "Glenda is leaving for the garage." She still found it amusing that they had chosen the name of the Good Witch of the East from the Wizard of Oz as her code name. She was sure that Helios was also designated with a code name from the same venue but as yet, she hadn't heard what it was. She just hoped it wasn't one of the flying monkeys.

Her thoughts, however, turned to Tom Hunt, her VP. Who was he? Was he the 'man behind the curtain' in the Land of Oz? Was she going to have to conquer the Wizard before she could get on with running the country? Her thoughts ran with the power of her mental comrade-in-arms, Helios. Strategies and contingencies began to race alongside thoughts about creating networks to keep the country moving forward. One of her campaign planks had been to re-seed the old forests east of the Mississippi and she wanted to build a task force for accomplishing that before her term was over. Even though it would take at least twenty years to accomplish the program, she didn't want it to linger until she had to win a second term. And the problem of the clean water supply to the whole country was still around, years after it had been declared an emergency. Chow-Ling Industries had come up with a technology that offered real hope but the cost was in orbit! And, of course, there was the pesky problem of...

"Madam President, your vehicle is waiting." The Secret Service woman in charge of her detail brought her back to the moment. Indeed, the limo was waiting with the doors open. Helios had already gotten into the back and was facing the seat directly across from the one she always used. Embarrassed that she'd been caught daydreaming, she smiled at the woman and gave her a slight bow. "Thank you, Lynn, mustn't keep the people waiting." As she slid into the spacious back of the ground limo, two burly men from the Secret Service got in the front and another hopped onto the rear-guard platform on the back. Four other identical vehicles drove with her out of the White House garage and sped on their way to the hotel suite where Starr Draper would be dressed, coifed, and painted to look presentable to the cameras as the new President of the United States of America.

≪ 5 ≫

The whirlwind of activity at the hotel was enough to distract Starr from the topics discussed in the president's private dining room. She had practiced her inaugural speech several times the night before and was confident she would be able to deliver it with all the energy necessary to set a tone for her first few months. By eleven o'clock, she was again in her limo and speeding to the designated entry tunnel for the Circle Plaza. Once inside, she was transferred to what looked like an old-fashioned golf cart and whisked along to the below-ground complex under the central stage. Everyone who was to be part of the ceremony was already there. But two people Starr hadn't expected walked up to her as she extracted herself from the silly looking cart. Lady McGuire and Trenton Hartford greeted her with smiles and finger touches. Lady McGuire spoke before Starr could say anything.

"Forgive us, Madam President for disrupting your schedule. But I felt it necessary to take another minute of your time before this important ceremony." Then she handed Starr a simple stick of incense, saying, "I bless you with the power of Air so that your mind is always clear." She produced a lighter and put flame to the tip of the incense, saying, "I bless you with the power of Fire so that you have command of your energies." Trenton handed a very small vial of clear liquid to Lady McGuire, who passed it on to Starr, saying, "I bless you with the power of Water so you my know the meaning and feeling of your life." Then Trenton passed what looked like a coin and the Lady handed it to Starr, saying, "I bless you with the power of Earth so you may know the value of the world you help to create." Starr looked at the face of the 'coin' and saw that it was a silver round with her face and today's date on one side and a pentacle on the other. When she looked back up at the Lady McGuire, she received an anointing on her forehead by the old witch with the words, "I bless you with the Spirit of all the gods and goddesses that shall accompany you through your life. May your heart be at peace and your soul be true to their will."

Starr was almost in tears after this marvelous surprise and she flung herself into the Lady's arms, laughing and trying hard not to smear her makeup. "Thank you, Maggie. Thank you a thousand times. I just hope I won't fail or disappoint you in any way. Goddess knows I'm as nervous as all get-out. I *will* carry out this duty to the best of my ability but, wow, do I wish I could see into the future." She laughed and hugged the woman even tighter. Then she broke away and hugged Trenton, thanking him as well. She put the incense and water on a table where various articles of hers were being piled. The coin went into her pants pocket. With a sigh, she gave her surprise reception party a grateful smile and turned, squared her shoulders, and walked into the ring of people who would be part of the swearing-in ceremony. A young woman dashed over and did something to her eye makeup, quickly brushed at her cheeks and smiled confidently. "You look like magic, Madam President," she said and then disappeared back into the crowd of people as Starr went to go over some things with the Chief Justice who would be administering the oath. Starr didn't much like Chief Justice Stella Moran, but she at least respected her office. And she would have to have more contact with the woman in the coming years, so she put aside her personal differences for the moment.

Above them, the venerable Walter X. Chu, the senior senator from Massachusetts was starting his introductory speech. That meant it would be another few minutes before Starr would be brought up to the central stage. She couldn't decide if she wanted the intervening time to speed up or slow down; it wasn't like her to be so self-conscious and nervous, but then she'd never been sworn into an office with over a billion people watching. The last time she'd felt this anxious was when she'd conducted the Solstice rite at the Circle of the Winds. How her life had changed since that day. Now she was to lead a nation and attempt to make the world a better place for everyone, all nine and a half billion of them.

She smiled to herself. *"What's the big deal? Hey, magic can, like, fix anything, right?"* She had actually said that to her Magic 101 teacher the very first day of class when she was only seventeen. She recalled the withering look Ms. Haines had given her over the incredibly naïve and stupid remark. Whenever she thought of the immense tasks ahead for her, Starr also remembered back to Ms. Underwear's (Starr wondered if the woman ever knew they called her that) first rule of magic: "Every spell begins with the words, 'I will.'"

Even though there was a double shielding of impenetrable spider-glass surrounding the central stage, Starr felt the sound from the half-million people crowded into the Circle Plaza as almost a crushing wave. She stepped from the platform and onto the stage amid the thunderous applause and marveled at the deafening power of it all. It was beyond anything she'd felt before. But then it died away to a silence that was equally incredible. Starr was transfixed by the raw power evident both in that welcoming applause and the sudden quiet. That she would hold that power and wield it as the president was as humbling as it was exciting.

The ceremony of swearing in the new President and Vice-President took less than thirty minutes. Then, for the first time as President, Starr addressed the people of her nation. The first half of her speech was mostly scripted by tradition: mention of the dignitaries, the outgoing President, her relatives and friends both on the stage and off, statements of gratitude and humbleness, and promises to be true to the ideals of the country and her campaign. Then she paused, taking a deep breath before delivering the real 'meat' of her inaugural address.

Facing not the cameras, but instead turning a complete circle to view the entire multitude, President Starr Draper let everyone know that what she was to say next would be the underlying theme of her term in office. "This grand circle is tiny when compared to the one that encompasses our planet. This nation has grown in ways completely unexpected by its founding fathers... and mothers." As expected, this brought a small moment of laughter. "In the previous century, we became a world power. Our economy and our military might were such that we could impose our will nearly anywhere on the globe and other nations would have to give way just to survive.

At the turn of this century, we had grown so arrogant that we hardly blinked when we tried to force our will again, this time in an area of the world that hadn't known peace for thousands of years. The result was that we lost any claim to having a moral superiority to anyone and we have suffered the consequences of our political and cultural arrogance. Today, we stand with many other nations... not as an enforcer or instructor, but as their equal. Our power can only be through our knowledge and humanity, never again through our ignorance and conceit.

"We are learning how to share power because we must not ever again allow ourselves to believe that we can't be wrong. We will question every move, not only of our global brothers and sisters, but most especially of ourselves... and most especially of our leaders.

"The office of the President of the United States of America is a great honor. But it is also a great trust. I will be your president, but I will not expect your trust unless I earn it. After the long campaign, some presidents have believed they have a mandate from their people. They have misused the trust offered to them. I will never assume such a thing. I will work on your behalf and assume only one mandate: that I must earn your trust every day.

"In the coming days and months, we will continue the previous administration's work on solving our water and energy problems. We will find better ways to educate our people and employ our skills for the benefit of all mankind. We will strive for compassion and aid for the sick, and find better ways to feed the hungry of the world. We will work in harmony with the other nations who share these worthy goals. We will not fight unless we know our cause is truly righteous, but we will maintain a highly trained and well-equipped fighting force that is capable of defending this beautiful nation. We will not bend our knee to any who think to conquer us. But we also will not try to dictate to them or any others who wish to live in peaceful coexistence.

"Tomorrow, in this same circle, I will have the honor of leading the celebration of the Summer Solstice. For those who do not honor this as a religious holiday, rest assured that it will be in the spirit of the brightness that day represents: that the warmth and light of our lives will give health, wealth, and good purpose to all our endeavors.

Just as the Winter Solstice represents hope for renewal, so does tomorrow acknowledge the good that can be found within each human heart.

"To the envoys and dignitaries from other nations who have graced this inauguration, I invite you to share this country's celebration of the light that shines on – and from – every person on our fair planet. Let it truly be a day where all come together in love and trust."

In the speech she had written with her two writers and practiced up until late the night before, this was to be the end. But back from the breakfast with the outgoing President, in the limo with Helios, she had made a decision and had mentally composed an addition to her prepared notes.

"Finally, to the millions of people in this country who work every day to better their lives and the lives of their loved ones, I give you my heart. Know that it beats in time with you and that I will work just as hard as you to keep this nation free and prosperous. I will serve you with every breath and every heartbeat. But all of our hopes and dreams cannot be made manifest without your help. I have decided to form a special team of advisors that will perform a vital task for all of us. These people will be my link to all of you because they will take your suggestions about anything... *anything* whatsoever that you wish to say to me in your email... they will bring the brightest and best of these to me and I will read them. This nation has some of the world's greatest minds, highly educated and innovative. *Everyone* has good ideas, sometimes even great ones. And as your chosen leader, I welcome them. Don't be afraid to speak your mind because not only is it your right, it is vital that I be told what you think. No one... and let me be crystal clear about this... no one will be punished for expressing their opinion about anything. I have just sworn to uphold the Constitution of this great land and freedom of speech is one of our greatest strengths. Of course, you may not threaten or incite to violence, but you can tell me exactly what you think without fear of retribution. I *want* to know what you think. All too often, leaders are fed words that people believe the leader wants to hear. I want to hear from the people; I want to hear from you. I want to hear from the first three words of our Declaration of Independence; I want to hear from 'We, the people,' because we... all of us... are the greatest body of free minds in the world. 'We, the people' are everything America is about."

She was going to add a 'thank you' but the cheering and applause would have drowned it out anyway. So she stepped back from the podium and acknowledged the crowd both in the Circle Plaza as well as the video audience. The applause lasted for almost a minute and began to lessen only when she turned and walked back to the platform that lowered her to the chamber below. She heard the band strike up *America the Beautiful* and Elizabeth Torun's glorious voice sing in such clear tones it melted the hearts of everyone. Even Starr, who was flush with the energy of the moment, let a tear fall over the intense emotion the woman put into the old song. Helios smiled at her in sympathy as she wiped away the escaping tear. She smiled back and whispered, "Gods, that woman can call the west anytime on my circle!" He laughed with her as they made their way across the lower chamber toward the carts that would take them back to the garage.

He leaned close as she sat down in her cart. "A small surprise for everyone, that last bit in your speech, what? You do realize how many people it will take to do that don't you?"

She gave him a meaningful look and said quietly, "I know. But I also know we can hide our political legal eagles in that pile of people and nobody will be the wiser. I want a team of three or four figured out before Congress gets back into session. We've got to find some way to collect them and keep them safe. Get Barnstead to help you. He'll find out what we're doing if he doesn't know already, so tell him I'm asking for his help." She settled more comfortably into their cart and turned to give him one last instruction. "And, Helios, I don't..."

"I know: you don't want any Wallys on that team."

She smiled broadly and copied the 'finger gun' the now former President had aimed at her that morning. "Bingo."

$$\text{\textcurrency} \; 6 \; \text{\textcurrency}$$

The rest of her day was a blur of activity and she finally got to her private quarters somewhere well after midnight. When she'd worked in the Senate, she had a staff of twelve who took care of her business. The press had kiddingly called it 'The Starr Grove.' She had hired not on the basis of what faith group each person subscribed to but on their skills in the position she wanted the person for. Technically, the people she hired were civil servants; they were supposedly hired by the government. But Starr had run a tight ship and if a staff member didn't measure up, they found themselves out the door and waiting in line for some other government job. The result was that Starr was used to a standard of work from her staff that greatly exceeded what was usually considered acceptable. She'd figured she might have to kick a little butt on her greatly expanded staff at the White House itself. To her happy surprise, she'd found them to be well beyond her expectations. In fact, it floored her how well they worked together. In the eight hours between the time the old President had left and she'd 'come home' from all the pomp and circumstance of Inauguration Day, the White House had been transformed from the furnishings of the old President to those chosen by the new one. Her wardrobe and personal toiletries were ready for use exactly where she expected them to be. She had declined using one of the historical and antique beds available and had told them she wanted the same utilitarian bed she'd used for better than five years. It was waiting for her, freshly made with a new summer weight comforter, when she finally was able to escape the clamor of the dozens of people who wanted her attention.

Fifteen minutes after closing the door, she emerged from her shower feeling almost alive. She pressed a button on the wall and told the answering attendant that she wanted her decaf with a shot of brandy and then she headed for the corner of her bedroom that held the computers and video screens. They never were completely turned off and she quickly typed a message to Helios about the next day's schedule and then another longer one to her father, who had insisted on staying at a hotel in DC rather than "sleep in some rickety old bed" in the famous Lincoln bedroom. She loved the old man dearly but sometimes had difficulty understanding his ways. By the time she'd sent her email off, the door chime sounded and her coffee and brandy was brought in by a tall woman wearing the White House standard medium blue pantsuit. Without looking up, Starr motioned for the steaming cup to be placed on the desk she was still sitting behind.

"Will there be anything else, Madam President?"

Starr looked up to reply when she suddenly realized who had brought her the coffee. She jumped up and skipped around the desk to hug the woman. "Lisa! Gods, but I didn't know you worked in the White House!" Then she held the young woman out with both arms and studied her a moment. "Or did Maggie work a charm and get you hired just so you could keep an eye on me?" Though Starr asked the question with a smile, she didn't think it entirely impossible that was exactly what the old witch had done. Lady McGuire was as cunning as she was psychic. During the campaign, Starr had seen the seer's great, great granddaughter only a few times but had come to admire the woman's savvy as well as her grace. Lisandra was much more than a beautiful woman and even the mildly lecherous Allen had treated her occasional input with respect.

Lisandra smiled, stepping back from the president. "No, Madam President, I don't work just at the White House. I work for the Secret Service and I'm in charge of the three A Teams assigned to you. So I go where you go."

At any given time, the Service had about a thousand people directly assigned to taking care of the president and, when applicable, the president's family. That Maggie's great, great granddaughter was the person in charge of the cadre they called the A Teams, that is, the three units of twenty-five people directly available to cover the president wherever she was located, was a great responsibility. Starr wondered if Maggie had pulled any strings to put Lisa in that position but quickly dismissed the notion. She knew that neither Maggie nor the Secret Service would do anything to reduce or jeopardize Starr's safety.

"So, do you also double as my personal maid or did you just happen to be in the kitchen when I called down?"

"Actually, I *was* in the kitchen then. I told Barbara I'd bring it up and tuck you in myself tonight. Thought you might find it a little disorienting here the first night and you could use a friendly smile."

The president was warmed by the gesture and thanked the woman. Then she said, "What I could *really* use is a good shoulder rub. It's been one grueling day, I can tell you."

"I can get Jimo up here in five minutes. He'll be happy to know his services are required." She spoke into her lapel mike before Starr was able to stop her.

"You mean there's a masseuse on call here? I can just order up a rubdown any time?"

"Absolutely, nothing's too good for your physical comfort. There's also a complete medical unit on duty twenty-four/seven in case the cook gives you a tummy ache. We even have a surgical theatre in the basement if it should ever be necessary."

The information was both comforting and disquieting at the same time to Starr. She knew that every president since Teddy Roosevelt had had somebody, sometimes more than one, try to assassinate them. It was almost a given that whoever was President was going to have at least one serious attempt on their life. She was also aware that there was a huge van that was an emergency room on wheels as part of the presidential entourage. And there was a special jet air-car that served the same purpose. That so much was invested in taking care of an assassination attempt if it were successful, or partially successful, was not a thought she wanted to linger over.

She asked Lisandra to stay while she got her shoulder rub. No sooner had the young agent said she would than the door announced the arrival of the masseuse. Forty minutes later, Lisandra was covering a snoring President. She paused in the doorway and gave the room one final check before leaving it all to the security computer.

Her first full day in the Oval Office started easily enough. Helios introduced her to some of the staff, the people she'd be dealing with the most. Then there was a thirty-minute briefing from the NSA and another from Frank Miller, the man she'd come to rely on for sorting out what was important in the news versus the 99% that wasn't.

Frank had about a dozen computers working in a dozen different languages looking through who knew how many news feeds from around the globe. She didn't understand the programming he'd created to pluck the important stuff out of the piles of data that crowded the planet-wide net, but she knew that she could depend on him getting the right information to her. His briefings were quick, easily understood synopses and whatever he started out with she knew was the most important for her to know.

The next few hours were filled with important Congressional leaders putting in their word and having a media show with the new President. By noon, she was ready for a break and told Helios she wanted fifteen minutes by herself. He nodded his head, but then said her father had been waiting to see her all morning. She had completely forgotten he'd said he wanted to wish her well before taking the Lift that afternoon to L5-B, the bio-lab floating over South America.

"Oh, gods! I can't believe I've left him waiting all this time. I'll bet he's been a pain in the butt for everyone, right?"

"Ah, well... ahem... no, not everybody. Actually, he's been flirting with Lisandra a good deal of the time. We've all been quite amused when she walks past and his head snaps around like a radar dish."

"Oh, yeah, that's my dad. It's nice to know some things don't change. Mom always used to jab him in the ribs whenever they went to the sky clad rites there in Java. Of course, he got back at her when they went to Tunisia on vacation. Mom said she only glanced at the man, but Dad said the guy was "hung like a horse" and Mom was staring right at his crotch for five minutes. They were both born in the twentieth century and even ritual nudity was somewhat rare. Please show him in, won't you?"

Starr's father was only eighty, but since her mother had died, he'd begun showing signs of aging quickly. That he still had an eye for the young ladies was good to hear in a way. She knew he'd taken it badly when her mother had finally succumbed from her fifteen-year bout with MPN, Morphing Pathology Necrosis, and she sometimes wondered if her father wasn't slowly letting go of life.

She was staring out the window at the oak trees on the lawn when she heard a low whistle. Turning, she saw her father standing just inside the door, looking around at the most famous office in the world. She walked over and hugged him tightly. When they broke, she guided him over to the seats in front of the old desk she had chosen to use for the office. "When do you have to leave, Dad? I'm sorry I've been busy, but," she waved around at the office, "it kind of happens fast and furious around here, you know?"

"Yeah, I figured that one out. But you've got a lot of people to help you. I hope you know enough to use them, Starr."

"You're right. And I know I've got a team that's going to work hard, Dad. Most of these people are veterans here and it's going to be a tremendous help when they all get into their own rhythm with each other as well as me. But let's not worry about that right now; let's just be family for a minute." She took both of his hands in hers. "How are you *really* doing, Dad? Is the work up at the lab going well? Are you getting enough sleep?"

"The work is going very well. We've narrowed down the DNA sequence of MPN and think we might have found the link that makes it change so easily. It's a smart critter, this bug, but before I kick the bucket I'm going to make it pay for killing your mother. You know we're still working off of her notes from the time she contracted the disease. I wish we'd never been put on that team to study it, but at least I know she'll be happy we're about to crush the damn thing. Do you know that MPN is now the number one killer worldwide? Takes a half a million people a year. There's a strain in Iran that's especially nasty. Even little kids are getting it. Of course, they die off almost immediately, less than a year, but not before it does its worst to them. It breaks my heart to see their little bodies grow those extra limbs that are completely useless and other growths that are without any known use whatsoever. How this monster bug came into being is still a mystery and I'm not sure I *want* to know.

"As for sleep, well, let me tell you that the older you get, the less sleep you need... at night. Of course, night and day are a little messed up out there. You'll be in total sunshine, look down, and the ground is still dark. Weird."

She noted the fierceness in his eyes when he spoke of conquering the disease that had taken her mother. And that was good; he needed something to keep him occupied and focused. But she wondered what would happen if tomorrow he made that breakthrough that spelled the end of the ravaging plague that had caused so much pain and heartache across the planet for the past twenty-five years. Her parents were highly respected scientists in bio-forensics and had been given a government contract to lead a blue ribbon team of scientists whose sole objective was to kill the MPN bug forever.

"I know you'll succeed, Dad. I know it. And, yes, Mom will be glad when you do. I guess, with her gone, I kind of worry more about you. You know I depend on you, don't you?"

"Ah, Starr darling, you don't have to worry about me. And I've known for years that you don't have to depend on anybody but yourself. You're 'strong in the Force,' remember?"

The phrase from an old video that had influenced quite a few people in the previous century had been used by her father many times while she was growing up. Now it seemed almost a joke, but it still had great meaning coming again from him. "Yes, Dad, I *remember*." She had to bear down to keep from betraying her strong emotions.

"And now, unfortunately, I need to get back to running the country. I've got a Solstice rite to conduct and it won't wait. I'm sorry you'll not be around for it."

"Oh, you can bet I'll be watching while the Lift is taking me back up from Macapá. You better deliver your lines right. Don't make me turn that thing around and come right back down to whack your backside." He smiled warmly and stood up to pull her to him again. Then he stepped back and they touched fingertips as he looked deeply into her eyes. "Merry part, Madam President. Keep the fires burning bright." He seemed to be about to say something else but instead turned quickly and left the room. But she'd seen the tears forming in his eyes and wondered about the feelings that had caused the unusual emotional display in her father.

8

In less than twenty-four hours, the Circle Plaza had been transformed into a sparkling clean field without the bleacher seating used for the inauguration. Starr had chosen to use Goldenrod, the extremely popular rock-chanter and teen idol, as her high priest. He'd flown in a few days before from London for the inauguration. Starr had asked him to act as her priest for the ceremony and he'd kindly accepted. But she hadn't actually met him in the flesh until today and was surprised to find that he dwarfed her by at least six inches. His long legs stretched out from his chair as if they were on the way back to London with the rest of him not going anywhere. When he stood up, she thought he wouldn't stop getting taller!

She knew Goldenrod was just his stage name, but it was an apt one for him. Today, dressed in a shimmering gold long-vest, pants, shoes, and with that signature gold hair, Freddie Macintosh, aka Goldenrod, was a perfect Summer Solstice priest. Of course, the fact that his last three music cubes had gone platinum two weeks *before* their release was another good reason to have him as her counterpart on the center stage.

She knew good theatrics was always a benefit when doing public rituals. And Goldenrod had performed in nineteen holo-vids, four of them as the lead male. And, unlike many teen idols in the vids, he could really act. His last was as a doctor facing the tragedy of his own son dying of MPN. The son was played by Barry Faydor and his wife by Suzette Guzett, the European sex goddess. Starr had seen it and was impressed by the intensity of Goldenrod's work. The scene where the doctor agrees to the euthanasia of his own son left her sobbing. It was that holo-vid that had caused her to ask him to be her priest today.

Like the day before, the stage was set with spider-glass screening. It would not only provide security for everyone on the stage but keep any stray breeze from blowing out candles or chilling the presenters. Above were four video sails that would provide a close view of what was being done throughout the ceremony. The giant screens were seventy-five feet wide and sixty tall, making it possible to see the video from as far as a kilometer away. Even though they were only two dimensional, few people thought of them as old fashioned. There were four of them, each facing one of the four cardinal points of the central circle, and the borders of the sails were colored yellow, red, blue, and green. Starr considered it a nice touch.

Starr noticed that Goldenrod had been watching Lisandra a lot while they were getting ready for the ritual. She knew that Lisandra wouldn't do anything to let her attention stray away from Starr, but she also didn't want Goldenrod distracted from the business of the rite. She drifted over to him while he watched Lisa move around the perimeter of the underground staging area and tapped him on the shoulder. Caught ogling the beautiful agent, he jumped a little when he realized he'd been busted by the president. She laughed at his embarrassment and said in a low voice, "I could arrange an introduction later if you'd like, but right now I'd like your attention, if you please."

His face got bright pink and he looked down briefly while trying to compose himself. "Certainly, Madam President," he muttered. Clearly he'd been hoping for more than an introduction, but she needed him to concentrate and stay focused on the upcoming rite.

Both the summer and winter solstice rites had become a tradition across the country since the amazing gathering of 2044 in Oregon. It was originally instituted as a way for Pagans to express their relief that the eruption of Mt. Rainier hadn't killed anyone. Lady McGuire had convinced the right people that the 'sleeping' volcano was going to give one hell of a bang with almost no warning and the Park Service had performed a miracle by gathering up people, pets, and camping gear in the park itself and transporting them a hundred miles to the north. At the same time, National Guard troops helped everyone south of the mountain to evacuate for a distance of two-hundred miles in a wedge shaped area. Just two hours after the last of the troops had reported that the area was as clear as possible, Rainier blew a small puff of smoke and then... nothing.

Scientists, Army Corps of Engineers, politicians, and about a billion Internet observers began to scoff after thirty minutes of holding their breaths. It had all been a big scare with no fireworks. Several million people began to get very angry with the woman who had perpetrated what some considered as the biggest fraud since the weapons of mass destruction fiasco of G. W. Bush, a president who had little understanding of international intelligence and even less of the national will.

And then it went off. It was later determined that it was the largest single volcanic explosion ever recorded. Its force was about three hundred times that of the strongest of the Mt. St. Helen eruptions in the early 1980's. The pyroclastic flow of dust and gas that covered most of southwestern Washington state had also made Portland as dark as night at three in the afternoon. It stayed dark for three days.

Though there were still traces of the eruption in the upper atmosphere thirty years later, the most notable legacy of the Rainier eruption had been the escalation of Lady McGuire in the public's eyes as well as a much better view of Pagans in general. It was estimated that she had possibly saved over three million lives. So when some local groups had asked to hold a public celebration of the summer solstice in a state park in central Oregon and a much younger Lady McGuire had asked the governor of the state to let it happen, the only thing left to arrange was who would call the quarters.

Even though the gathering wasn't well advertised, in the two-week time between getting permission and actually occupying the site, the word had spread to every corner of the continent and the park was overflowing with almost a million Pagans of every sort coming to the ritual. Commercial campgrounds, motels, bed and breakfast houses, and nearly every bare patch of land that could accommodate a tent for seventy miles around the park had Pagans dancing, singing, making love and merriment galore. Unlike the rock festival in the previous century known as Woodstock, however, there was very little cleanup needed afterwards. From that time until the present, solstice celebrations had become part of the American tradition. Now, many non-Pagans took the day of, the day before, and the day after the solstice as almost a national holiday. Some employers had actually told their employees that they wouldn't expect them into work until two days after the solstice. Then they'd close up and go to one of the thousands of circles that had come to dot the land.

Now the president would lead the huge solstice gathering in the heart of the nation's capitol and there hadn't been even a ripple of objection from any quarter. If ever there was an indication that Paganism had 'made it,' it had to be this very celebration, Starr thought. But this success also was perhaps a sign of troubles to come. What was once a Bohemian spirituality had obviously become a popular fashion. She thought of the accusations from Stamper and his cronies about how the Paganism of today was 'impure' and knew that most of the solstice celebrations conducted today would pander to the not-very-spiritual populace. She had to admit there were at least a few grains of truth to his rantings. But she was determined that this circle would be true to the ideals and spiritual sensibilities of the Pagan populace of her country.

It had nothing to do with her election to the highest office in the land that she was to lead the celebration today. Or at least, it had very *little* to do with it. It was a given that whomever was chosen to serve as high priestess had to be well known. Holo-vid executives wanted viewers, and celebrity names helped do just that. Starr was flattered that she had been asked. The fact that this solstice followed the day after the third Saturday of June made it all the more noteworthy and H-V execs had capitalized on the event. But that wasn't any reason for it to be entirely a commercial event in her mind. Yes, they'd signed up Goldenrod and the girl acting as Maiden would be a young and beautiful starlet from one of the H-V evening drama series. But Starr had sat down better than a month before and discussed her take on the event with the six other people who would be presenting the nationally broadcast celebration. She had come away from their teleconference feeling confident they were all on the same page concerning the importance of the spiritual aspects of the rite. It was refreshing to know that everyone was dedicated to this being a beautiful and moving experience. She had previously made several recommendations to the writers and director of the event. Thankfully, they had listened to her and some of what she considered gratuitous or frivolous had been either changed or eliminated. She'd had to give way to their demands to break for a commercial right after the rite, but the one thing she wouldn't back down from was her stand that each and every person on the circle would be Pagan. She'd told the producers that if she wasn't satisfied with the people who would be tagged for the other positions, she'd back out in a heartbeat.

So there were four quarter/Element callers, the Maiden, High Priest, and herself... seven people who would have the honor of presenting a holovized broadcast of the National Solstice Celebration. Waiting for the cue to take their places on the staging elevator, Starr strove for inner clam and focus but it was difficult. MaryAnn Harris, the young actress from the show, *A Small Circle of Friends*, came over to her, smiled, and took the president's hands in hers.

"A little exciting, isn't it? But you've been on the holo plenty of times before and you were great yesterday at your inauguration. Why so nervous today?"

The girl was so composed, Starr was humbled. The youngster's natural poise wasn't an act, of that she was sure. And the president had to admit it was contagious. The simple act of touching and *being there* for the president had made a magical change in Starr's energy. She smiled back at the elf-like starlet in thanks and said, "You're right, I have been on the holo lots of times. And I've performed this rite for thousands. But today, it all seems so *important* to me. I guess I'm not very good at staying grounded for things like this, sorry to say."

The girl cocked her head and raised her eyebrow. "Of course it's important. And if you didn't care, you wouldn't be nervous. My thespian coach says we need to use that nervous energy to get deeper inside of us, to reach down to our core where all things are possible and to find that one perfect piece of us that completes the moment. It works, you know. The Goddess is in each of us and we just need to find the right part of Her to do the right magic, to complete the moment. They chose you for High Priestess because the Goddess is so close to the surface in you. You hardly have to reach, I can see it."

Starr couldn't believe that such beauty and wisdom could be gifted to her through this daughter of the Goddess. Here she was, the president of the United States and a young girl was a thousand times wiser than she about what was happening. She had to fight back tears as she pulled the girl close to her and hugged her tightly. "Oh, MaryAnn, thank you... *thank you*," she murmured into her ear. "You are the *perfect* Maiden for me."

When they broke apart, a makeup person came over to the president and admonished her for smearing her makeup at the last moment, then did a quick touch-up and floated away. Right then, a bell sounded and the director said, "Places, places everyone." The seven presenters quickly moved to their spots on the elevator and the guardrails came up around them. As it rose, they jockeyed around a little, but by the time the platform was level with the great stage, they all were ready for the rite to begin.

Each presenter had both throat sound pickups as well as an earphone in each ear. The left earpiece was for the director to give orders if necessary and the right one was to hear exactly what could be heard from the other presenters' throat devices. Special contact lenses, invisible to the audience, allowed each person to read their lines if they hadn't memorized them and the production computers kept every contact in sync with the others. The system worked perfectly for such productions and it was usually impossible for anyone to know if a presenter had read the line, or just knew it by heart.

Goldenrod stepped off the platform first and held up a hand to quiet the cheering audience in the great plaza. Just as the day before, the resulting silence seemed almost unnatural to Starr. She waited for the Priest to deliver the traditional lines that would signal the beginning of the ritual. They were the same words spoken on that solstice celebration in Oregon many years before.

"There is no greater magic than Love; there is no truer act than Trust. Let all who come to this circle do so in Perfect Love and Perfect Trust."

The traditional response from the spectators came back to them like a wave: "SO MOTE IT BE!" Then cheering erupted from what was probably half a million throats as the rest of the presentation team stepped off the platform and assumed their places. As soon as the Maiden picked up her broom, the crowd quieted to hear the sweeping chant she would use.

"Sweep away pain,
Sweep away strife.
Sweep away the strain
Of a suffering life."

"Sweep in the love,
Sweep in the light,
Sweep in the energy
That will win the fight."

Though the lines were simple, Starr marveled at MaryAnn's delivery. The girl made the words seem like something from Shakespeare and she appeared almost to float around the stage. So soft and flowing were her movements, it seemed she never touched the ground. MaryAnn was a lovely young woman, but today she was the total... the *complete* Maiden. Starr smiled to herself as she recalled Lady McGuire's comments about exciting the 'old goats' when she was young. MaryAnn quite possibly was doing even better than that.

Having made her sweep both widdershins and deosil, the Maiden returned the broom to lie under the central altar. As she did so, the woman who had taken up the position at the eastern quadrant of the circular stage stepped up to the altar and lit a yellow candle there. She picked it up and turned out to the audience.

"May this light of inspiration brighten the path for all on this solstice day. Let your mind be free and your wonders great. With this light, look ahead to a world at peace and in harmony with the forces of nature."

Again, "SO MOTE IT BE" was the response. The east quarter caller returned to her position at the perimeter as the young man guarding the south quadrant stepped up to light the red candle. He too turned and addressed the audience.

"Every thought, every question must have energy behind it or it disappears with the wind. Let us all be energized by the sunny days ahead and by the promise of the bright future we all work for."

The west caller lit her blue candle and said, "Precious water, essence of all life, we ask you to forgive the ways of our ancestors. We know now the true meaning of the clear brooks and sweet rains and ask that you flow again in great abundance."

The roar of, "SO MOTE IT BE," was nearly a crushing blow from the people. Starr shared their distress over the terrible problem of usable water. The whole planet was hurting because of it.

Finally, the earth quarter stepped up and lit his green candle. "We all are made from earth. The Earth is our Mother; we must take care of her. Walk lightly upon her face and respect her ways, for though we travel to other parts of our solar system, this is our home, our life, and our only hope."

This time, a somber and more subdued, "SO MOTE IT BE," was heard from the people, a mere murmur compared to their response to the words from the western caller. But this perhaps was the most heart-felt response of all.

Starr let the moment linger. Even though this ceremony was to be a celebration of life and light, the troubles faced by everyone on the planet because of the irresponsible actions of just the last few hundred years were dire. Without acknowledging those problems, there would be little hope for a brighter future. That sort of willful ignorance was exactly what had gotten the planet into the mess to begin with.

Finally, when the people surrounding the center stage began to stir again, Starr stepped to the altar and picked up the last candle, the white one. Holding it high and walking slowly around to get fire from each of the other candles, she spoke to them all. "No matter your faith or how you perceive the gods, the brightness of this day, the longest day of the year, serves to brighten the hearts of us all. With the mid-day sun giving us its warmth and light, we come together in companionship and good will. No matter our differences or disagreements, for at least this one night let us put them aside and recognize that we are all one people on our planet. We are all brothers and sisters, mothers and fathers, children of the same ancestors. We all seek the same goals of health, wealth, and wisdom and none of us will know real peace until *all* of us can achieve those goals.

"Just as this Spirit candle shines with the fires of each of the Elements, so too must our lives shine with the balanced light available only through one another."

She placed the candle back on the central altar and turned. Slowly she approached Goldenrod, her priest for the day, and placed her fingers softly on his temples.

"By the light of the rising sun... by the warmth of the human heart... by the power of our collective will, I call upon the divine that dwells within us all to come forth through this child of the light. Let him see with the vision of truth. Let his heart beat with the power of our combined love. Let him speak with the wisdom of the ages." Lowering her hands and stepping back to bow before her priest, she said the final words of the invocation. "And let him carry the greatness of our people in his soul for the fortune of us all."

The central stage was the very model of the most current technology, complete with holo-projectors, an enormous variety of lighting gadgets controlled by computer to thousandths of a second, and audio capacities from below to above the range of human hearing. But much of it was not in use for this event. Even though such devices might have been able to achieve something grand, they never would have been able to duplicate what happened next.

The change that Goldenrod manifested was more than theatrics. It appeared as if he grew not just in height, but became larger in every way. His eyes seemed to glow with a strange light and his skin... she would swear it had become like red gold!

He smiled at her, then turned to the audience and the cameras. "I am the heat of passion and the brightness of a child's smile. I am the fire of love and the warmth of a long friendship. I am the ease of summer days and the whispered promise in the dark winter's night. Use this, the longest day to forge peace and cooperation among you. There is no greater magic than love for the Earth and all of its creatures.

"And if you make a wish upon my reflection in cool, clear water, know that your true hearts' desires will be made manifest. My fires consume, transform, and empower your lives now and evermore and all my energy is at your command so long as you live in harmony with The Lady, your Mother, the Earth.

"Live each day at peace with your neighbor and in harmony with the Earth and you will feel my light and warmth in your heart every day of the year. I will shine through you and upon you. For you all are children of the Earth and the Sun, loved equally and fully."

By now, he was actually prancing around the stage just as a stag would for his harem. Though Starr had seen many priests who could channel this sort of energy well, she'd never before seen such a keen understanding of how to show the masculine energy of the god. She noted how MaryAnn watched him and smiled to herself knowingly. She hoped they waited until they got back to the hotel before starting anything.

Her priest was nearly done with his lines and he came back to the central altar and gathered up the large snifter glass filled with a golden wine. Facing out again and slowly turning, he delivered the final invocation as he saluted them with the glass held high. "All that is dreamed may come to be; blessed are the Blessed Be! Live, laugh, and love in my name and you will give true worship to me this day." In one draw, he downed the entire contents of the glass and then walked over to the Maiden, captured her in his arms and gave her a ravishing kiss that was in no way mere theatrics.

The audience went wild, cheering and shouting them both on and Starr wondered if the whole broadcast would have to be blacked out in only a few more moments. Fortunately, both Goldenrod and MaryAnn had to come up for air. Amid the roar from the audience, they each looked deeply into the eyes of the other, making Starr fervently hope the stage was fireproof.

The energy between the two was so powerful and raw it almost could be seen as a physical light. The moment was stretched as far as humanly possible and then stretched a little bit more. Slowly they parted and the people eventually quieted until a hush settled on the entire field and stage. Goldenrod turned to the audience and raised the now empty glass again to them all and shouted, "So mote it be!" Though many shouted back with "SO MOTE IT BE," it was nearly drowned out with the additional cheering and stomping from everyone.

From overhead, two hoverflats rushed over the crowd dropping chocolate 'sunshines' wrapped in gold foil. Everyone cheered and dashed around to catch as many of the disks as possible as everyone on stage watched the energy that had been built to such a peak get grounded with laughter and good spirits. Starr was standing closest to the northern element caller who was laughing and pointing to a trio of two young women and an obviously lucky man not far from the spider-glass barrier. The women were smearing the chocolate all over the young man's chest and face and licking it off in a most erotic way. She knew there were possibly much more explicit things going on in other parts of the gathering and decided it was time to finish the rite before it devolved into something the tabloids would find a way to attach to her and her office. She stepped to the edge of the stage and began to walk the perimeter, speaking in calm and measured tones.

"And now it is time to end this rite. We thank the Elements and the Sun for its light. With laughter and love we will celebrate life and to all our relations we offer the magical three: 'Merry meet... merry part... and Blessed Be!" Then, amid more cheering and applause, the people on stage gathered the props they'd brought with them and stepped onto the platform that would lower them to the space below. As was the tradition, Starr had to carry the white candle that would burn until the next dawn. Because of that, she missed the first lowering of the platform and had to wait with two of the element callers for it to rise again. When she finally did make it down, she wasn't surprised to see that Goldenrod and MaryAnn had disappeared ahead of the rest of the people involved in the event production.

Lisandra approached her as soon as she stepped off the platform. "That was really powerful, Madam President; congratulations." Then she leaned closer and said, "I thought Mr. Macintosh was going to nail MaryAnn right on stage there for a moment."

"Or she was going to get him. I take it they both have left?"

"Oh yes, indeed they did. I don't think they bothered saying good-bye to anyone; they just jumped in one of the carts and zoomed out of here. Probably set a new land-speed record. I think I heard a sonic boom about two seconds after they rounded that corner there."

"Ah," the president sighed, "there's nothing like true lust."

❧ 9 ❧

It took only a few more minutes before the president was being whisked back to the limo that waited for her at the entrance to the Circle Plaza. A short time later, Starr made a show of carefully carrying the shielded candle into the White House where it was placed in one of the windows so the press could see that it was still burning.

She went immediately up to her private rooms to change for the upcoming meeting with the Joint Chiefs. The two hours she'd spent on the Solstice ceremony had taken a surprising amount of her energy and she poured a large cup of coffee as she refreshed herself and put on a tan blouse, darker brown skirt, and burgundy jacket. She walked over to the vanity in the large washroom to pick up the gold necklace she'd chosen earlier that day for her outfit and was surprised by a small red envelope sitting on the vanity's top. It was addressed to "Madam President" with a paste-on label similar to the return address tags used for a hundred years.

She was quite sure the envelope hadn't been there that morning when she left and she was equally sure it should never have been put there by anyone who had access to the rooms. A small but urgent alarm went off in her head and she backed away from the table as she spoke to the computer system that always listened. "Security! Come to my rooms immediately."

She'd exited the washroom only two seconds before the door to her private rooms was thrown open and three armed men and Lisandra rushed in, looking everywhere at once and immediately surrounding the president. Then a whole squad of six people swarmed in and started checking every room, closet, and, yes, even under the bed. Lisandra turned to the president and asked, "What is it?"

Starr pointed to the washroom. "The washroom... on the vanity... a red envelope. It wasn't there this morning." Lisandra motioned two agents to investigate and then started ushering the president out of the area as she called for a bomb sniffer to be brought to the rooms. In less than a minute, the president was in what everyone called the Panic Room, a subbasement chamber in the White House that was supposed to be able to take a four-ton direct hit and a bowl of water wouldn't even show a ripple. It was lead-lined and had its own electrical generator and sanitary facilities. Fortunately, it also had plenty of room for comfortable seating for the president and her cadre of guards.

It was a tense and quiet twenty minutes before the speaker unit on the wall buzzed. Lisandra spoke with someone in the upper levels and then said to Starr, "They've cleared everything, Madam President. You can go back up whenever you wish." Starr looked at her watch and nodded. "Was there any note in that thing?"

"Yes. They're checking it over now out in the van. If it checks out, they'll bring it back right away. I assume you'll want to know what it says?"

"Just show it to me on the monitor in the blue room. I'm going there now for my meeting. But ask the Joint Chiefs to give me a moment before showing them in, please."

"Certainly, Madam President, I'll see to it." Lisandra spoke quietly into her pickup as she left the president at the elevator and walked quickly down the hall to wherever chief agents went under the circumstances. Starr wasn't afraid as much as she was angry. That her security could be breached in this manner was more threatening than anything that might be in that envelope. She was sure that Lisandra was going to have a few heads on a platter before the end of the day.

When she walked into the meeting room, there were two Service officers still there. "Is there still a problem with this room or is it clear, gentlemen?" She didn't want to share whatever was in that red envelope with everybody just yet. She reached to turn on the screen at the desk on the east wall. She waited until the two agents had exited before speaking. "This is the president. Give me the PTAT guys." The presidential Threat Analysis Team was an integral part of the Service's coverage of the president. No matter where or when, they had the ability to analyze any kind of evidence connected with a real or perceived threat to the president. Ten days before the inauguration, President-elect Draper had been thoroughly briefed about most of the security measures that would be her constant companions while in office. She'd met the fellow who was the head of the PTAT (pee-tat) group. He could easily have been the poster-boy for Nerds International but she had liked him immediately. Now Franklyn F. Franklyn's face filled her communication screen almost instantly. Wearing old fashion eyeglasses that he was constantly pushing up his too-narrow nose, he smiled like a shy schoolboy at her.

"Yes, Ms. President," his White House etiquette was not the best but it didn't matter to her. She wanted to know what... if anything... was in the red envelope. Fortunately, 3F (what everybody called him behind is back) didn't have to be told that was what she wanted to see. "I've put the card under the SARPA" (she had no idea what that was) "and both of the Mann machines" (again, no clue) "and there's nothing there... just printer paper and ink... we'll see if that leads anywhere, but I personally doubt it; of course, we might get lucky on the paper; sometimes that happens, but, of course, we got some oily stuff that probably isn't part of the ink and maybe we'll get a hit on that and there's a funny shape to the 'y' and 'a' and that could nail the dummy who printed it but the best part is the envelope itself... probably a specialty paper... and I'm glad to report we couldn't find any poison or bio-stuff, but maybe you shouldn't be exposed to it just to be on the safe side, don't you agree?"

She was sure he could continue his monologue for another five days if she didn't interrupt him. "I need to see what the note said, Frank. Put it on, will you, please?"

"The note? The note? Oh, yes, of course." He looked around as if it was now the last thing he expected her to ask about. Then his face lit up and he moved off the screen for a few seconds. The view changed and she was reading what she presumed was the card that had been inside the red envelope. She read through it several times, getting angrier each time.

"Send a copy to me in the Blue Room, Frank. Thank you." She was about to switch off but then said, "Connect me to Helios, wherever he is."

Fifteen seconds later, her CoS appeared on the screen. "Yes, Madam President?"

"I need to meet with Allen and Maggie, and you, too. Keep it on the QT, but make it tonight." She didn't wait for an acknowledgment; it was obvious she was going to have to address the Stamper problem sooner rather than later. In the greater scheme of things, this wasn't nearly as big a problem as the water shortage or any number of other issues she was concerned with. But it was in her face and she wanted to deal with it now so it didn't grow into a larger problem.

❧ 10 ❧

They were gathered in the same dining room Starr had been in the morning of her inauguration. She had automatically taken the same place the outgoing President had used when they'd had that meeting. She recalled him saying that the problems they'd discussed were going to be her problems, not his, and he was obviously pleased he could finally pass the scepter. She idly wondered if he'd gotten his fishing rod out yet. Maybe he was at this very moment sitting on the end of the dock at his Florence Lake cabin in California's High Sierra country, watching the stars come out, truly relaxing for the first time in eight years. She already was beginning to envy him and it made her chuckle.

Maggie looked up from reading the message and raised an eyebrow. "I'm afraid I don't see what's funny, Madam President."

"Oh, nothing about *that*, Maggie. I was just recalling something my predecessor said just yesterday. Believe me, I don't find *anything* humorous about *that*." She pointed to the copy Maggie was passing to Barnstead. Starr had asked Lisandra to join them as well as her Chief of Staff. Although she was a Secret Service agent, Starr thought it useful to get Lisa up to speed on the Stamper situation and hoped the agent's people had perhaps found out who had placed it in the president's private quarters.

Allen passed the page on to Helios and shook his head. "What I can't figure out is why they went to so much trouble to send this to you in the manner they did. I mean, why even bother? It all seems so childish in a way. If you've got any sense, you don't warn a person that you're going to bring them down. Not in this town, anyway."

Lisandra spoke up then. "Ritualized behavior. Stamper's people are formally declaring the president to be their target. At least, we're assuming it's connected to Stamper. This is the equivalent of a slap in the face with a glove, as it were."

"A challenge?" Lady McGuire wondered if that was the only reason. "Maybe, but I'll bet it also was meant to intimidate and force the president's hand. Stamper, or whoever arranged this, might be trying to see how she'd react. He might think she doesn't know about his little game, though I doubt that he's that foolish. It's the opening salvo in a mind-game. It's a challenge, a warning, and a bit of war-psych all in one."

Helios read one of the lines out loud. "*You have made the waters impure and will suffer your own poisoning.*' What kind of stuff is that? It sounds like a bad vid script."

It was Lisandra that responded. Of the five of them, she had studied the note the most. "Read it from the top, Mr. D'Amico. Most of what's written there has some very complex meaning if you're Wiccan. It might sound like it rambles around but it's pitch perfect to a witch."

Helios read the note again, as Lisa had instructed. He too knew it wouldn't have made much sense to those unfamiliar with Wicca. But he wanted to see if he could find any more meaning from the note, any further clue about the sender or what it might portend.

"*The farce of the public Solstice was a very bad idea.*
Your power as president will wane with the fading light.
You have made the waters impure and will suffer your own poisoning.
Though you eat well and have much wealth, you will be buried by your foolishness.
Despair and wail, for your ghost will forever wander the Wasteland.'

"It still reads like something out of a B video. The only line that seems even halfway sane is the first one. Whoever wrote this is certifiable."

"Don't dismiss this so easily, Helios," Lady McGuire cautioned. "It's a carefully worked piece of magic. The person who created this knows their stuff. Each line comes from one of the Elements. The first is Air; the 'bad idea' and reference to a particular *time* is all part of the Air Element. The second line is Fire. It refers to 'power' and light. The third is obviously Water. In fact, I think it is a twist on the old Spell of Making warning about how if your Water is impure, you'll be poisoned. That's pretty obscure but it may be a clue about where the writer is coming from. The fourth line talks about things from the Earth Element. And the last is all about Spirit."

"So this is a curse, is that what you're saying, Maggie?"

"Exactly, Madam President. It follows the standard formula for that kind of spell. And I would be very surprised if the envelope, paper, and ink hadn't been subjected to some sort of spell craft as well. Of course, that wouldn't be detectable by any sort of laboratory analysis, but if we got the original pieces to a psychometrist, I'd wager they'd be able to tell us a lot more about our perpetrator."

The president looked over to Lisandra. "Find one, a *good* one and get those pieces to them."

The agent nodded and wrote something on her pad.

"Anything from the surveillance cameras?" Starr knew every inch of her new home was constantly being watched by computer controlled electronic eyes. Even the bathrooms. While it might be uncomfortable to know that you had not even a hint of privacy, she also knew that no humans would ever see much of those more private areas unless it was absolutely necessary. But she was sure that Lisandra had to have pulled the last twenty-four hours worth and put them through careful computer screening to find out who had access to the dressing table where the envelope had been placed.

The agent lowered her eyes and shook her head. "Nothing, Madam President. The cameras went dark in much of the residence areas six hours before you found the note and for some reason the computer never gave us an alarm. I've got a tech trying to figure how, but, so far, we're stymied there. And we haven't gotten any hits on DNA tracing for the envelope or the note inside." Starr noted that Lisa looked ashamed at these negative results but she was sure it wasn't due to any mistakes or lack of diligence on the part of the Service.

Next, she turned to Barnstead. "You've been remarkably quiet throughout this whole meeting, Allen. I'm sure all of us would like to know what, if anything, you've managed to make of all this."

He looked up at the president, then over to Lady McGuire and Lisandra. Finally, he looked to Helios, who was sitting next to him. He looked back at the president again, and spoke quietly." Forgive me, Madam President, but I've been trying to pick up on anybody who might be worried about what we're all doing here tonight. I wanted to see if I could find any stray thoughts that might be suspicious."

"Surely you don't think one of us in this room had anything to do with this, do you? If so, speak up, man."

"No. No, I don't have any reason to suspect anyone here. But there're about fifty other people in this building that I've tried to read. Some of them have remarkable shielding; others are as transparent as glass. By the way, Helios," he said to the Chief of Staff with a grin, "be careful of the communications tech in the president's office. She's got a bad crush on you." The psychic smiled at the look on Helios' face but then turned back to the president. "As far as I can tell, none of those people had anything to do with this incident. But as I say, some of these folks are well shielded. And some of them aren't here tonight, of course. Also, I can't be sure I've been able to get everything from a lot of them because they keep getting too far away. They come back for a moment and then take off again. It's difficult."

She thought for a moment, then said, "Lisa, Helios, see to it that Allen has full clearance to walk around here tomorrow morning. Allen, I want you to give me a report by noon on anything you *might* consider suspicious." She rose, signaling their meeting was over. "Thank you all for coming at this late hour. I appreciate it."

Lisandra and the two men walked out, but Lady McGuire stayed in the room with the president until they were gone. Starr gave the older woman a look and raised an eyebrow. "You had something to add, Maggie?"

"Yes, I do Starr. This," she waived the sheet with the words from the note, "is not to be taken lightly. It's a curse, a spell. And it's working. It's gotten you to act in a very predictable way, a way I'm sure the maker of this spell had to be able to foresee. I can't help but think that, knowing pretty much how it would be acted on, it might be a distraction. While your mind is set upon the note and its contents, something else might be going on the spell crafter doesn't want you... or Lisa... to notice. Be very, *very* careful. I seriously doubt that we're playing with an amateur here. By your own estimate, you're a mediocre magic worker at best. Trust very few around you."

The president studied the woman closely and said nothing for a few seconds. "Do you *see* something, Maggie? Are you trying to warn me about something but don't want to disclose it because doing so might actually make it happen? Is that what's happening here?"

A hint of a smile touched the older woman's mouth for a moment. "You're not as *un*-psychic as you think, Starr Draper." She patted the president's hand and turned to leave. But just before she went through the door, she looked back over her shoulder and said, "You're best when you use that talent, Madam President. Go with your gut; it works a lot better than you think."

Starr stood there, thinking about the seer's words a moment longer. Then she squared her shoulders and walked back to her office. There were still about a hundred other things that required her attention that hour besides this mystery. She had a country to run and it needed her full-time attention.

~ 11 ~

When the fossil fuels started to look like they were going to dry up in the late twentieth century, everyone began to look for alternative sources of energy. At the time there were several contenders to take the place oil had played in making personal transport continue as the most common form of getting from point A to point B. In the latter half of the twenty-first century, public transportation had gained in use nearly ten-fold. But use of personal carriers had not gone away. Roads still crisscrossed the land and under the oceans. Oil was used only for a small list of industrial applications now but substitutes were being found for most of those on a regular basis.

Automobiles, considered a staple of twentieth century commerce, were now much smaller and safer than their ancestors and they no longer ran on fossil fuel; they ran on water. Technically, they ran on the same principle as the old gasoline engines: they exploded. That explosion was contained and used to drive a shaft that made the wheels turn and the vehicle move down a road. Because the basic mechanics had not changed too radically, the H_2O engine was less expensive to build and maintain than some other possible designs. And it had the subtle advantage of making the public feel comfortable with the new technology; the new engines ran mostly like the old petroleum ones. They had much the same look and feel, and wasn't it wonderful that they had zero harmful emissions?

It took nearly twenty years for the world to recognize that though the engines expelled water as their only emission, that water was not the life giving liquid that every living thing on the planet required. For several years, it wasn't even known how the water from the exhaust of an H_2O engine differed from the kind everyone used in their cooking pots. Though he was the bearer of very bad news, the person who actually discovered the truth received the Nobel for his work. The water from hundreds of millions of automobiles was a strangely married molecule formed from three normal water molecules. Though it contained all of the atoms of those three, it somehow could not be used by any living cells on the planet. And the amount of 'dead water' in the atmosphere was increasing rapidly. In 2067, the UN announced that it was above 5% and growing rapidly.

As usual, politicians wrung their hands and looked around to see who could be blamed. But the common people of the world were just as irresponsible. They kept on buying autos that ran on water and then would drive to rallies to protest the effects of those autos. The only 'good' news about the 'dead water' was that it could still operate as fuel for their cars. The bad news was that the irony of that was lost on most people.

Though engines using water as fuel had been around for nearly a hundred years, the H_2O engine departed from the previous concepts in one important way. Instead of breaking down the water to extract hydrogen and then burning only that with oxygen from the atmosphere, the H_2O engine broke the water apart and then recombined it in the cylinder. The result was slightly less power than burning just hydrogen, but the technology needed to do it was a hundred times more simple and cheaper. It came from Mars.

The first flight to Mars that also returned with soil and atmospheric samples brought with it some very big mysteries, not the least of which was a strange *porous* crystalline deposit the media quickly dubbed the 'impossible crystal'. This combination of carbon, boron, nickel, and silver was, according to modern chemists, impossible to make. Every chemist in the world tried to understand how the crystalline structure was possible as well as why it was so abundant in the surface layer of soil brought back from Mars in 2021. Scientists all over the world studied the material and scratched their heads.

It was in 2025 when a junior chemistry major at the small University of Gröttenburg made a most amazing discovery about the 'impossible crystal': it was a fantastically efficient catalyst for separating water into hydrogen and oxygen. His discovery was made into a revolutionary technology in just eight short months. If the 'impossible crystal' could be obtained in sufficient quantity, the 'IC' (impossible crystal) fuel injector would make water engines work almost exactly like a gasoline-powered engine. An extremely small sphere of the IC in a fuel injector similar to the ones used for gasoline would separate the water into hydrogen and oxygen as it was pumped into the cylinder. The two gases would explode and water vapor exhausted. Though it wasn't as powerful as a hydrogen-only engine, it was much cheaper... if you could get the crystal, that is.

Commercial space flight had already begun mining on the moon and industrial giants had set their eyes on Mars before the IC injector had been invented. But its introduction made a demand for Martian dirt that would not go away. Venture capital and funding for Martian mining made for some very risky investment opportunities. And, as always, the greater the risk, the more that could be made for those willing to take that risk. Eric Stamper was able to put together a consortium that financed the first real mining ship to Mars and his fortune was made on its return. A little better than forty-five years after that momentous adventure, Stamper was still in control of most of the shipping to Mars and back. His empire was also stretching into the asteroid belt and speculation about how that would affect his net worth was universally positive. The so-called 'Wizard of Mars' would never have to worry about useable drinking water; he was rich enough to buy it even if it were the very last drop.

Simply eliminating the IC would stop the problem from growing, of course. But the economics of such a move were almost as bad as the problem itself. The public kept hoping for another impossible crystal, one that turned the dead water back into life-giving water molecules. But so far, that was only a wish. Estimates of when the good water supply would be 'drowned out' by dead water ranged anywhere from fifty to three hundred years. In other words, nobody knew. Subsequent explorations of Mars confirmed speculations about the water supplies that had been discovered lying under the surface and at the poles: they were nearly a hundred percent dead water. Every nation on Earth was desperate to solve the problem. Unlike land or other resources, the water supply was not going to be any better in the country next door than it was in your own country. Global warming had taken a great deal of the glacial ice from the extreme north and south areas of the globe and even the trillions of gallons of water still available in what remained would delay the problem only by a year or two at best.

Few people appreciated the problem more than President Draper. Though her campaign had been a long and sometimes acrimonious fight, one thing both she and her two opponents had agreed on was the importance of solving the water problem. Her approach was a balance between alternative engines and finding a way to raise water from the dead. For her, the problem was the most important one the country... indeed, the world... had to solve. But it wasn't the most imminent. The job of being the president was in some ways a crazy mix of fluffy ceremonial events that had nothing to do with the country's welfare and crushing responsibilities at the center of various crises. When she arose the next morning, Starr didn't have time to think about the red envelope from the day before. There were many more things that had to receive her attention and direction. Only a few days into her office and the workload was already enormous.

On a three-masted sailing ship, built to look like an eighteenth century schooner, Eric Stamper lounged with his feet propped up on the stern rail twenty feet above the water. He gestured with the same hand that held a glass of pale wine as he spoke to the man and woman seated next to him. "It's not like there isn't any sort of history to check against. Wicca is what it is, not what some people think it should be changed into. You can practice whatever way you want to, but don't tell me it's Wicca unless you can show me the lineage and the ritual that goes back to Gardner. The rest is just a bunch of wannabes who have their head where the sun don't shine." A white-coated waiter silently refilled his glass because most of the wine had sloshed out with his last sentence. The man and woman who listened knew Stamper would probably be done with his favorite rant in a few minutes and they could get on with business, so they politely smiled in agreement and grunted appropriately.

"Now we've got ourselves a president who insists on making a spectacle of herself, pretending to be a Wiccan priestess. I mean, have you ever seen such a phony stage show as that thing she did in D.C. on Sunday?" He spit over the rail to show his opinion of the broadcasted solstice ceremony. "It's high time we stopped this farce. Honest witches don't prance around a stage and wave to the crowd. That's no way to act, making a mockery of it." He banged his glass down so hard it shattered, throwing pieces of glass everywhere and his companions flinched. "Ah Hades!" Two waiters immediately swept away the mess. Stamper hardly noticed. "Mark my words, these phony witches are going to find out it's wrong to make fun of the gods; you just watch. They'll know better than to make our rituals into a freak show. Pretty soon, they won't dare to poke their noses above ground. You just wait and see."

"Mr. Stamper..."

"Oh for the love of Isis, Cassie, we sleep together. Call me Eric."

The man had no idea how unsettling he could be, but Cassandra Whatcom was used to it and she was impossible to rattle. She continued as if his interruption hadn't even happened. "I was going to remind you that the Armstrong is due to arrive next week and this strike is going to cost us millions if we can't find a way to settle it soon."

"Well, I'm not going to give in to those South American ingrates and that's it. Tell the crew they're going to have to go into orbit until I can get this Juncito what's-his-name to bow to my terms."

"But sir," the heavyset man spoke up, "they're only asking for a one percent raise."

"*And*," he held up three fingers, "three extra holidays a year! Do you know how much that'll cost, Carter?"

"They're Catholic holy days, sir. And they're offering to work the solstices and equinoxes in exchange."

"Exactly, Carter. They're a bunch of damn Catholics. They can practice whatever faith they want, but not on *my* time. If they can't accommodate my schedule, I don't see why I should accommodate theirs."

"Because it will profit us, sir. They're asking for three days off and giving back four. Even if we give them the raise, we'll be gaining. Keeping the plants up and running during the holidays saves us a bundle. Bob Willis, your top accountant, he figures a half-percent gain, sir. Parking the Armstrong in orbit for just two days will cost more than that."

"I don't care! It could cost ten times that and I'd still do it. You may not understand this, Carter, but it's the *principle* of the thing. No damn Catholics are ever going to dictate terms to witches ever again! It won't happen!" He stood up and paced a few steps away from them, then turned back and pointed to Carter. "Get this guy, Julio-or-something to me at the house tonight. I'll put it in words simple enough even he'll understand them." He turned to look at the wheelman and yelled, "Turn this sucker around and get me back to 'Frisco pronto, Charlie." Then he stomped across to the ladder to the lower decks and disappeared below.

Carter followed the man with his eyes until his head was below the deck line. Then he turned to his companion and started to speak. But before he was able to say anything, she held up her hand and shook her head. "You're not going to sway him, Paul, and don't ask me to do it either. Call Bossett and get Juanito Bolar up here tonight." She saw Carter was again about to say something so she stood and leveled a gaze at him. "Just do it, Carter. I'm going to see if I can't calm him down some. He's got high blood pressure and I'll bet he hasn't taken his meds. I'll make him take his pills even if I have to tie him down. You get hold of Bossett." She strode over to the same ladder her boss had taken and went below.

Stamper was pacing back and forth in front of the 2D wall screen that was tuned to a news station. It was re-showing the solstice rite done in the nation's capital the day before and he was throwing glances at it and muttering. Cassandra couldn't make out what he was saying but she knew it probably wasn't nice. She brushed past him and pulled open a drawer. Sure enough, the morning dosage of medications he was supposed to have taken was still in its container. She grabbed it and then went over to the bar to make some iced tea, adding plenty of sugar.

Turning back with the drink and meds, she was glad to see he'd stopped pacing and was now seated, talking to somebody on the personal communicator resting on the table in front of him. Rounding the couch, she noticed the PerCom was dark; the person Stamper was talking to wasn't letting their video through. That was unusual; Stamper normally wouldn't speak with anyone if they didn't show their face. She placed the tray down and then went to the other end of the room to work at her own PerCom for a few minutes. But she kept a wary eye on her boss and was satisfied when he finally upended the tablet container and took a big gulp of the tea she'd prepared. He continued to talk to the blank screen for another ten minutes before sitting back and looking out the stern-facing windows. It was sunny and warm, perfect for relaxing and enjoying the day on the Pacific. But, true to his nature, Stamper didn't appear to be enjoying any of it. The scowl on his face frightened most people but she knew it was his normal look. In fact, since he wasn't grumbling, she guessed he was in a better mood than earlier.

He must have sensed her watching him because he turned his head and caught her eyes. Squinting a little, he held her gaze a moment longer. Then he asked, "What – *exactly* – is your take on our new vice-president, Cassie?"

Without having to think, she answered the question. "Vice-President Hunt is one of the most accomplished and qualified men elected to that position. He has always demonstrated a true understanding and empathy for the common soul and I believe he is that rarest of commodities: an honest politician."

Stamper kept his eyes on her while slowly nodding his head. She began to feel slightly uncomfortable under his prolonged scrutiny. But just as she was about to find a reason to get up and break eye contact, he turned back to look out the stern windows at the western horizon. So she turned back to her desk and was about to make a note on the file she had accessed when she was startled by a horrendous crashing noise. She jumped and turned toward the sound. Stamper was standing over pieces of the coffee table that had been in front of him only a moment before. He was rubbing his right hand and saying the same thing over and over again in a low tone that Cassie knew signaled he was furious.

"Damn, damn, damn, damn..."

Eric Stamper was famous for being cranky. But few people had ever seen him lose control. Cassandra Whatcom hadn't risen to her present place of power at the side of the great Eric Stamper because she'd slept with him, but she'd shared his bed long enough to know that if she tried to leave now, tried to escape from being in the same room, he'd turn and strike out at her like an enraged tiger. Seven years of knowing him intimately had taught her what to do. Others would probably have thought it extremely dangerous, but instead of fleeing from his dark mood, she moved towards the man.

As expected, he snapped his eyes around the instant she started to move. She met his gaze evenly and with assurance, keeping her eyes locked on his, not as a challenge but in respect... and trust. When she was close enough, she reached out without hesitation and surrounded his hands with her own, still holding her eyes steady. He'd stopped mumbling only seconds before and she saw him flinch as she touched him. Yes, Eric Stamper could be afraid. And like a wild animal, he was capable of violence without mercy if not handled correctly when he was like this. Cassie somehow had always known how to sooth the beast within Stamper. It was just one of her many magical talents.

She silently fed him energy for several long seconds, allowing him to put the wild animal back in its cage before speaking to him. "What? What's wrong?"

He didn't answer at first. She saw the inner war still going on behind the hooded eyes and let him take his time. Finally, he took a deep breath and let it out slowly. "Did you know that your answer was word-for-word exactly like two others I've asked today? Did you know that?"

"No, I didn't. But why are you so angry? I would assume that I and whomever else you asked probably got the wording from some campaign ad or something. What seems to be the problem?"

"From a campaign slogan? This late after the election? Everyone remembers *some* of those ads for a while, but *exactly* the same words? What are the chances, Cassie?" He pulled his hands free and said, "Computer: tell Paul Carter to come to my office."

"*Yes, Mr. Stamper. (pause) Done, sir.*"

"Now I want you to go back and sit at your PerCom and act uninterested. But keep your ears open." He patted her hands and gave her a slight push in the right direction and a smile of gratitude.

Paul walked in a minute later, puffing a little from having to move fast. Cassie thought he really needed to exercise more and shed about forty pounds, but she reminded herself that it wasn't any of her business and tried to appear casual while focusing in on Paul's voice.

Stamper had gone back to sitting on the couch, the pieces of the coffee table still on the floor in front of him. When Carter arrived, he rose, gestured toward the table and offered a grin. "Your boss is getting clumsy as hell, Paul. I think I'll replace this thing with one made out of spider-glass." He chuckled and walked over to put a hand on Paul's shoulder. "Paul, you know I value your opinion on a lot of things and you are a tremendous help, even if I don't say it all the time. I know I'm hard to get along with, but I also want you to know I want you to be as open and candid with me as you can be. We might not always see eye to eye, but that doesn't mean I don't want to hear what you've got to say. I guess what I'm saying is I don't like yes-men, Paul. You've shown some spine and I appreciate it. So, with that having been said, I've got to ask you about something that's been bothering me lately."

Carter was flattered by his boss's words; they were a great confidence builder and much needed after Stamper's gruffness with him earlier. He wanted the man's approval and felt validated by his words. "Certainly, sir, what is it you want to talk about?"

Stamper had just told his man that he appreciated candor, but he knew that what he'd really done was reinforce Paul's tendency to agree with most everything his boss said. Now was the test. "Paul, I want to know your opinion on T. J. Hunt, our new Vice-President. I'm wondering if he isn't some sort of flim-flam artist. You know what I mean?"

There was hardly any hesitation before the man replied. "Vice-President Hunt is one of the most accomplished and qualified men elected to that position. He has always demonstrated a true understanding and empathy for the common soul and I believe he is that rarest of commodities: an honest politician."

Stamper smiled and turned to catch Cassandra's eye before continuing his words to Paul. "Thank you, Paul. I'm sure what you just said is your honest opinion, even if it might not jibe with mine. I appreciate it. Now, is that fellow from Brazil coming in tonight?"

"Yes, sir. His flight should land in about four hours. I told him you'd see him at eight. I hope that will be okay, sir?"

"Excellent, Paul, excellent. Well, we'll have dinner a little early and then wait for him to be there at eight." He lightly slapped Paul on the shoulder. "What would I ever do without you, Paul?" The man's dismissal wasn't subtle, but Stamper believed that most messages needed to be obvious with Paul.

When Carter left the room, Stamper turned back to Cassie and lifted both eyebrows. "And that makes *four* today... the exact same words. Still think it's coincidence or a campaign slogan that's especially memorable?"

"Well... no, I guess that would be unlikely. But what do you make of it? You've had plenty of contact with Hunt, especially in the last two years. You certainly gave him a lot of money for the campaign, even after it was obvious he couldn't get the number one spot. Are you now saying you distrust him somehow?"

"Actually, part of me *wants* to trust him. I, like you and Paul, think of TJ as a true-blue patriot and a very accomplished fellow. If I wasn't fighting it, I'd probably say the same things you both said. But think about it for a moment, Cassie. What exactly has Hunt accomplished? What *are* his qualifications? He's been in politics for about thirty years and, frankly, I can't remember anything he's done that is important. Sure, he's won elections. And he knows how to slip-slide out of problems like a greased snake; look what happen with the Detroit Stadium deal when it collapsed. I can't list his qualifications for any office he's had. It just seems that every time he runs for office, he wins. And he's fantastic at raising money. The first time I met him, I wanted to back him. *The first time!* Is that like me, Cassie? Is it?"

"No, it isn't. In fact, you had some rather unflattering things to say about him before that meeting. I was surprised when you both came out of that office. You were shaking hands with him, remember? Well, everybody knows Hunt's reluctance to adopt the five-point greeting. But for *you* to be shaking his hand, well that *was* a surprise."

He snorted and then walked over to stand looking out at the sea. After a minute, he turned back to where his Personal Communicator was sitting on the floor amidst the pieces of the destroyed coffee table. He folded it up, put it in his pocket, and then walked to the doorway that led to the rest of his personal quarters. "Wake me when we tie up. I'm going to get a nap before I see that young Brazilian buck." He closed the door very carefully when he left, which she knew meant he was still exercising tight control to keep from showing his anger. She sighed and called for someone to clean up the pieces of coffee table. Then she walked to her own quarters to get a shower and change into more suitable business attire for their move to the land office. Eric Stamper was a complex man and she didn't pretend to understand him completely, but she loved him. She didn't have any illusions about them as a couple, but she still wanted him to have some peace in his life.

The rest of the world saw him only as an extremely rich man, an iconic figure. But she saw the man underneath that image. He tried so hard to understand the world and to make it fit in with his ideas about what things meant in a more cosmic sense. It just wasn't in his nature to try it the other way around. His stubbornness about changing himself to fit into the world was what had made him rich and powerful... but it had also made him very alone in that world as well.

She had a makeshift altar next to her bed which she now sat in front of. She darkened the room and lit a votive to have a spot to concentrate on. It took only seconds for her to become relaxed and centered while letting her mind roam free. In less than a minute, she began seeing the possible future take form from the energies about her. She resisted the always-present temptation to push those streams of energy into recognizable shapes; such impatience would provide only one possible future and it would be tainted by her own hopes and fears. She waited for the ghostlike forms to select their own meanings. It required discipline, but she had been practicing her art for a long time. She knew the process, and would wait for it to give her what she needed.

◈ 12 ◈

Five days after her inauguration, President Draper was fully immersed in the chaos of running the political business of the country. The pace that was merely hectic at first had quickly evolved into nearly crushing. But Starr Draper had surrounded herself with very capable people and she kept reminding herself that there really was some kind of order to her life, just a matrix of energies that made each moment seem impossibly important or endlessly banal. And sometimes both at the same time.

The red envelope incident had receded into the background and she had put it into the mental pile of things that didn't require her attention because others of better capabilities were doing what was needed. She was in the Oval Office with her Chief of Staff, discussing the agenda and talking points for the upcoming World Water Conference when her secretary notified her Agent Morgan was asking to see her.

She brought with her a very old man who looked like a dwarf from a fairy tale. He was dressed casually in jeans and a red western shirt with silver-tipped collar points. His hair was all the way down his back and she could see a shiny silver streak that looked almost unreal braided in with the glossy black. "Madam President," Lisa said, "I'd like to introduce Dr. Chester Silverwolf, a psychometrist and healer from the Snohomish tribe in Washington State. He has some interesting things to tell us."

The president raised her hand to give greeting, but the man didn't return the gesture. Instead, he looked down and said in a small voice, "Forgive me, but I can't return your greeting in that manner; it would not be wise." She noted that he was wearing gloves and realized the man was protecting himself from unintentional contact. His refusal to touch fingers with her was most likely protection not only for himself but her as well. State secrets should not fall into the wrong hands, especially ones that could discover so much simply through touch.

"Of course; I didn't think. We appreciate your discretion. Agent Morgan says you have something to tell me, doctor."

"Yes. Your people asked me to read an envelope and piece of paper to find out things about who had sent it or at least who wrote it. I've spent the last few days with the objects and I believe I've extracted everything that can be read from them." Though the fellow was diminutive and maybe somewhat comical in appearance, the president recognized a strong inner power in the man. Most people, when they entered into the White House, and most especially into the Oval Office to stand before the president, displayed a great deal of nervousness. But Dr. Silverwolf seemed to be relatively unaffected. Starr guessed the man was used to power in many forms and had made friends with all the Elements a long time ago. A person with such command of self could pose a threat but she knew the Service would have cleared him before letting him get his hands on the envelope and card, let alone come near her. Besides, her own instincts told her the man was truly at peace with the world and didn't have a mean bone in his body.

"I can assure you, Dr. Silverwolf, that everyone here is more than appreciative of your efforts. Please tell us what you have been able to read from the objects." She gestured for everyone to sit as she settled on a nineteenth century French settee near her desk. Lisa, as usual, remained standing. The small man sat carefully on a hassock instead of the chair behind it. He reached into his jacket and brought out a single sheet of paper, which he handed to Lisa to give to the president. But before Starr had a chance to read it, the psychometrist began to speak.

"At first, the envelope was the more interesting of the two objects. It was apparently not subjected to as much energy to clear it as was the card inside of it. The person who wrote on it is a male about my age: sixty, or so. He is not in good health. He has something wrong with his blood but I can't tell you what it might be.

But he doesn't seem to know about the problem or he doesn't care. He is the first born in his family and has a younger brother. Despite the circumstances that Agent Morgan has apprised me of and the obviously cursing message inside the envelope, I didn't get any sense of hostility behind either the envelope or the message card themselves. It was that oddity that made me try to probe deeper on both of the objects.

"When I did, I got a sense that the person who actually wrote the message wasn't truly the author; he was doing it under the direction of another. And the writer may even have not been consciously aware of writing these things. That, of course, was a clever way to disguise the true author of the message. And it would have worked beautifully if that had been the only method of avoiding detection. But the mysterious puppeteer behind all this made a mistake. They did another thing to hide their presence; they tried to clear the energies from both the note and the envelope." Starr noted a look of triumph in the little man's eyes as he glanced around to his audience.

His index finger went up to emphasize his next point. "She, and it *was* a she, left a signature energy all over and through both of the objects as she tried to clear them. Of course, I can't give you much in the way of details about her, but I would recognize her energy if I encountered it again."

"Is there anything you can tell us about this mystery woman? You've provided much more than we were able to get from laboratory analysis, but I'm curious if you found anything else."

"Only that she identifies herself with Wicca. In fact, she's very proud of her identity as a witch. I'd guess she's probably a third or fourth generation witch. At the very least, her parents were. I don't get any great age, so she could be anywhere from twenty to seventy and I'd not be able to read it. But the skill level involved in what she's done isn't something you learn in your first magic classes, that's for sure. So I'm guessing she's likely to be at least over thirty-five or forty." He looked out the windows behind the president's desk a moment, then shook his head and said, "I'm sorry, President Draper, but that's about it on what I've been able to see." He looked downright apologetic when he offered this last remark.

Starr stood and closed the few steps between them. Instead of making the same mistake she'd done earlier, she bowed before the man and said, "You have given us a great deal of very valuable information, Dr. Silverwolf, and I assure you that you have nothing to apologize for. I assume the Service will compensate you for your work in a very generous way," she glanced at Lisa, who gave a nod, "but I'd like to offer you a token of my own to show you my deep appreciation." Walking behind her desk, she opened a lower drawer. From it she lifted a wooden box dark with age and carried it back to the man. She laid it on the floor before him and opened the lid.

"This is a personal treasure of mine. It belonged to one of my ancestors who once sailed alone around the world. The sextant has not been used since but was passed down to my father many years ago and then to me. My own name, 'Starr,' was in honor of this feat. I am sure that you will learn much from this object and I freely give it to you as my personal thanks." She saw the man was about to object and knew that only a moment before, when she'd opened the box, he'd shown considerable interest. "Please, Doctor, accept this small gift from me. Though it has been in my family for years, nobody else in the Draper family has wanted to go to sea. So we haven't had much use for it except to pass it on. With you, I think it will find a better use. There is nothing I can offer you that expresses my gratitude and appreciation more for your gifts and how you have helped not only me, but by extension, the country. We owe you much more than this."

He studied her for a moment and then nodded his acceptance with a smile. Picking up the box, he stood up. It was obvious he was about to be escorted out so the president could carry on her other duties, so he bowed slightly and said, "There is no debt between us, Madam President. May you live in peace with all your relations."

After he'd gone, Starr turned to Lisandra and grinned. "I think he'll find a great deal to work on with that sextant. My great grandfather was quite a rascal. His daughter, my paternal grandmother, used to say he had 'wives' in every port. Dad wouldn't confirm that, but from what I remember of great-grandpa, it's likely he had more than *one* 'wife' in every port. It's possible I just gave Dr. Silverwolf a piece of psychic erotica." She turned serious again as she spoke to her Secret Service Commander. "I also happened to show that sextant to T.J. not more than a month ago when he told me one of his pastimes was sailing. Perhaps handling it will give Dr. Silverwolf some added insight for us. I trust you'll follow up on Silverwolf's information?"

"We've already begun. Although he was able to read quite a bit from the envelope and card, we still don't have much more to go on. I will, of course, advise you of anything new as soon as we have it, Madam President."

The president relaxed again on the settee after Lisa had gone. She sighed heavily. "This whole security thing and Stamper's fundamentalist views are more of a distraction than anything else, Helios. What I find really annoying is Stamper's actually the one responsible for this mess with the dead water. I don't think he had any foreknowledge about the problem but he's still bringing down IC and it's still going into injectors. More dead water is being created every day. Everyone, and I guess I'd have to include myself in that list, is hoping for some kind of magic bullet to cure the problem."

"The ionic screens still seem to be our best solution so far."

"Yes, but they can only reduced the problem, just slow it down. And they won't be mandatory until two years from now."

"And," Helios was shaking his head, "no mandatory retrofits. What were they thinking when they wrote that bill?"

"Their political backsides, of course. I voted for it only because it's the only solution currently available. The amendment to make retrofitting mandatory went down in flames in both houses. 'Too costly' was the label they slapped on it from the beginning." The president rose up and slapped the desktop in frustration. "Great Mother, when are we ever going to put the health of this planet first? Nobody seems to think it's *their* planet! It's always somebody else's responsibility!"

Clearly upset, the president paced back and forth. Helios remained seated. He knew she would calm down in a short while but had to pace out her aggravation so they could get back to work. No words passed between them for nearly five minutes, but he quietly fed her soothing energy while he worked on his PerCom, making more notes for the conference scheduled that weekend in Mexico City.

Finally, Starr sat down behind her desk and took several deep breaths. Helios recognized a different energy in her before she even spoke. "I wonder: what would it take to get Stamper to come to this conference?"

He was surprised by this turn in thinking, but part of his mind started working on the problem while he asked her, "What good do you think that could do?"

"Well, it would allow us to gauge directly how much he hates me. And it would allow everyone at the conference to see the face of the man most responsible for the dead water problem. The psychic pressure alone should make him realize he's not immune to its impact."

"All the more reason for him to stay away, I'd say."

"I know. So we'll have to figure out something that would make him *want* to come there." She became still a moment and then smiled at him. He felt a surge of adrenaline as an idea began to take form. Before he fully saw it in his mind, the president gave it voice. "What if there just happened to be a rumor that the IC was going to be replaced by something else? Something that worked ten times better and didn't make dead water? What if it was rumored that the conference was going to go public with this new 'magic bullet' after we figured out how to outlaw the IC everywhere? *And* the heads of state were going to work together – for a change – to hammer out the details and sign the pacts this weekend? Hmmm?"

He thought silently about it a minute. Then he spoke up. "To make this believable, we'd have to 'leak' it just right. And the timing would have to be close. We can't be direct; he'd smell a rat immediately."

"Arranging a document leak is better..."

"A snitch would never work..."

"Too obvious."

"Something that looks like it covers up the 'real' purpose of the conference..."

"Something that gets to him through someone he already trusts..."

"And something else that *might* be construed to be the 'real' reason we're holding the conference..."

"That comes to him from another source..."

"So he'd have to reach his own conclusions but couldn't avoid being alarmed."

"I love it."

"Me too."

They both were wearing wolfish grins and the air between them almost crackled with energy as details wordlessly raced back and forth between them to flesh out the magic.

"Get hold of Trenton tonight. We need the sneakiest SOB on the planet to work this spell and my vote is for him. If he needs *anything*, make sure he gets it. We've got maybe a day before all this has to start happening."

Helios typed something on his PerCom and punched the 'send' button. Then he sat back and stared up at the ceiling a moment longer, tapping his teeth as he thought. "Paul Carter... he has a penchant for college girls. What if we got one of the younger D.C. pro's to leak this to him? Or part of it, at least. Somebody who'd 'bump' into him and spill something enigmatic she'd heard from one of her clients."

"Hmmm, no, it's too clumsy and unlikely. We can't be that direct. Find out what Stamper's doing and see if we can insert this 'magic bullet' rumor to him through someone he's going to see in the next two days." She too was looking at the ceiling with eyes unfocussed, the better to see the plot that was being hatched between them. Then she leaned forward and looked at her CoS. "'I hereby declare 'Project Magic Bullet' to have officially begun," she said with a tap of her fingernail on the desktop and they both grinned. Helios rose and left the Oval Office without another word.

⟨ 13 ⟩

In a room that was hidden to all but the most carefully screened, the magic worker rocked back and forth before a beautiful rosewood altar. Two oil candles scented the air and gave a soothing, flicker-free glow. The only other items on the altar were two small God and Goddess statues. The worker's mouth moved silently with a mentally repeated mantra:

"By the power of the Goddess, bring forth the Air of truth, the Fire of purification, the Water of cleansing, and the Earth of manifestation.

"By the power of the Goddess, bring forth..."

For each recitation, the hand moved over a small piece of jet on a string thirteen-times-thirteen beads long. Only with the last bead did the words finally change:

"By the flaming sword of the God, I pledge my life to your sacred way. Help me destroy the false ones, your enemies, and clear The Path for your Truth. So mote it be.

Ever since that night atop the hill at Cornwall with the Beltane fire blazing high, this had been a nightly ritual. The gods had spoken that night and the memory of that fire — and the hundreds, even *thousands* more across all of Britain — had been the vision that powered the work ever since. The Wicca would be made pure once again. It *would* be so.

.

❧ 14 ❧

The president didn't need (or want) to know how Trenton Hartford managed to do it, but by Friday, Eric Stamper had demanded that he be included in the conference in Mexico City. The self-invitation from his office that had been sent to the committee in charge of the event announced that he would appear at the door to the Ciudad Centro at 11:30 Saturday morning. The note didn't even bother to say that he expected to be allowed in without any problems; of course it would be so. The fact that he and his entourage would be the only 'civilians' there was hardly a reason for him to be blocked from the conference and... again... the note didn't bother to address the matter. Eric Stamper operated from a base of complete confidence in himself, which made realities other than his totally irrelevant and unacceptable... to him. The fact that he had been doing it for more than twenty years with virtually no opposition was 'proof' (to him) of the correctness of his attitude.

But the president nearly fell out of her chair at the imperious wording of the copy relayed to her from the committee's office. In the current world, it might be argued that she was *perhaps* 'important' enough to make such haughty assumptions about herself. Even if she'd had such delusions, though, she hoped she would have enough sense to keep from so blatantly displaying them in any kind of written record.

Waiving the sheet at her Chief of Staff, she couldn't stop laughing while speaking. "I'm beginning to wonder if 'inviting' this man wasn't a mistake, Helios. It's possible that we won't get anything of substance done with a comedy act like this in the middle of things. I mean, could he really be this arrogant?"

Helios had read Stamper's letter and was amused by its wording as well. But time was short and he was needed for many things before they left for Mexico City. He merely smiled and gave a brief look of pity to the president and left her to see to the remaining ten thousand details. As the door closed behind him, her PerCom chimed and a message that her father was calling from the Gates Lab above Brazil flashed on its screen. Starr immediately entered her code and her father's face filled the screen. The response time between them was slowed due to the multiple security filters and systems on the White House PerComs, but his face lit up as soon as he saw her on his unit. Before she could say a word, he spoke with an excitement she hadn't seen in him for several years.

"We've done it, honey! We cracked that sucker's code wide open. We ran a second series just two hours ago to confirm it, and we've got the damn thing on the run now. MPN is gonna get its butt kicked, you just watch."

She assumed he was referring to the DNA link he'd mentioned only a few weeks before when he was visiting her from the orbiting research lab at the end of the space elevator tethered in Brazil. Starr wasn't a forensic biologist, but she'd spent her first nineteen years living with two of them and she knew exactly what a breakthrough his excited announcement represented.

"That's wonderful, Dad!" She was actually bouncing in her chair and clapping her hands like a schoolgirl. And though her every move was being recorded by the security computers, she didn't feel embarrassed for her display of pure joy at her father's news. "Who else knows? Have you talked to the WHO yet? Does the UN team in Egypt know?" Her father's group wasn't the only one being funded to find a cure for the horrific disease. Even though they were in a kind of competition with one another, by international law every research team had to share all new knowledge with one another without delay. Nobody wanted the science teams to fail and keeping any information that might prove of value to any of the people trying to find a cure for MPN was out of the question simply on moral grounds.

"Not yet, but Dr. Ng is calling them right now to transmit the data. But I can *feel* it, Starr. This is what's going to put an end to this damn bug." His face lost some of its childish glee and he looked away for a second. When he turned back, she saw a totally different person, a much more somber man than the one who had called her. Rather than ask him what was going on, she waited patiently for him to say it his own way.

Just when she thought he might not tell her what made him suddenly grow more sober, he finally spoke. "Starr, honey, I didn't want to tell you this just after you were inaugurated; you had so many things on your mind." He paused again, obviously reluctant to go on.

"What? What is it Daddy? What were you trying not to tell me?"

He gave her a wan smile and then held up his right hand to the screen. Then he turned the hand around so she could see the back. She didn't understand at first, but then she noticed a shadow on the back of the hand where the pinkie and ring finger joined. It looked like a small, extra knuckle. No…

It looked like the beginning of another finger.

Everything in her world stopped as her brain registered what that bud on his hand meant. She froze. Part of her mind screamed to look away but she couldn't move and her eyes were locked on the image of her father's hand. She couldn't breathe and felt as if her heart was going to burst at any moment. For some reason known only to the gods, her father, the man who headed the team of scientists who had made such a wondrous breakthrough in conquering the most horrific disease the human race had ever seen, was himself infected with it. First it was her mother and now her father! Her mind was in such shock she couldn't even get to the inane question of why.

Then two things happened at the same time: The door to the Oval Office opened without any announcement and her father's hand began to move on the screen once again. Awareness slammed back into her like stampeding buffalo and she felt as if her body was beginning to dissolve while her consciousness watched from somewhere else.

For some reason she couldn't quite understand, the office was filling with dozens of people, all of whom were crowding around her and making sounds. They were touching her and they even got between her and the image of her father's face now filling the screen. One of the faces between her and the screen was that of her friend, Helios. Only instead of his usual strong and confident look, he was frowning and his mouth was moving in time with various noises she couldn't understand. And even though she had never before had an out-of-body experience, she was pretty sure she was having one now.

She could see the scene from the physical eyes in her own head but she also could see it from somewhere above, up near the ceiling. There she was, seated in the chair at her desk with people all around her. People were still trying to come into the office even though it was obvious there were already too many. She even could see the area immediately adjacent to the Oval Office; it was as if it was all a holo-vid and she was sitting on a director's chair high above the set that had no roof over it. She saw three people in white jackets plowing their way through the crowd that had formed outside of her office. Just in front of the three was a lithe woman dressed like a Secret Service agent... she recognized her as Lisandra, Maggie's great, great, granddaughter. The woman was shoving people aside like they were made of air. The team of three white jackets and Lisa entered the Oval Office and even Helios was swept aside as the three slammed their equipment down and began to pull out odd gadgets the president didn't have a clue about. Hands lifted her out of the chair and placed her flat on the floor and began to open her blouse.

That shouldn't happen; she was the president! Didn't they have any manners? How could they possibly be doing such an outrageous thing? And what was that thing they were putting on her chest? What were they going to...

LIGHT!!!

"Nothing. Again."

LIGHT!!!

She was looking up into a pair of hazel eyes that held nothing but concern and confidence. They were set in a head with the most wonderful wavy black hair she could ever recall seeing. And she couldn't see anything except what was in the range of her physical eyes now. *Pity,* she thought, *it was really neat there for a while.*

And then she remembered. Great gods: Daddy! She tried to sit up but she heard somebody say, "Please be still, Madam President.

Your heart stopped and we need to get you to the infirmary." As she registered the words, hands began to slide under her and she rose up into the air and started to move horizontally.

"Stop!" She barked out the order like a drill sergeant. And it worked; everyone stopped in their tracks a moment. But then she began to be moved once again. "I said STOP!! That means you guys carrying me. You're violating my civil rights and abducting the president of the United States, so you bloody well better stop now or I'll give you a reality check that bounces better than a Loony K-ball before the day's end!"

That seemed to do the trick for the moment. Hazel eyes leaned over her and gave her a wonderful smile, filled with teeth so perfectly white they nearly blinded her. "Madam President, please. You've had a cardiac incident and we need to find out what's going on before something *worse* happens." He gestured at the two husky agents at either end of the rolling bed they had her on. "We're all trying to insure your health and safety, and you must allow us to do our jobs... *please*."

By now, she was back in command of her senses and she lifted her hand and hooked a finger at the handsome man. He leaned a little closer and she reached out and grabbed his tie to pull him close enough to smell his aftershave. Projecting as much will power behind her words as possible, she spoke very quietly. "That was a fine speech; you ought to go into politics. Now, I swore to uphold the Constitution and the laws of the land. And one thing I know is that in there somewhere is something about patients can't be denied their rights, one of which is we get to choose whether we get cared for or not. As long as the patient is not mentally incapacitated, they've got the right to walk out of the hospital or wherever. So, Dr. Hunk: *LET... ME... UP... NOW!*"

Great Hera, did she just call him Dr. Hunk?

He smiled down at her and confidently looked over her head to check a monitor. After a few seconds, he nodded to the guys at either end of the rolling medical platform. "Help the president up, will you please?" He stepped back and observed how she reacted to being vertical. His eyes kept shifting to the monitor screen every few seconds. Then he took her hands and helped her stand, again

94

watching the monitor. Ever so slowly, he stepped away and watched as she began to test her legs. Suddenly she realized that she had no shirt and was standing in the middle of the Oval Office in her bra! With as much poise as she could muster, she turned to find Lisa. The agent was only two feet away. "Could you find me a blouse, Lisa?"

The woman smiled and said, "Already on its way, Madam President."

"In that case, would you please explain to me exactly what has caused all this, this... fuss!?"

"The security computer alerted us that your heart had stopped, Madam President. A Code Three was transmitted both to the Medical Team and the Service. The alarm also sounded in the outer office and, well, everyone responded."

"I see." Turning to the doctor and his team, she said, "Thank you for your quick action, people. I apologize for being a bad patient." They all smiled, as if it happened every day for them. "I just received a... bad emotional shock and I guess my body didn't react well. I appreciate your quick work." Turning to her Chief of Staff, she waved her hand at the still crowded office and said, "Would you get all these people back to work, Helios? I believe the local crisis is over and the world is still in need of their efforts."

As the office began to empty, the doctor and Lisa remained. Somebody came in with a dark red blouse for the president. She frowned at the color and style choice but beggars couldn't be choosers, so she put it on with as much grace as she could. The doctor was trying to convince her that she needed to be fully checked out but she ignored him and went back to her PerCom. She re-established the connection to the Gates Lab at L5-B and asked for her father. When they were finally connected, a look from her sufficed to quiet the people remaining in her office. Her father had already been briefed about had happened and why the link had been cut off so quickly. He looked at his daughter with concern in his eyes for her just as she was worried about him. After about a minute of them arguing about how he would need to get back dirt side and start treatment, he finally gave a long sigh and said, "Starr, why aren't you laid out in a bio bed? How come you're sitting there talking to me?"

She thought his question was an attempt to divert her from making him see reason, but she answered him anyway. "Because I'm fine right now and there's other things I need to do. Like getting you down here to start treatment for that 'little bump' of yours!"

"You've 'got other things to do' that are more important than looking after a little ol' heart stoppage? Other things to do?! You see, that's *my* argument. *I've* got other things to do, too. You're afraid I'm going to die. Okay, I don't like the idea of that myself. You're afraid I'm going to be a freak in pain for months or years before it does me in. And I'm not fond of *that* prospect either; I watched your mother go through that and it scares the hell out of me just to think about. But I've got other things to do besides worrying about what might be. Besides, when it comes to treating this thing, there's hardly any better place for me to be. We've got the very best minds and equipment up here and I intend to use every bit of it.

"I'm going to beat this." He held his hand up to the screen, "And this is my biggest motivator right here. Now, with all due respect, *Madam President*, I'd like to get off this link now, because *I've got other things to do*."

She wanted to argue more, but he'd taken away any strength from whatever she could say. So she gave him a long sigh and, with love in her heart and respect for the man that had sired and raised her to be just as stubborn as he was, she said, "You know, sir, I believe it's against federal law for non-politicians to use the president's words against her." That brought a smile to his eyes. "And if you don't start *beating* this bug, and *soon*, I'm likely to come up there myself and start kicking some butt." Then she held her splayed hand to the screen, "in love and trust, Daddy... love and trust."

She quickly switched off the PerCom before he could see the tears in her eyes and swiveled her chair around to face the windows rather than let the other people in the room see her that way. She knew they were giving her time to compose herself and she appreciated it. It took only moments, but the office was as quiet as a tomb except for the ticking of the antique grandfather clock against the north wall. Finally she turned back and looked directly at the doctor. "I'll give you thirty minutes, Doctor..."

"Watson, Madam President. Dr. Elliot Watson."

"My goodness, I wonder if he has any friends named Sherlock?" She refrained from speaking her thoughts, but a slight smile started to form. "Thirty minutes from right now," she stabbed the desktop with her finger, "and I'm back in this chair doing what I need to do... got it?"

He smiled that unbelievably white smile and said, "Got it, Madam President. Now, if you'd just sit over here, we'll need some blood and I'd like to monitor your heart for one minute, please."

It took only fifteen minutes. She was put through a battery of tests that were a total mystery to her. True to her word, she cooperated fully and even sat for another five minutes while the doctor and his team mulled over the results. Finally he turned and gave her his trademark smile again. "It would appear Madam President that indeed your heart is healthy and that your self-diagnosis of a stress induced heart stoppage was correct. Perhaps the security monitor over-reacted in assuming you were experiencing a true heart attack. In most of these cases, the heart resumes beating on its own after only a few seconds, as yours did. The computer only knew that your heart wasn't beating for over ten seconds and it assumed the worse. Our own diagnostic monitor also interpreted your heart's fluttering as tachycardia so we shocked you. It didn't return to normal so we hit you a second time. I apologize; I've been told the sensation is not pleasant."

"Not pleasant... humph! It felt like I was being blown up. I'll forgive you only because I want to believe you were doing what you thought best. I would suggest, though, that from now on you don't believe everything a damn computer tells you, doctor."

The entire incident had thrown her off her pace and schedule and, as she had told her father, she had other things to do. Besides, she found the doctor's presence disturbing for all the wrong reasons and she hardly needed distractions at the moment. So she sent everyone packing and tried to recall what she was supposed to be doing before she was interrupted by her father's call. She was, of course, elated at his team's breakthrough. But the fact that the disease had her father in its grips now terrified her. Wrangling with a cocktail of emotions that had already caused her a... what was it Dr.

Hunk had called it? Oh yes, a 'cardiac incident' was what he'd said. Oh, goodness, she'd just called him Dr. Hunk again! She had to get her mind on something else... and *keep* it there. She picked up the rundown on the country's upcoming tri-centennial celebrations and began reading. Thankfully, her participation had been kept to a minimum because of the conference in Mexico. It was more important that the country saw a fourth centennial than for her to make a show out of the third.

❈ 15 ❈

At one time, Mexico City was the most polluted city in the world. You could cut the air with a hatchet and sell it by the pound. That was, thankfully, many decades before and now the whole country had some of the most stringent carbon-factor laws in the world.

Though the air was now refreshingly pure, it was what Starr would label as "thin." The city's elevation was much higher than Washington DC and she felt her entire body trying to adjust as soon as she arrived.

It was not by chance that Mexico City had been chosen to host the conference; it had no IC automobiles. Even cargo trucks were banned from its vast stretch of streets. Instead, the city had built a unique form of transit coaches that ran on electricity. Every street had buried cables and switches that allowed each coach to travel without personal steering or stopping except for pedestrians. Every personal coach had a computer that allowed the user to select their destination and then sit back and relax or talk with family and business associates without having to worry about congestion or even parking at the end of their journey. Once dismissed, the coach would automatically go to the nearest terminal and recharge. Calling a coach was easily done on a PerCom or on thousands of stations around the city and a surprisingly small fee was deducted from the user's account for each kilometer. Coaches came in various sizes, from one- to eight-person capacities and everyone over the age of twelve was allowed to use them. For a distance of fifty kilometers around the sprawling borders of Mexico City no vehicle other than a 100% electric one was allowed to be used. Violators weren't just given a ticket, they were *jailed*. The USA had some cities trying to imitate the system with varying degrees of success but Starr envied the beautiful system Mexico City had been using for better than eighteen years. Not only did the city's carbon factor come very close to zero, there had not been a traffic related death within the system's domain for better than a decade. There were still children and others who insisted on running out into traffic, but the city had programmed in speed changes and other safety efforts that made even these accidents result in manageable injuries, not deaths or serious disabilities. Even though the official population count of the city was over forty million, life in Mexico City was considered to be among the best in the world.

Not every nation represented at the World Water Conference allowed IC water engines within its borders. Some had made the shift to all electric transports before the IC injectors had been invented and could boast about their innocence in contributing to the dead water situation. But that didn't mean they'd ducked the bullet and had nothing but good water within their borders. Many of those countries had clamored for the USA to find a solution as well as pay the bill for their attempts to purify their water for their people. Each of those countries had sent representatives to the conference and Starr knew she'd have to endure their anger. She'd have to stand there and take it from some of the more vocal ones. And she'd do it because she knew they were in many ways right; America *had* been the most responsible for the current water crises.

The problem existed for everyone on the planet, not just those in countries that drove millions of autos using the IC injectors. Dead water molecules evaporated the same as regular water and had no trouble falling back down on the 'innocent' countries along with its life-giving brethren. The president of the United States would be the favorite target for most of the delegates' finger pointing but Lisandra Morgan was more concerned about other possible implements making the president a target and the Service had over five hundred agents on site and involved in her security. The transport that carried the president from the military airport just south of the city was a heavily armored model that ran strictly on electricity... under normal operation. What the public wasn't told was that it also had two IC engines that could be engaged in less than a second that would, if necessary, allow it to speed away from danger at a top speed of over a hundred and seventy kilometers per hour. But even when her charge was safely in the suite reserved for her, Lisa was nervous. There had been both public and private threats made that the Service was aware of and, she feared, some that she wasn't. She felt disempowered having to sit in the central control unit stationed outside of the conference center. Logically, she should have felt just the opposite. She was in contact with not only every Service agent assigned to the security detail, but also to the city's forces and even Mexico's armed forces who were ready to respond if needed. But the inactivity of sitting with dozens of monitors and banks of communication equipment wasn't easy on her. Every few minutes she'd get up and pace the short length of the command center and back again to burn off her pent up energy. Lisa didn't think she'd inherited any of her great, great grandmother's seer's abilities, but she had a gut feeling that nothing about all their preparations would prevent a dedicated terrorist's attack if one was out there. And so she got up to pace once again.

True to his letter, Eric Stamper made his grand entrance to the conference at precisely 11:30 Saturday morning. There could be no mistake about his arrival; his entourage consisted of four eight-passenger autos for his staff and an outrageous 'stretch' electric for himself and two others. Watching it all on her monitors, Lisandra shook her head and kept silent with her thoughts about the over-the-top display. However, 3F, who was helping to keep all the equipment (including the air conditioning, thank the gods) working and coordinated, looked over her shoulder and snorted what passed for a laugh.

"Hermes-with-a-hernia, you'd think he'd sneak in the back or something. There's probably not a single soul out there who doesn't think of him as the devil incarnate. Talk about gutsy!"

She smiled and said, "Not Eric Stamper. He can't miss out on the audience, good or bad. He might not approve of the president's show at solstice, but he's a publicity whore through and through. Look at him: walking casually up to the entrance doors as if he doesn't have a care in the world. He knows there's about five

101

thousand security people here for all the other delegates and the likelihood of him being shot is lower here than on top of Mt. Everest. Quite the showman."

President Draper was at that moment watching the broadcast of Stamper's arrival along with several other representatives in a small meeting room in the upper floors of the huge complex. It was a little too warm in the room for her but it was Stamper's blatant playing to the cameras that made her the most uncomfortable. However, there wasn't anything she could do about the man's giant ego. One part of her even admired his chutzpah for the show he was making.

If all went as intended, she and Stamper would meet later that day. Her plan was simple: beard the lion and see how he reacted. She'd tell him that she knew about his plans to 'purify' the party and put an end to the 'immoral' and 'irregular' practices of the 'renegade' Wiccan groups. Wasn't that how he'd characterized it in one of his speeches two years before? She'd also accuse him of conspiring to threaten her in the form of a letter that chastised her performance of the national solstice celebration. She knew Dr. Silverwolf had said the card was the work of a woman, but Starr believed Stamper was behind it and she wanted to confront him with the bold accusation and see how he reacted. She'd arranged to have Barnstead in a room adjacent to hers in the hope that he would pick up something at the moment of her accusation. It wouldn't be the first time that a momentary shock or surprise had opened up somebody's psychic defenses.

Of course, Stamper wasn't the only one to make a grand display of arriving. Many of the dignitaries, especially ones from countries that blocked the IC engines, arrived with a good deal of fanfare that insured their constituencies knew they were at the conference trying to improve their country's conditions. It was inevitable that these shows made it impossible for the conference to open on schedule. However, the official beginning was put off by only fifteen minutes. In the security van, Lisa kept a weather eye of the broadcast on one of her monitors while keeping in touch with her security team. She knew the rest of the afternoon would be mostly speeches and vids condemning the IC injectors and the plight of the world as the dead water problem increased. Although it was a terribly serious problem, it wasn't hers at the moment. Her job was to keep the president safe and that was exactly what she was going to do.

Finally, at 5:30, the conference broke for dinner. As usual, nothing of substance was done at the conference except to make a public show. The real activity of politics would begin with the meal and then there would be some shuffling around of representatives until the private talks began. The meeting between Stamper and the president was scheduled at 8:30 that evening. The president had made it clear that she wanted to meet with him 'alone' with only her Chief of Staff in attendance. Stamper's people had said he'd bring only his second in command with him, Cassandra Whatcom. Lisa knew Ms. Whatcom was an adept reader, a part-time scientist, and a devout Gardnarian, but little else was on record about her other than an enviable steady rise in Stamper's businesses over the past few years. Apparently she now occasionally shared Stamper's bed but Lisa knew it was unlikely an exclusive arrangement for Stamper.

Only two days before, Lady McGuire had called Lisa and informed her she should pay close attention to Whatcom. Lisa asked why but her Granma Maggie hadn't 'known' anything more than a faint feeling that the woman was 'important' in some way. That was enough for Lisa. She had assigned two agents to shadow the woman from the moment she arrived. According to their reports, she'd gone to the rooms assigned to Stamper and hadn't left until just before dinner. She sat next to Stamper during the dinner but so far had offered little in the way of conversation. Lisa had nothing to indicate why her elder relative had felt the Service should be alerted, but she would continue the surveillance nevertheless.

The video from her agents at the dinner wasn't the best, unfortunately. At first, they'd thought it was faulty cameras; the ones they had dated back to 2060. But as soon as they brought them back to the van, they worked perfectly. There was something in the building that made reception bad. But while at the dinner, there wasn't much to see anyway, just a bunch of politicians posing and providing 'spontaneous' quotes for their respective audiences. As used to it as she was, Lisa still wondered how anything got done by politicians.

Though Stamper was as welcomed as a fox in the henhouse, he still was the center of attention, both earlier at the conference and now during the dinner. Lisa knew that he was wealthier than some of the countries represented at the conference. But even that didn't stop many from seeking an audience with him during the meal, no matter how briefly he might speak with them. For many, Stamper was the devil incarnate as 3F had said, but they still courted his attention. Lisa noted that Whatcom always paid very close attention to the people who came by to speak with her boss. *Very* close attention. And when they departed, the woman sometimes would lean over and speak quietly in Stamper's ear. He hardly ever seemed to react to whatever she said except to perhaps briefly smile a little more. Grudgingly, Lisa had to admire the man; he was a fantastic showman. Stuck in the middle of a hundred people who hated his guts and he acted as if he was at a country club filled with long-time friends. It was amazing he could pull it off and everybody else bought it. For probably the fiftieth time that day, she smiled to herself and shook her head.

"Something's wrong," 3F said from beside her. He pointed to a feed from one of the agents standing near the west doorway into the dining area. On the screen there appeared a strange hazy spherical shape that seemed to hang in the center of the picture. It looked for all the world like a miniature round cloud, about the size of a grapefruit. It was moving away from the lens in the agent's lapel which meant it was moving toward the middle of the dining hall. Lisa instantly punched a button and spoke to the agent who was closest to the weird cloud.

"Max, what is that thing?"

"Unknown, boss, it just came past me in the door a second ago."

"Get POTUS out... NOW!" POTUS stood for President Of The United States and every Secret Service agent assigned to Washington for the past hundred years knew the acronym. Her command was given to every agent in the building at the same time and it caused an amazingly well choreographed set of activities to begin instantly. Lisa wanted more than anything else to jump into the hall and whisk the president away herself but she was over a hundreds of yards away and would never have been able even to get in the building guarded by security teams from around the world in less than five minutes. It was up to her subordinates to perform their job and her to do what she was there to do. But while part of her was watching every screen to analyze and determine threats, another portion of her mind was weaving a protection spell around the president.

Once she'd given her command, it was nearly impossible to make sense out of the videos coming from the lapels of the dozen agents in and around the dining area. She turned her attention to the screens that fed information from the stationary cameras situated high up in three corners of the large room. They fed pictures to all of the security forces at the conference as well as the news pool covering the conference. Lisa watched with dread as the mysterious cloud quickly moved directly toward the president. She knew it would reach POTUS before her agents could. Five Service agents converged on the president but now other security teams were running to cover their respective charges and the view from high above the scene looked like a circus act of clowns all running around and getting in each other's way. Lisa could only groan as the cloud reached the president.

And passed right by.

Lisa saw one of her team bodily lift POTUS from her chair and whisk her away less than a second after the cloud had nearly brushed the president's hair. She was relieved to know they had managed to reach the president and were now carrying her (literally) to safety, but she still kept a watch on the cloud as it seemed to move even faster toward its unknown target. And then, she just knew: "Stamper! Oh goddess, it's going after Stamper," she said in a whisper.

In back of her, 3F was pacing quickly, feeling useless while watching the various feeds and listening to the now screaming delegates. But he'd heard Lisa's remark and he stopped and looked at the camera feed that was pointed almost directly at Stamper's table. He and Cassandra Whatcom had just a second before begun to rise out of their chairs and look for the best path to leave the hall. No security people were coming to their aid and what appeared to be wave after wave of burly, black-coated, dark spectacled linebackers were rushing around them to secure their own various dignitaries, blocking the two from being able to escape the foggy ball only a few yards from them and now obviously coming straight for Stamper. At the last moment, it was Whatcom who probably made the best move available to them; she threw an arm around Stamper and pulled him towards her as she dove for the floor.

When the cloud reached the table where they had been sitting, it 'exploded.' Lisa heard a faint 'pop' from the audio feeds and the sphere changed color from light gray to greenish-yellow and dissipated. The surrounding area became covered with the sickly color proportional to the distance from the cloud when it 'exploded.' For a moment, those who were still in the hall stopped and stared where the cloud had been only a second before. Most of them hadn't even heard the faint sound it had made; they'd only seen it suddenly change color and begin to dissipate. It was so anticlimactic, many got a quizzical half smile on their faces before they realized that they could be too close to what might be a chemical or biological agent. Then panic reasserted itself and they started the screaming and running all over again.

Lisa heard one of her men say something but it was garbled. "Say again, Tom." She heard coughing at first. Then, "Oh god, it smells awful! Like rotten eggs (cough)." She heard what she was sure was him retching for several seconds. When he spoke again, he sounded weaker. "It's a damn *stink bomb*!" Then she heard him retching again.

Lisa didn't think for a moment that what she was seeing was a kid's prank. Turning to 3F, she said three words as she pointed to a pack hanging against one wall of the command post. "Bio-hazard kit!" He knew what to do and popped the bag's flap to allow several pieces of gear to spill out. They both donned the coveralls and breathing masks designed to protect them and expected the team that carried the president would be doing the same for her and then themselves. Then 3F reached down and picked up what looked like a normal workman's toolbox and ran out of the huge van holding the box in one hand and his identification tags in the other. He was going to get a sample of the cloud's dust from the dining hall before anybody had a chance to tamper with it. Lisa would once again have to stay behind to coordinate what was going on with the president. Every muscle in her body wanted to run and jump into the middle of the activity but she had a job to do and she would. She knew her people would take care of business and everything that could be done to protect President Draper was being done in the quickest and safest manner possible. She had to let them do it without getting in the way.

⋖ 16 ⋗

"Put me down and we'll *both* make better time!" The man over whose back she said this probably could carry three times her weight and still bull his way through a cement wall. And he *was* making damn good time, but Starr wasn't used to being carried over anyone's shoulder and, now that they were out of the dining hall and probably safe from whatever it was that had been thrown from behind her, she wanted to be put down on the ground. A couple of seconds later, that was exactly where she was. The big man who had run with her simply popped her down on her feet and opened the door in front of her. She looked up at him as he held the door and he returned her gaze with an easy smile. *Damn him*, she thought, *he isn't even winded*. She turned and looked out at the chamber a couple of yards from the open door. There was a plastic covered walkway stretching from the doorway to the boxlike structure and her linebacker-turned-rescuer was gently urging her forward with a ham-sized palm between her shoulder blades.

Starr knew what the chamber was: a decontamination unit. Whatever that thing was back in the dining area, they obviously thought it some kind of toxic or radiological threat. She sighed in resignation; when it came to the security of POTUS, the president had absolutely no say. She knew what she had to do and no amount of complaining would change it. She walked through the door and into the first chamber. When her guardian closed the door, she started to undress and begin the first of three showers.

Less than ten minutes later, lathered, scrubbed, rinsed, scrubbed again, and nearly boiled, the president ended up sitting on a bench wrapped in a white bathrobe with the presidential seal over the left breast. A door opened to her left and two people in what looked like space suits shuffled in. One of them turned to a bank of screens and switches next to her and the other came over and shined a bright light in her eyes. In the white hazard suit, she could hardly see much more than part of his face, but she guessed who he was.

"Dr. Watson, I presume?" She couldn't resist using the line. Her answer came swiftly; the smile he showed at her words was as telling as a picture I.D. She wondered if he'd had them coated in some kind of porcelain.

"And your presumption would be correct, Madam President." The words were coming through a tinny sounding speaker somewhere at the base of his suit's 'head.' But the bad fidelity from the speaker couldn't hide the humor in his voice. Looking at part of his face showing in the clear front of his hood, she wondered again why he wasn't in the vids or something. The gods had been very generous with his looks and she still mentally called him 'Dr. Hunk.' She felt herself blush and quickly tried to think of something else. And at exactly that moment, he was gently pulling one side of the bathrobe open enough to place a sensor patch over her heart. That made it even more difficult to think of the *right* 'something else.'

"What was that thing, do they know yet?"

"Ms. Morgan informs us that they haven't completed the analysis of the dust left by the object but, so far, there doesn't seem to be any biological or radiological threat to it. Unless," he cleared his throat, "you consider the odor factor. Apparently, it smelled extremely foul. Enough so that most of the people in the area when the object, uh... 'exploded,' lost that delicious salmon dinner."

"Hmmm. I'm glad I missed that part then. But I have to tell you, I now know what it's like to be a sack of potatoes. I don't know the name of the Service agent that packed me out of there so fast, but I can tell you it was an experience."

"Ah" he said, looking at her now and flashing that super smile again, "that would have to be Hump."

"Hump?" There were some names that just made you think of strange things.

"Humphrey Addis. Half superman, half tank, and former all-star rusher for the Mars City Crushers."

Starr knew the Crushers were a popular K-ball team. Low-G Kinetic-ball was *the* sport on both Mars and the moon. Players needed great strength because of the 'ball' used for the sport. Played on a circular field about one-half kilometer in diameter, it was vaguely like the football that was still played on Earth. But the 'ball' was a relatively small sphere of titanium-clad lead weighing (on Earth) forty-five kilos. In low gravity, it was easy enough to carry but damned hard to lift and throw. And *catching* it was dangerous. Having a nearly hundred-pound sphere come at you at around fifty kilometers an hour wasn't exactly like catching a spit-wad.

It was officially called Kinetic-ball but almost everyone called it *K-os, chaos-ball,* or simply *K-ball.* The game started with twenty players to a side and the ball dropped from a hundred meters over the center of the field. The object then was to get the ball into one of the small goals. Each team had two goals located half way between the center and the edge and they alternated around the circle. The final score was always one to zero because the first team to score was the winner. The ball was always in play unless it was out-of-bounds. Then it was dropped again in the center and the chaos would begin all over again. Players could hit, stomp, kick, and otherwise abuse their opponents as long as they didn't damage or try to damage their life support systems. That was a foul and the person inflicting it was out of the game with nobody coming in as a substitute. That pretty much constituted the whole of the 'rules.'

Games had been known to last for days or be over in minutes. When a player needed to replenish his oxygen or do anything else, he simply went to his team's designated spot at the edge of the field and switched tanks. The game kept going while that player waited for his tanks to get changed. The game had originated on the moon about a dozen years ago in one of its craters but had spread to Mars and there was a huge audience for it on Earth. Lunar K-ball (sometimes also called 'loony-ball') was played on a larger field but everything else was mostly the same. Starr remembered the 'big event' the media made out of the fact that one of the K-balls from the moon had been 'accidently' kicked into escape velocity and was going to burn up in Earth's atmosphere. Huge crowds went out to see the 'fireball' from Luna. A small selection of penguins and villagers in lower South

America got to see a one-and-a-half second dull glow in the evening sky and the 'big event' was over. In spite of the month-long hype before its arrival, there wasn't much mentioned about it after it had burned its way into the history of sports.

Starr had watched holo-vids of matches from the moon and decided it wasn't something she was particularly interested in. But she appreciated the strength 'Hump' had displayed a few minutes before. Being carried over his shoulder was probably one of wackiest things she'd experienced in her political career and it was definitely one she'd have to include in her memoirs after her term in office.

The doctor continued to probe and thump and otherwise make her feel like a bug under glass for a couple of minutes. She tried to weather through it all by thinking about what the incident meant and how it would affect the rest of the conference. When it seemed he was finished, she looked over and asked, "Well? Am I going to live?" His back was to her and she thought she heard him talking in low tones to whomever it was assisting him. But a moment later, he turned back to her and pulled the seal on his suit to remove the head covering.

"Indeed you are, Madam President. We just received the 'all clear' from the Service. Agent Morgan is coming here to brief you in just a moment." He turned back to the samples he'd collected and began to place them in a small sealed box. Once it was closed and sealed, he placed the box in a transfer chamber in one wall and flipped some switches. She heard a hum and then a whoosh as the two lights above the hole turned green. She guessed her biologicals had just been transferred to somewhere for further analysis. Dr. Watson then went to the door he'd come through and punched in a code to open it. When it swung open, there on the other side was Lisa carrying a largish box. She made her way over to the president and put her package down beside her.

"These are the clothes you removed in the first decon station. We've checked them and they're fine. I've got 3F analyzing the powder from the device and for now it seems it really was nothing more than a stink bomb. Helios tells me he thinks it's a good idea for you to appear as quickly as possible so everyone understands you've not been harmed."

The doctor and his assistant kept busy writing notes on their computers as Starr began dressing and listened through the details of what had happened and what was known about the incident, which wasn't a great deal. Lisa produced some makeup and a comb and the president repaired things as best as she could.

"Well, how do I look?" She turned around in front of the Service agent and tried to put on a serious and non-flustered look. She'd been told by a very senior Senator only couple of years before that there were two faces a politician *never* used in public: fear and confusion. Starr had practiced in front of a mirror after that bit of advice and trained herself to know exactly what those two faces felt like so she'd know without thinking what facial muscles *not* to use.

"Perfect, Madam President. Helios says the media is clamoring to see you and President Corrientes and he will set up in the entrance hall. Can I tell him you'll be there soon?"

"Absolutely. Tell him I'll be available in fifteen minutes if he can set it up that fast." She checked the time as she put on her watch. "Did El Presidente come through okay?"

Lisa smiled conspiratorially and leaned close. "Yes, except his Vice President barfed all over him."

Starr tried hard to keep her face neutral. "Well, there never was any love lost between those two anyway. I doubt if Juan could hate the man any more than he does already." She looked over to the doctor and said to his back, "Thank you once again, Dr. Watson. We do have to stop meeting like this, though."

He turned and gave her another flash of white teeth. "Indeed, Madam President. But you have been a most cooperative and gracious patient. It's been my honor." He gave a bow of the head and turned back to his notes. Lisa noticed the president's lingering look at the doctor and made a mental note. She may not be much of a psychic, but she knew how women thought and the doctor was a most appealing man. The fact that Starr Draper was not married had been a hot topic all during the campaign. And she knew that any news of the president being attracted to anyone would cause a great deal of trouble not only for the president but for the Service as well. It was Lisa's job to see that problems were taken care of *before* they happened.

Unfortunately, today had proven that such a task wasn't able to be accomplished all of the time. Whatever it was that had made the dinner into a disaster was a demonstration that she and her team had missed something. Though it hadn't harmed the president this time, it did show that they had better improve their methods by a great deal. Lisa would be brainstorming with her people far into the night and perhaps several nights to come.

Since the whole conference had been threatened by the strange 'cloud bomb,' as the media had already labeled it, some of the other dignitaries were at the hastily called press conference. But it was Presidents Draper and Corrientes who got the most attention. Starr wondered at the fact that Stamper hadn't shown up. Not only did she think he wouldn't miss the drama of it, but it had appeared that he was the actual target for the 'bomb.' Starr kept looking around, expecting him to make an appearance, but he never did. When the media show was over, she asked Helios if he'd received any word the scheduled meeting with Stamper had been postponed or cancelled. He assured her that nothing had been communicated to him about it.

"Good," she said. "Then we'll play it just the way we planned. Make sure Allen is in place at least twenty minutes ahead of time and you and I will be fashionably late." Turning to Lisa, she asked, "You have the chip?"

Reaching into a pocket, the agent pulled out a memory chip incased in a clear holder and handed it to the president. "Right here, Madam President. And I have a back-up if required."

Starr pocketed the chip and proceeded to her rooms, there to stay until the scheduled meeting with Stamper. She had much to take care of and she sat for the next hour working with her people back in Washington, catching up on the business of running a country. She also found time to send her father a message letting him know that she was perfectly fine and that the whole affair was probably going to be exaggerated by the press and he wasn't to worry.

Pausing with her finger over the 'send' button, she thought about the irony of her sending him a note that said not to worry. She got a lump in her throat every time she thought about him now. MPN was a horrible disease. It made its victims into terrifying looking people and there was a great deal of pain as well. Caregivers and family members alike were strained to be around its victims, both because of the possibility of catching it and the guilt over their natural reactions of repulsion and fear when the advanced stages of the disease had done their damage. Starr thought of the leper colonies of old and knew that these reactions were not new. But the degree or scale was somehow greater with MPN and there was hardly a person on the planet that wasn't closely connected to a victim of the disease. All that fear and guilt and pain was just as big a problem as the dead water situation because it killed the spirit of humankind. And without spirit, nothing ever survived.

❧ 17 ❧

The meeting took place in a suite of rooms on the sixth floor of the conference center. It had a beautiful view of the city's skyline and the last trace of the sunset had given way to a clear canopy of stars that seemed brighter than any other place Starr had been. The lighting in the rooms was not too bright to block the glorious spectacle and when Helios and the president arrived, Stamper was standing inside the doors to the small patio looking up at the sharp points of light that shone down on the city. As they entered, he turned away from his stargazing and greeted the president.

"Madam President, it is a great honor."

She had decided ahead of time that she'd play 'bad cop' to him. Although this meeting was exactly what she'd hope for, she had arranged it so that Stamper would have to ask to see her, not the other way around. In that way, she had leverage she could use against him, which was just the way she wanted it. She pretended to be disapproving of him from the moment he spoke. She didn't offer her open hand when he held his up. Instead, she walked straight to the chair at the long end of an arrangement around a coffee table in the center of the room. Without even acknowledging Cassandra Whatcom's presence, she sat before speaking.

"Cut the bull, Stamper. What is it you want?"

She noted a slight look of tension on Whatcom's face, followed immediately by the beginnings of a smile and a spark in her eyes. They looked across at each other, each silently, each studying the other and waiting for Stamper's response. They didn't have to wait long. He obviously wasn't used to being treated in such a curt fashion, but he wasn't intimidated by the president's manner, either.

"I was under the impression that you wanted this meeting as much as I, Madam President. I'd hoped we could be of benefit to each other, not adversaries."

Starr slowly turned her head to look into Stamper's eyes and to give her next words as much chill as possible. "If I had wanted to speak with you, I would have let you know. Now what is it you're asking for?"

Helios knew the president was putting on an act; that this wasn't anything like her. But he was impressed that she could carry it off so convincingly. He'd never seen her so... so... well, *bitchy*... as what she was pulling on Stamper. But he wondered if Whatcom was buying it. She seemed almost to be enjoying how the president was treating her boss. Or maybe Stamper had some kind of ace up his sleeve and she was just waiting to see it sprung. Whatever the case, Helios was ready to help the president in any way he could. For the moment, however, the best thing for him to do was simply to remain observant.

"You and," he waived his hand to indicate everything and everyone at the conference, "several others consider me the devil, don't you?" Starr just stared at him in answer. "Well, I'm not. I want a solution to the water problem just as much as you and the rest of these people. Do you know I've put over four billion dollars into trying to find a solution just in the last year? That's more than what your Congress coughed up in the last *three* and I'll bet most of *that* money was used to print posters against me instead of being put into real research. And you can be sure that if my people do come up with a solution, it'll be on the market *and affordable* before you can say 'boo.' I'm not the monster here, Madam President.

"For some reason, your people fed my people some cock and bull story about this conference being where some new technology to solve the problem was going to be introduced. That was an... *interesting* development. Because if such a thing existed, I'd know, believe me. I decided to come here to announce something myself. But since you seemed so intent to 'lure' me here, I figured we ought to have a nice chat. So, Madam President, once again: what is it that *you* want?"

He sat and made a show of waiting for her reply. Starr exchanged glances with her Chief of Staff and picked up a glass of water to drink slowly. Nobody said anything. Finally, she looked at Stamper and spoke.

"Eric, I'm sure you aren't 'the devil.' But I also know that you've put a lot of energy into trying to 'purify' the Earth Party, making it solely a party of 'real' Wiccans. I take it you don't approve of me or my brand of spirituality."

"That is correct."

Well, Starr thought, at least he doesn't deny it. She thought to surprise him with her next words, even though they were mostly a bluff.

"And I know that you're behind a not-so-veiled threat to me in the form of a note in my boudoir."

Looking first at Whatcom and D'Amico and then back to the president, Stamper smiled. "Your *boudoir?* This is a joke, right? And even if it isn't, what has that got to do with the water problem?"

"It doesn't... directly. But if I have to be concerned about your fundamentalist views being a threat, it takes away from the really important things, such as this conference. Your efforts to 'purify' our faith will weaken us all and history will bear me out on that."

"Excuse me, Madam President, but I've got to correct something here before you go any further. First, I never sent any note to you in any form and certainly not to your – how did you phrase it – your *boudoir?*" He smiled. "I love that term; it's so... *classy.*

"As for my views about Wicca and how the religion has been bastardized, I'm not about to apologize to you or anyone else. Fundamentalist? I don't think I'm being a fundamentalist to require some sort of test for those who call themselves Wiccan, madam. Since you believe my views personally affect you, let's begin there: What exactly *is* your lineage? Can you trace your so-called initiation back to Gardner? Or do you follow a line of people who have no idea what our founder stood for?"

"Our spirituality is not simply one line of thought and belief Mr. Stamper. It has evolved in the last hundred plus years and is still evolving. It..."

"Evolving! That's just a fancy word for every Tom, Dick, and Mary making up new stuff as they muddle along because they're too damn lazy to learn or uncomfortable with the original rituals and laws! The *real* Wiccans of this world are constantly being marginalized because of such inane and pretentious activities of the unfaithful. My work to weed out the pretenders is based on the laws that Gardner himself wrote: 'No one shall know our rites or learn of our meetings unless they have been *properly prepared* and in a magic circle *such as the one I am in now.*' It isn't rocket science to know what 'properly prepared' means, Madam President."

Starr had more self-control than to say some of the things she was thinking at the moment. Also, she wasn't going to be drawn into some argument over what was or wasn't the 'one true religion.' But she had to respond to the man's tirade at least to leave a thought with him.

"You've memorized the laws from Gardner's Book of Shadows?"

"Indeed I have. Many years ago."

"Which one?"

"I beg your pardon?"

"Which Book of Shadows did you learn from?"

"From Gerald Gardner. Didn't you just ask me that?"

"Well Eric, there's been some question about who actually wrote a lot of those books. There's been several turn up that seem to be in his hand but aren't the same as ones that are dated earlier. There's also the obvious infusion of things Doreen Valiente wrote for his group and the addition of material that may have been copied directly from the Golden Dawn and O.T.O. of that time. I was just wondering which Book of Shadows you're using."

He appeared to be forming a reply but she had more to say. "It really doesn't matter what book you're getting it from, Eric. The very fact that Gardner himself made changes underscores the fact that our spirituality embraces change. It can *evolve*. And I seriously doubt that quoting scripture was part of his or anybody else's idea of what Wicca was all about back then. You're views are using *dogma* to justify the narrow-mindedness and inflexibility that Wiccans have always run from. Dogma creates hate, stifles learning, thwarts

118

adaptability, and kills beauty and love Eric. If your faith doesn't worship love, then I'm thankful you don't include me in it."

Starr watched the man's face turn red. She sat back and changed the pace as well as her tone of voice. "Now, there are two things I want to settle before I have to leave. First, if you didn't send me this note," she put the memory chip in the reader for the wall display and an image of the note popped up, "at Solstice, who did?" Stamper studied the image of the note for several seconds. But Whatcom, the president noted, looked at it only briefly.

"Also, you said you had come here to announce something yourself. I'd like to know what that might be." She sat back with all the grace and calm she could muster. By shifting gears, she sent a signal that she was in control of the meeting. She doubted he much liked it but she was the president of a very powerful country and he wasn't.

Stamper just pointed at Whatcom. She seemed to know his meaning and responded to the president's question while her boss attempted to get himself under control. "Madam President, Mr. Stamper has come to announce the end of his shipping of the IC crystal material to Earth as of the 10th of September, which is one week after the *Aeries* is scheduled to arrive from Mars. Until a solution is found, he will not bring any more of the material in. But we would appreciate it if you didn't let this be known until Mr. Stamper has given his speech tomorrow at noon."

This was news to Starr and she didn't bother to hide her surprise. As welcome as the announcement might be, though, she was sure that the price of IC would skyrocket the moment the announcement was made. She'd bet the entire federal budget that Stamper had already positioned his holdings to take full advantage of the jump in profits the last shipment would produce. She just nodded her head and turned back to Stamper. She once again shifted the conversation so as to keep him off balance as much as she could. "And the first item I mentioned? The little spell that was left for me in the White House? What do you know about *that*, Eric?"

She watched as he composed his face before answering. "About that, Madam President, I know nothing; I swear it by the gods. I don't hide behind veiled threats and I don't cast spells on presidents." Starr's eyebrow twitched upwards at the last statement. "I don't think you know how much your activities on the solstice saddened me, Madam President, but I wouldn't interfere in such affairs of state, even if you were a bible-thumping Mormon."

To her credit, Starr didn't burst out laughing at the man's reference. She was sure he hadn't thought much about the Mormon religion before using it. Nevertheless, she also regarded him in a new light. She'd have to consult with Barnstead, but she was of the opinion that Stamper had just spoken the truth. So she once again did the unexpected.

"I will honor your secrecy concerning the IC shipments, Eric. And I will accept your words concerning the threat I received because I assume you are a man of honor." She stood and offered her splayed hand to Stamper. "Let there be peace between us." She held her hand up and waited for him to respond. She'd purposely but rudely not accepted his greeting earlier, but she hoped he would accept her 'peace offering' now.

To his credit, he immediately rose on his long legs and touched her fingertips with his, saying, "May the blessings of the Goddess be yours always, Madam President." Then, still touching her hand, he leaned closer and said, "And I hope you catch the sneaky bastard that invaded your... ahem... *boudoir*." She noted the twinkle in his eye every time he used the word, confirming his reputation as 'a randy old goat,' and smiled back at him.

As she left the suite, she acknowledged the two Service agents waiting outside the door and turned to the elevator that carried her to her rooms. Minutes later, Helios brought Barnstead in. As expected, Allen hadn't picked up anything from Stamper. But he also reported that Cassandra Whatcom seemed to be very good at shielding as well. The only time he was able to get inside her head was for just a moment before the president had walked in. "I can tell you that she is very protective towards Stamper. In fact, I believe she loves him. Other than that though, I got stumps. Sorry."

"I believe you're right about Whatcom. And perhaps Stamper loves her as well... in his own way. We may never know who wrote the note, but I'm guessing Stamper didn't know about it until I mentioned it. What I'm a little confused about is this announcement he says he's going to make."

"I'm not surprised by it," Helios said. "He's shrewd. I'll bet he's just about hit market saturation and wants to squeeze more money out of the crystal he's got stored. Plus, he's getting into asteroid mining. That means he'll need his fleet to be redirected or else have to build more ships. Even with his money, those things aren't cheap. He's just using his resources wisely."

Allen was nodding his head. "And he may be closer to figuring out how to fix the dead water emissions than anybody else. I hate to admit it, but he threw more money into the problem than we did when it was discovered. That means he's got more of the really smart guys in his wallet. He was there first and he's paying them royally to keep them working for him."

Starr was feeling tired and she didn't have anything else that needed her immediate attention. So she finished her meeting with D'Amico and Barnstead and got ready for some much needed sleep. But just as she was about to tell the room to dim the lights for sleep, her PerCom buzzed. It was Lisa Morgan. The president switched it to the wall screen and sat down in a rocker.

The Secret Service agent was surprised to see the president in bathrobe and slippers so early in the evening. Most times, she didn't get to bed before midnight. "Excuse the intrusion, Madam President, but I thought you'd like the latest intel about the stink bomb event earlier this evening."

Starr mentally shook her head at the young woman's drive. She knew the agent had been up earlier than the president and yet she was obviously hard at work and appeared to have plenty of energy even this late in the evening. In fact, Starr thought, the woman almost seemed to have *more* energy than earlier. "Go ahead, I was just going to try for some extra sleep tonight, that's all. What have you got?"

"Well, 3F thinks it was a magnetic membrane with the gas trapped inside until detonation. He figured it couldn't have moved on its own, so there had to be something that attracted it. And, sure enough, we found a strong electromagnet hidden in Stamper's chair that could be switched on or off wirelessly. We found several of them

121

around the room once we looked closer. They weren't detectable when switched off unless you knew where they were hidden."

"All right. So what's a 'magnetic membrane'?"

"He tells me it's like a bubble made out of magnetic currents flowing in the pattern of a sphere. It seems the first one was produced clear back at the turn of the century but very little has been done with them simply because nobody ever thought they had much use. Apparently, you can't keep them coherent much longer than a minute or so, depending on their size, and it takes a lot of power to make one. We're looking to see how one could be made here in the building. Poor Franklyn is all excited about it," she said with a chuckle. "He's got a bad case of techno-lust over the thing."

Everybody in the presidential detail knew that 3F was a geek through and through but they all relied heavily on the fact that there wasn't much about modern technology that he didn't know. Starr was amused by the man's quirky behavior as much as amazed at his knowledge. It seemed Lisa felt much the same way, judging by the smile she displayed when talking about the man's enthusiasm for anything techno.

"Well, keep me informed. But right now," a big yawn interrupted her sentence, "I've *got* to get some sleep. Thanks for the update." The next day was going to be a busy one and she was asleep almost immediately after her head hit the pillow. Unless something required her to be awakened in the middle of the night, she might get almost seven hours of sleep, a rare luxury for any president in office.

✦ 18 ✦

Starr wasn't used to having nightmares. In fact, she rarely remembered her dreams more than a few seconds after waking, if at all. And though she remembered having a few times where she awoke feeling threatened or frightened, so-called 'normal' reality always dissipated the irrational images quickly enough. She usually slept without interruption from her subconscious or any other part of her mind bothering her enough to cause her to wake up in the middle of the night. But this night was a glaring exception. When she asked, her PerCom told her it was 4:53 a.m. local time, which was a most inconvenient time to be awakened. It was slightly over an hour from when she normally would get up, which made going back to sleep almost not worth the effort. And it probably wouldn't have happened anyway because her brain was obsessed with the strange dream that had awakened her. She could remember her dream vividly, but she couldn't make sense out it no matter how hard she tried.

As in most dreams she had remembered, she wasn't sure of exactly how it had begun. Dreams weren't like regular stories; they didn't necessarily start at a logical point. A dream never started out with, "Once upon a time..." Her dream had begun at some point she was sure was in the middle of some 'story.' She remembered already understanding and being engaged in the events and environment of the dream. But other than that, it wasn't anything like a sensible sequence or story:

The greenish-yellow haze was in some ways like thick syrup; it wasn't easy to move through and it seemed to stick to everything. She could sense several presences around her in the haze, though most weren't visible or making any sound. Every once in a while, she had to get out of the way of disembodied wheels that came out of the haze randomly and from every direction to quickly roll past her and disappear back into the fog.

When Starr was a child, there had been a big construction project not too far from her house that had been stalled half-completed and where many of the neighborhood's older children played on summer days. Aside from some stacks of bricks that might have injured anyone unlucky enough to have them fall on them, there weren't many dangerous things at the construction site more serious than a bent nail. Starr had played there many times and used to love going into a huge section of metal pipe nearly six feet in diameter which had been left on the property. She'd listen to the sounds of the other children as they played outside of the big cylinder and wonder at the dynamics of the tube as it echoed and distorted them into what she imagined to be a musical score. But the most fantastic experience connected with the pipe was when somebody would take a rock or, better yet, a two-by-four and smack the outside of the pipe. The bell-like quality to the tone was more than sound; it was a pressure wave that made her entire body resonate.

That same tone began to surround her in her dream. At first it seemed far away but it kept getting closer. And it was getting more intense and more frequent as well. It soon was beyond the delightful internal tickle of her childhood and she somehow knew that if it kept up she would be shattered into individual atoms. To confuse things more, an internal 'voice' seemed to be telling her to look for some sort of code to stop the sound before it killed her!

Just as she was sure she was about to disintegrate, a box slammed down on a table that appeared before her. By the light emanating from the fog surrounding her, the box looked a reddish-gray and had definitely had been ill treated. Cracks and gouges were everywhere on it and it was slightly warped and out of square. Her hands reached to open it before she even could wonder how the table and box had suddenly come into being in front of her.

As soon as she lifted the lid, the terrible gonging sound stopped. Inside the box were several envelopes like what she remembered from her childhood when people would send letters written on paper. She reached for the stack inside the box and pulled out several of them. The writing on them was faded and they had little stickers in the corners she remembered were called 'stamps.' As she held them, they began to fall into dust until only one envelope remained. She very carefully opened it and extracted a single sheet of paper. Then she turned the envelope over in her hand and it too began to disintegrate into dust, but not before she saw an initial along with a faded return address in the upper left-hand corner. Where there would usually be the sender's name, there was only the initial 'D'. And the only part of the address she could read was "London."

She'd read the handwritten letter from its beginning in her dream, but she couldn't remember most of it. Even now though, several minutes after waking up, she still recalled exactly the words of the last paragraph.

"This is not the way of freedom, G. Do not let it be your legacy. The magic is too great for words to bind it. For the sake of the Goddess, do not create what you can not destroy. My priest, my love."

Starr sat in the dark for several minutes. Though she might not have classified her dream as a nightmare, it troubled her. She could almost conjure up the smell of the aged paper and box. When first she had awakened, she was positive she still held the page in her hand so powerful were the sensations from the dream. Indeed, even now when she again looked at her hands, they still were formed as if holding the page. She smiled at her foolishness and decided to get out of bed and enjoy more than a minute under a steaming hot shower. She didn't know what her dream meant, but she did know she needed to relax the tension in her back and shoulders before the rest of the day's activities.

She managed to get a full quarter of an hour under the hot spray and took another forty minutes getting dressed. Then she notified her people that she was ready to get to work and ordered a light breakfast. Ten minutes later, she was reading her morning briefings on the wall screen while eating her huevos rancheros with some kind of Mexican sausage and rich, dark coffee. She was looking at a synopsis of some trade figures when she saw a note in the corner of her screen being entered by Helios. She tapped the PerCom in the desk and spoke to him directly.

"Good morning, Helios. What have you got?"

"*Winds of the West*, the San Francisco e-paper, ran an article about the stink bomb incident and coupled it with news about a wild drop in Stamper's stock this morning. It got me to thinking. Why did that thing target Stamper? And isn't it strange that such a sophisticated device – and 3F assures me that it was something *really* unusual – why such a device was used to deliver what essentially was nothing more than a nuisance payload? I mean, it was just barely beyond an insult. So I put somebody on trying to find out who might be involved in developing such a device."

"I'm sure the Service is looking into that for us already."

"Yes, but I've asked the person who most wants to find out about it to look long and hard for us. I just wanted you to know personally because I told him not to discuss it with *anybody* except me and you."

She stopped with her fork half way to her mouth. "Am I reading you right? Are you saying that he's to not talk to the Service about this?"

"Yes, that's exactly what I'm saying. I know it didn't sit well with him, but I gave him the order and told him I'd confirm it with you later this morning."

"Who is this person? Oh, wait a minute; you're talking about Franklyn, right?"

"Right."

"But he's part of the Service, Helios. I mean, you're essentially telling him to cut off communication with the people he's there to work with. Why? If he does as you've asked, sooner or later somebody who works with him will notice something's amiss. And if he goes against your orders and confides in anybody there, then he's committed some other sort of foul and it's another kind of mess."

His face remained neutral, but she could feel the emotion behind his next words. "Don't you think it strange that both the note in your rooms and that stink bomb were able to sneak past some of the best security in the eight planets? I'm not pointing fingers here.

I'm just saying that I can't be sure about anything or anybody until I'm sure. I'd like your backing on this."

"And you're *sure* about 3F?"

"Yes, I am. Other than some really awful driving incidents in his youth, our Mr. Franklyn has not shown any tendencies towards any terrorist activities. And, to be brutally blunt, the man hasn't the imagination to be dishonest or sneaky. He's so committed to being a techno-geek, he doesn't have time for anything else. He eats and sleeps science and technology. I don't even think he could be used by outside forces because it simply doesn't fit into his belief structure that the good old USA isn't the Promised Land for techies. I wonder sometimes if the man even sleeps. Maybe he's got a chip in his head or something."

She wanted to reassure her Chief of Staff that she'd back him on this move but she couldn't shake the feeling that it was just another complication to a problem that made things more difficult. Nevertheless, she'd relied on the man's intuition for years and it very seldom turned out wrong. "Okay, you've got my backing. But let's hope nothing bad happens because of it. I don't want to think the castle is going to fall because of the guards." There had been a wildly popular comic holo-vid a few years back about a medieval kingdom run by a bumbling king and a bimbo princess that had been 'attacked' by even more bumbling guards. It was stupid and completely unbelievable, but it had tickled the funny bones of billions of people and still had a devoted following. Her reference to the castle falling because of the guards would have been understood by almost everyone on the planet and Helios smiled appropriately.

Bowing his head slightly, he replied. "Let us hope, Madame President." The communication block winked out and she went back to reading the morning's briefings. The rest of the morning went by quickly and she spent some time making appearances around the city, spending nearly half of the time at a local MPN hospice, offering sympathy and possibly some hope to the victims. With her mother dead of the horrible disease and her father now infected, the whole time in the presence of the wasting victims was a terrible strain on her. But to avoid the visits would have been unthinkable. So she put on a brave face and visited with as many as she could in the allotted time.

All the way back to the conference center, she kept up the appearance of a brave and hopeful dignitary. But once back in her suite, away from the crowds and the reporters, she gave into the waves of emotion that had been gnawing at her inside and she spent the next half hour repairing her face after she'd bawled like a child for fifteen minutes. Looking in the mirror, she was horrified to see that her eyes were still red as strawberries and she called Lisa. The agent arrived less than twenty seconds later. The president wondered how the woman always was so quick to show up. Then she looked at the agent and saw that even though she appeared perfectly neat and proper, she was breathing a little faster than usual.

"Yes, Madam President?" The voice was calm and the agent looked completely in charge of things, but, yes, she did seem slightly out of breath.

"Find the doctor for me, Lisa, and see if he can make my eyes not look so inflamed, will you?"

"Of course." She took out her PerCom and quietly spoke into it for a few seconds. Replacing it to her jacket pocket, she looked back at the president and asked, "Will there be anything else?"

It had been completely unnecessary to call Lisa for such a mundane chore as finding the doctor. She could have gotten him there herself in less time. But the whole business her CoS had brought up earlier that morning was still weighing heavily on her mind. Despite her giving Helios her backing, she wanted to get a different perspective from the woman she trusted the most.

"Well, I did want to talk to you about something, Lisa. Let's sit down a moment, can we?"

The agent cocked her head a little but took a seat on the couch across from the president. Lisa let the president take her time with whatever she was going to say.

Starr went through it in her head before speaking but finally sighed and began. "I wanted to ask you about 3F, Lisa." The president noted a small change in the agent's expression, a subtle look that might have been fear. And that was something Starr considered completely out of character.

She began to fidget. "Oh," she said in a small voice. "Umm... I didn't know that you knew yet, Madam President." The agent began to speak more quickly. "I was going to tell you when we got back to Washington. Actually, I was considering the possibility of maybe you performing the ceremony. That is," she looked down at her hands, which were fiddling with each other, "if you could find the time, that is."

Now it was Starr's turn to be confused. "What are you talking about, Lisa? Perform what ceremony? I'm talking about Franklyn here; what are you talking about?"

The agent gave the president a blank look for a moment. "Oh, oh, oh my goddess... I've messed it all up, haven't I? I'm sorry, Madam President. I thought you were speaking about something else. I'm sorry... I..."

Now Starr was completely mystified. She had to find out what had been going through her Security Detail Chief's mind. "All right, let's do this the other way around. Exactly what did you think I was going to talk about?"

"Well, I thought..." the agent now looked like a schoolgirl caught doing a love spell in the back of the class. The president had never seen her detail lead so nervous and she was becoming alarmed. "I thought you'd learned about Frank and me. But it was only last night he proposed and I... Well I thought maybe Gramma Maggie had called you and said something or maybe somebody else knew something or..." She let her voice die as the president absorbed the woman's words. "You didn't know anything about it, did you? Oh stumps! I knew this would be difficult and I've blown it to hell already, haven't I?"

"So 3F... I mean Franklyn..."

"It's all right, he doesn't mind the nickname; he thinks it's kind of funny himself."

"Okay, so 3F *proposed* to you? Last night? And I take it you said 'yes'?"

"Yes. Yes, I said 'yes'. I mean, I *did* say 'yes'. Yes I did."

The president gave Lisa a lopsided smile and said, "Careful; I'm beginning to lose faith in you as the most unflappable person on the planet, Lisa. You really love him, don't you?"

"Oh, yes, I really do. We've been very professional, though. About the job, I mean. I want you to know that we haven't..."

The president just smiled and waved her hand as if to dispel the idea. "I have no problem on that score, dear girl. I just think you should stop and take a breath before going on about him, that's all. Gods, woman, you are a total mess over this, aren't you?" The big smile on the president's face made it clear that her 'reprimand' was *not* a criticism, merely a girl-to-girl offering of shared joy. "How long have you two been dancing around this?"

Lisa actually *blushed* before answering. "Well, we've been working together for a couple of years. But we didn't go out together, you know, on a date, until I asked him out last Winter Solstice. And then, on Beltane, there was this ritual 'hunt' and I captured him and put the horns on his head and then... well, you know..."

"You bleeped his brains out, right?" The president was enjoying Lisa's awkwardness and just had to push it a little. The woman was so charming when she was talking about it; Starr had to get her digs in when she could.

"Uh, yeah. In fact, for the whole bleeping night! Gods, who would have thought he had it in him, right? I mean, you look at him and he looks like some kind of string bean until you get his clothes off. But *then*..."

"Uh," Starr interjected quickly, "I don't think those details need to be discussed right now, Lisa." The president stood up and offered both hands to the agent. "I would be absolutely delighted to perform the ceremony for you both. Just one caveat though: *No skyclad rite*. We'll do it in the Rose Garden if you'd like. And if it rains, we'll put up the dome for you."

The doctor arrived then and Starr had him put a few drops of a clear liquid in her eyes so she didn't appear to have been crying. She engaged him in some small talk for a few minutes but she had to return to her work so she could attend the last half of the conference. Then she would return to Washington and probably spend another few hours before getting time for sleep. She and Helios watched Stamper announce the end of the shipments from Mars on her wall screen and she was busy with a parade of dignitaries from various countries for another two hours after that.

The rest of the day was filled with the usual non-stop activities that always surround gatherings of heads of state and Starr was exhausted by the time she climbed aboard Big Bird, the nickname for the flying fortress that would carry her back to DC. She slept the entire seventy-five minutes after takeoff and awoke only after they had taxied into the armored hanger. Another ten minutes by ground and the president was back in residence once again.

She finally got a minute alone with Helios and told him about Lisa and 3F. In light of the circumstances, she didn't think they could expect 3F to keep anything under wraps and still make any progress. D'Amico reluctantly agreed and said he would contact the man in the morning and undo the promises he'd gotten from him the night before. As Helios was leaving the office, his PerCom buzzed and he stopped near the east door to answer it. A second later, he turned back and quickly went over to one of the wall displays and switched it to the feed from his hand unit.

There was Eric Stamper talking with the top newswoman from *National Open Wire*, the sensationalist e-paper for the DC area. Helios sat by the president and said, "My man at the media center says Stamper is saying the stink bomb was designed to discredit and humiliate him and even though he didn't directly name the White House, it would have been impossible to not get who he was blaming." They picked up Stamper's comments in the middle of the interview.

"... rampaging against the values that my faith has held sacred since before the dawn of time. If these pretenders think they can sway me from trying to protect our Mother Earth, then they don't understand Eric Stamper, by the gods."

The newswoman, known mostly for her flaming orange hair and huge... tracks of land... smiled at the camera and asked, "But Mr. Stamper, your business has been almost the only source of the Impossible Crystal which is the cause of the global water problem. How can you say you want to protect the environment when you're one of the people who has helped damage it so badly?"

Stamper gave the woman a fatherly smile. "That's not quite true, Mie-Ling. When I first got into Mars shipping, nobody knew about the devastating effects IC would have. In fact, it wasn't until five months ago that the UN commission declared it was positively the cause of the Dead Water problem." The UN commission he mentioned was more than a couple of years late in their conclusions, Starr thought.

"And as soon as it announced its findings, I initiated plans to stop the flow of IC forever, or at least until some kind of technology is invented to overcome its insidious effects. As I announced at the conference a few hours ago, the last of my shipments of materials from Mars will be the *Aries*, which is on its way to Earth as we speak. To try to turn it around isn't possible because of fuel consumption, so to keep the crew safe I'll allow this last load."

And make a bundle on it, Starr thought. She knew Stamper could order the cargo be dumped in space but she didn't expect that would happen. Nor did she expect it to be questioned in this interview.

"When it arrives, my involvement in IC will cease and I'll pursue other interests, chief among which will be a way of overcoming the catastrophic rise in Dead Water that has us all worried."

"And do you believe we'll be able to create that technology?"

"I've been working for a long time, even before the UN commission declared IC to be the cause of the problem, on just such a technology, Mei-Ling. And, the gods willing, I will be able to announce success at some time in the near future. I'm sure that every true Wiccan will join me in putting energy into this vision. In fact, I've arranged to have a mammoth circle at the magnificent Yellowstone National Park this Autumnal Equinox to create just such a vision and give it energy from the faithful the world over."

"Ooo, it sounds exciting," the woman said in a reasonably good imitation of a breathless Marilyn Monroe. She thrust her chest at the camera and cooed, "Will you invite me to your circle, Mr. Stamper?" To show the world how much she wanted to attend the rite, she suggestively licked her lips with the tip of her tongue. The effect on the male audience was undoubtedly worth the effort. It was commonly known that Stamper's rites were *always* skyclad. The president was sure that the prospect of the huge tracts of land carried by the newswoman would ensure a good turnout of males for the planned event.

With what was undoubtedly the greatest restraint he could muster, Stamper smiled and said, "Well, of course you can. I will personally sign the invitation." He was obviously having a difficult time keeping his eyes above the reporter's chin and his smile now seemed to be frozen. Starr figured he was trying hard to keep it from becoming a drooling leer.

She was enjoying the show and idly wondered if Stamper had ever thought of growing a handlebar mustache so he could twirl the tips when delivering lines such as this to pretty young maids. Helios, as usual, was in synch with his boss. He chuckled and said, "Gods, he is *such* a letch. He should grow a mustache so he could twirl it at times like this." Her CoS's words matched her own thoughts so well they both ended up laughing hard. So much so that they missed part of Stamper's next remarks. When they returned their attention back to the screen, they both sobered quickly.

"... with the Vice president's backing to introduce a bill to permanently change the method by which candidates are chosen by their parties. The massive amounts spent on the hodge-podge, state-by-state races that wastes money and begs for special interest corruption makes the elections into a circus rather than a real democratic process. There's hardly a single American who doesn't have access to the Net and one or more devices for posting their thoughts to the candidates. Why should Americans spend their time, money, and resources on what has become a dog and pony show that lasts two years and serves only to confuse issues? The process itself makes behind-the-scenes deal-making the way in which power is gathered and directed."

"Wow. That sounds really important, Mr. Stamper. You're working with the Vice President?"

Leave it to The Brain to nail the most important part, thought Starr.

"The political parties themselves need to clean up their act. You're part of the news media, Mei-Ling, part of the so-called fifth

133

estate charged with keeping the public informed. Can *you* tell me a single plank of the platform of *any* party in your last election?"

Starr was pretty sure the woman had trouble telling time. She almost choked watching the momentary flash of terror that crossed the woman's face. However, she recovered quickly and put on a rather unconvincing show of seriously considering Stamper's question. From Helios, Starr heard a disdainful moan.

"Well, now that you mention it," the reporter said, "I can't. It was quite a while back, and there's been so much happening since then." *Yeah,* Starr thought, *like the last time she got her nails done.*

"Don't feel bad. I'd bet there isn't more than a hand full of people who are aware of the current administration's agenda as set forth in the Earth Party's platform, Mei-Ling. They've managed to distract everyone with fancy shows and carefully spun news bites."

Together, the president and Helios sat up strait at this. They both sensed Stamper was about to throw a political grenade. Of course, it didn't surprise either of them; they had been expecting some kind of move to be made by him for quite some time. But the question wasn't whether the big bad dog was going to bite; it was where and when it was going to bite and how big a chunk it was going to take out of their political hides before they could get its jaws pried back open.

"President Draper and the Earth Party made it part of their platform to help solve this water problem. Yesterday and today, as I'm sure you know, I attended the conference in Mexico that was supposed to be an international conclave to set up priorities, coordinate information, and allocate resources relating to this situation. I have to say it was disappointing, Mei-Ling, to watch the political antics of nearly everyone there. It was two days of politicians posing and strutting and making speeches, nothing more. Oh, maybe *one* thing more: There *was* the childish prank of setting off a stink bomb that ruined my dinner and one of my best suits." Stamper smiled at the camera almost like a grandfather who had caught one of his grandchildren stealing cookies. "And I'm sure the world will remember President Draper being carried out like a sack of potatoes by an ex K-baller." He turned his grandfatherly smile into a derisive smirk and the interviewer giggled right on cue. The president was not amused.

"And I know this is going to sound self-serving, Mei-Ling, but I'm going to say it anyway. I think the only worthwhile action taken at that conference was when I got up and announced that I would stop shipping IC from Mars. Did anybody else make any kind of move or announce any real action they or the countries they represented planned to make? No. I was most disappointed by President Draper's failure to make any kind of difference, to put forth any sort of plan that would help the situation or show some real leadership.

"I'm a citizen of the UN, as I'm sure everyone in your audience knows. But I have long thought of the United States as kind of a foster-country for me. Starr Draper technically isn't *my* president but she is supposed to be a leader of the country that collects a lot of money in taxes from my companies. And the party that backs her, the Earth Party, sets itself up as a collective of people concerned with saving this planet from the destructive elements our species has inflicted upon it for centuries. Although it doesn't limit itself solely to participation by members of only one faith, its core ideals are inspired by and geared to Wiccans. Now, I'm proud to say that I'm a true Wiccan. But I hang my head in shame when I see what the Earth Party now is doing in the name of Wicca, Mei-Ling. It's completely upside-down from the beliefs and tenants of real Wiccans. President Draper should be ashamed at her attempt to portray Wiccan beliefs and practices by acting as priestess for that sideshow they called a national Summer Solstice celebration. And her lack of leadership at the World Water Conference shows she doesn't really uphold the values real Wiccans support. The fact is I've gotten no support at all from President Draper for election reform."

This was true enough; Starr hadn't been approached by Stamper or anyone else concerning election reform. The topic had forever been a political football and she wondered if Stamper had any real interest in the matter. She suspected it was only a smoke screen for other activities he was working on.

"Obviously, she doesn't believe in true democracy any more than she believes in making a real change in our environment. Instead of running away from the problem, like she did at the conference, she should be standing solidly against the degradation of our planet and the moral decline that allows it."

By now, Stamper wasn't talking just to the comely interviewer; he was looking into the camera and speaking directly to the audience. "I'd like to encourage every *real* Wiccan to send a message to President Draper that they expect better than mere theatrics; they expect her to live up to the moral code she claims to represent. And I'd also ask them to force their congressional representatives to do something about the Dead Water problem. I've put more money into research to solve this problem than the U.S. Congress has! What have they really done?

"America was formed by people who knew the value of individual action. The ideals expressed in the writings of Franklin, Adams, and Jefferson, the men who helped frame your Constitution were Wiccan ideals. The Masonic lodges of their time were the stronghold of the Wiccan people who had been driven underground by the Burning Times."

Helios turned to the president and said, "I wonder what history books he's been reading?"

Keeping her eyes on Stamper, Starr just shrugged and replied, "I wonder what he was smoking when he read them."

Stamper was on a roll and continued his speech making after another dazzlingly inane remark from the interviewer. "As you say, Mei-Ling, the American people are the ultimate leaders when it comes to the policies of their representatives. They need to demand that their Congress pass the laws necessary to control the problems the lax policies of past lawmakers, and now the current administration, have created. If Congress doesn't make that happen, then true Wiccan circles should band together as a voting block and elect public officials who will. Wiccans should run for office and become the leading edge of policy decision makers. It's their duty as citizens of their country as well as members of this huge faith group."

"Oh boy," Starr said in a low tone. "Here we go."

"I will gladly give support to any true Wiccan who cannot afford the cost of organizing campaign blocks to help spread the information about what it means to live a truly moral and patriotic life. I've spent money for such endeavors in the past and I'll gladly help where I can now. I can be reached through my PerCom site at real_wiccan dot UNWeb dot wzrdwrld." The site address appeared in blue letters below Stamper's image. Anyone interested in accessing it needed only to hit a few buttons on their PerCom. Starr was positive anyone contacting the site would immediately be placed on a mass mailing list for later influence peddling. But she couldn't fault Stamper for doing the same thing her own campaign had done to help her into office. The tactic had been around for nearly a century and hadn't even been started by politicians. E-vertising was a constant in every economy and as long as people used their PerComs to find out about what was going on in the world, data mining would be a fact of life.

Starr was sure that Stamper had thrown the political ball about as far as he dared for the moment, so she muted the sound. "See if you can find out anything about what Stamper says he's talked to TJ about," she ordered her CoS. "And let's get somebody in with the people who are setting up this big circle in Yellowstone. It'll be interesting to see what exactly is planned and where the energies will be directed."

Helios rose and said over his shoulder on the way out, "I'm on it; I'm just as curious as you are. I'm also going to check our little conclave of web-watchers to see what the general reaction to Stamper's interview might be."

One thing Starr was sure of was that there would be plenty of response. After all, Stamper might not be the shrewdest of politicians but he knew how to throw the political K-Ball. Now it was up to her and the Party to see how they might be able to block him from scoring. Starr knew from her history books that the Christian Fundamentalists did exactly what Stamper was urging Wiccans to do: Flood the politicians with demands to align the entire country with the 'values' of the 'upright, devout, and patriotic' people that supposedly were represented by the Fundies. And get the 'true believers' elected to all the political offices you could in every town, county, and state. It always fell back on the interpretation of an arrogant few as to what those values might be. But if you could get enough people believing that was what everybody *else* thought, then you had a power base that could influence not only the politicians but society as a whole. Of course, it would eventually fall like a house of cards, but not until it ran over the freedoms and aspirations of millions of people.

Lady McGuire was right... as usual. This has all the earmarks of becoming the Armageddon for Wiccans if we can't stop it early. Starr picked up her PerCom and dialed the person most responsible for her becoming President. It was time for a war council.

❧ 19 ❧

The image of witches that had prevailed in people's minds for over a thousand years was largely perpetrated by superstitious people who had little or no idea what they were talking about. Combined with the Inquisition, these images were enhanced and exaggerated by literature and, later, moving pictures that created a mythology of a half-demented and haggish woman who made noxious potions and cast evil, debilitating spells on all who displeased her. It's doubtful, if not completely unbelievable, that such creatures ever existed beyond the imagination of some clever writers and film directors. However, it is only human to look for scapegoats and easy to blame beings who don't conform to widely held social norms. And even if those scapegoats don't exist in reality, it matters little to those who think they can escape consequences by trying to shift blame. When the modern magical movement began early in the twentieth century, many followers of Gardner, et al, tried to overcome the engrained image of a 'witch' and claim the label for themselves. Whether there was any real value or reason to do this, the definition ingrained in the minds most people was too much to overcome. It served no real purpose for people of serious spiritual purpose to continue fighting to change the word's meaning to be almost the opposite to that of the public's understanding.

For several decades the battle over what word would be used as a general descriptor was waged within groups as well as between those groups collectively and society at large. Early in the twenty-first century it looked like the term 'Pagan' would succeed in becoming the group name. However, through a strange twist of literary whim, 'Wiccan' came to be used more and more as the umbrella label for the rapidly growing faith movement. Raised to the level of an iconic descriptor, the word became capitalized forever more and was now used to cover a large number of belief systems and practices. To say one was Wiccan was not very specific about what methods of practice or beliefs the individual employed.

There were, however, some who still claimed the term 'witch' and held on to it with a death grip. These people tried to justify their insistence, some being less believable than others, for using the word to depict their faith group. But the important aspect was that they were nearly always at odds with others who used 'Wiccan' to describe themselves. According to the smaller group, 'Wiccan' either was being applied improperly or was a copout for those 'afraid' to use the less popular 'witch'.

One aspect of the old image for the 'typical' witch was actually closer to the modern day reality than might have been expected. It related to the potions brewed up by the hags of the old literature and woodprints. These were probably based on the real medieval alchemical practitioners who were in many ways the cutting edge scientists of their day combined with the wise women of Middle Europe who knew the magic of herbs and other natural items. Modern Wiccans were also interested in science and technology, some of them even at the very forefront of those disciplines. In fact, the holder of the prestigious Hawkings's Chair at the Palo Alto College of the Physical Sciences was an avowed Wiccan who claimed that the so-called 'Philosophers Stone' of the ancient alchemists was in reality a dimensional flux mechanism named the Weaver String and that it was responsible for the ever increasing speed at which the galaxies were traveling away from one another.

So it was little surprise that many Wiccans were attracted to the sciences. And, in the basement of a California mansion, a lone magic worker was carefully working with an eclectic assortment of mechanisms that most universities would've loved to have. The person who had paid for all of the cutting-edge technology was rich and powerful, but the one engaged in the use of it all was not the same person who had purchased the equipment. This work was a magic much more refined and technical than what most Wiccans could understand and the person who labored in the room wasn't like the media image of days gone by. She was neither half-demented nor fooled by superstitious pseudo-science. However, there was a slight similarity between the modern witch and her dramatized counterpart of old: She muttered to herself and even occasionally chuckled at her own wit.

Amid the hushed sounds of some of the equipment, a steady hum was slowly growing stronger. An ever-changing screen displayed readouts indicating the progress of several complex energies working together to construct what the sorceress thought of as her best spell craft. Modern science would have considered it a wondrous piece of technology but the potential for fame and riches through the device wasn't why she had developed it. Tonight's work was solely about justice. If she could make the magnetic sphere to the size she'd worked out, it would be the perfect tool for vaporizing two square blocks. Not just any two blocks either; the target she wanted to obliterate was the White House. And the president who lived there, of course.

The prospect was so exciting it took every bit of her concentration to keep her hands steady. If they weren't, she might lose control and the sphere would disappear into some other dimension. Or so the theory went; her understanding of the process didn't extend quite that far. But her understanding went much, much farther than anyone else's.

The control necessary to coordinate all the energies was as much art as it was technology. Magnetic spheres hadn't been studied much until she had resurrected some old information about them and married it to several modern theories. So far, after several years of study and planning, she'd managed to produce only six stable magnetic spheres.

The first one had been an accident. What she'd thought would work had kept failing for reasons she didn't comprehend. All the theories seemed to say the same thing and the physical mechanisms needed to produce the sphere had been calibrated and balanced to manipulate the energies in accord with her careful figures. And yet, for two frustrating years she didn't produce even the tiniest of magnetic spheres. Then, on a night that had stretched her patience and worn at her self-control, her hand had slipped on a control during a vital intersection of energies. And there before her eyes appeared the first magnet sphere the world had ever seen. It lasted for nearly twenty seconds before winking out of existence with a small popping sound. But that was long enough for Cassandra Whatcom to get enough information from her sensors to allow her to produce the next sphere. And the next.

By now, she was sure she could produce a larger sphere and keep it contained for a longer time than the one in Mexico City. The so-called security there had been more lax than where she would next utilize her invention, but that was a hurdle she would work on later. For now, she just wanted to produce the larger sphere.

The humming grew louder and higher in pitch and she was grateful she'd worn sound dampeners. As the process neared completion her excitement grew, but then a quiet 'pop' interrupted everything and the only sound left in the room was that of the ventilators. Cassandra released her grip from the control panel and slumped in her seat. The cork-out-of-the-bottle sound marked another failure. The last few hours' effort had resulted in nothing but frustration... again. She was exhausted and allowed herself a short moment to wonder if she'd ever be able to accomplish her goal. She let her self-control briefly slide away and the weight of the failure wash over her. It threatened to crush her spirit but she was made of tougher stuff than to let the problem get the better of her. She'd suffered setbacks before; this was only a small disappointment in comparison. She reminded herself that she'd already accomplished what other scientists had declared impossible and her back straightened as she methodically and confidently rebuilt her shields. She would try again after studying what had happened this time to prevent the size of the bubble from expanding beyond what seemed to be an arbitrary size limit.

Three other times she'd tried to produce a sphere over the size of the one she'd used in Mexico and three times they had ended like the one tonight. And the size at the time of disintegration was almost exactly the same for all of them. She'd bet tonight's ball was within a few tenths of a millimeter from all the rest. She had to get the magnetic sphere beyond the third of a meter size that seemed some kind of barrier for her.

It was more than just a scientific challenge for her. And it was more than a simple grudge or act of revenge that motivated her. A terrible injustice had been perpetrated on her, her family, and the entire country. Starr Draper was never supposed to be the next president. Just thinking about the woman running the country for the next few years made Cassie nauseous. By the president's own admission, her psychic abilities were next to zero. Cassandra believed that real power was psychic power. The leader of the greatest nation in the world needed to have psychic control of the people that served him or her. It was an open secret in Washington that Lady McGuire and Allen Barnstead were the real power in the Earth Party. That was totally unacceptable because neither one of them were true witches. Her father was the only person that really deserved to occupy the White House and if he wasn't in control, then it was up to her to rectify the situation.

And it was obvious to Cassandra that not only was Draper not a psychic but she didn't take her religion seriously. Eric's response to Draper's attack when they'd met in Mexico was more than disappointing. If the president had tried the same thing with Cassandra, she would have been furious. How Stamper could stomach such blasphemy was disgusting and she'd lowered her opinion of the man because of it. Her father never would have behaved in such a simpering fashion. How or why Eric could act that way defied her understanding.

Whatcom left the laboratory, turning off devices as she went, and locked the door. She was done for the evening and needed rest. Climbing the stairs slowly, she went over every detail of that night's efforts, trying to understand the elements that still eluded her. She wouldn't be beaten by this. She was a scientist and a witch; she needed to control the energies around her. And by the gods, she would.

❧ 20 ❧

For some unknown reason, people loved to hear bad news. Nearly everyone would deny it, but there was no other explanation as to why e-news feeds that ran so-called 'good news' failed and the sensationalist, holocaust-in-two-minute-bytes newscasters flourished. But if you believed that every day was filled with disasters, constant political problems, rampaging crime and corruption, flagrant disregard of common morals, and threats to the health and welfare of every human on the planet, perhaps your own miseries or problems didn't feel so bad. Political leaders learned early on to disregard much of the panic promoted on a daily basis by those in the business of selling hype and over-the-top bad news. If the world everywhere was as horrible as what those programs seemed to imply, it would end at 11:30 every evening.

However, the president needed to know what was really going on all over the world and how it might threaten the welfare of her nation and its people. Her morning briefings were mostly bad news. In some cases, so bad that if it ever leaked out and become general knowledge, it probably would cause panic in the streets and generate even more trouble. There were some who thought the public had a right to know everything, that there should be no state secrets or hidden information. Anyone who sat in the president's chair had learned the harsh truth that this was more than naive, it was delusional. Some dangers demanded a level of control that would be impossible to achieve when in a state of panic. And, though it was a sad comment on just how far the human species had *not* advanced, there was a constant supply of problems and challenges that would literally cause chaos if known by the general populace. It was the job of the government to act as a barrier between those forces and the people who were ill equipped to handle them.

No president, no leader of any nation could possibly solve all of the problems. Reducing them or even just delaying them was a mammoth job. Creating groups of people – bureaucracies – to tackle them sometimes worked. But more often than not, such agencies usually only proved to be a way of changing the face of the problem or hiding it better from the public. However, the bureaucracies of all the world's governments provided one overriding benefit: they kept the governments on a steady roll. Without them, no nation could survive and no government could function. They were an unfortunate necessity.

Nobody knew how many bureaucracies existed and drew life from the federal government. In many cases, it would have been impossible to determine simply because there were bureaucracies within bureaucracies. Minor officials always were trying to establish control over bigger groups while also attempting to gain more control of the people and powers they already were in charge of. The lines of energy were constantly shifting. But even though there was a constant paper war of boundaries, there was also an upward flow of energy from these battlefields of bureaucrats. And that energy usually made its way to the top officials within Congress and the White House. One of the chief jobs of a president was to direct the way in which these energies were applied. That work occupied most of Starr's time and she had to have the most accurate information about world conditions that was available. For this she had to rely on... a bureaucracy. But Starr Draper also had others who could advise her on specific situations and to whom she turned for advice and perspective. These were individuals she believed she could trust in many ways more than any bureaucrat or politician. Her relationship with Helios D'Amico as one of her most trusted advisors and his job as Chief of Staff was an example of how much Starr valued his input.

Lady McGuire and Allen Barnstead were two others Starr could turn to for advice and assistance whenever she needed and she had grown to trust them far more than most. Not simply because of their unusual psychic abilities, but because she knew them both to be people of exacting and unquestionable honor. And they gave her something many leaders had a hard time finding: the candid truth. It was inevitable that leaders attracted those who wished for more power, sycophants who would feed answers to the heads of state they thought their leaders wanted to hear rather than the real information needed to make good decisions.

It was always important that the Emperor knew when he wasn't wearing any clothes.

Now the four of them, President Draper, Helios D'Amico, Lady McGuire, and Allen Barnstead sat around the low service table that had been brought into the Oval Office. It was best to nip the problem in the bud and Starr wanted her most trusted friends to help brainstorm the situation.

"I'm the last person to say Stamper should not be allowed to state his opinions. But I'd like to find a way to make him look more ridiculous than he's made me look. After being carried off 'like a sack of potatoes,' as Stamper put it, I can hardly expect the public not to think his ideas might be true. This is a war of words; the note and the stink bomb were all designed to make me and the Secret Service paranoid and overreact. I want to strike back in some way and put his 'spiritual purity' notions where the sun don't shine."

Maggie smiled at the president's choice of words and spoke up. "Well, the Service is *always* 'paranoid,' I'm afraid. Granted, that wasn't the most graceful exit that could be made by a president. But I've seen the vids and I have to say that man really moves well, even when carrying a sa..." She saw Starr's look and revised what she was going to say. "... carrying a person. Be that as it may, you're right that Stamper has the edge right now and it seems he knows exactly how to capitalize on it. And, as I'm sure you all will agree, if we can't turn the tide of opinion his words will likely cause a bad change within the Wiccan groups. Once that happens, it's only a matter of time before the non-Wiccan public begins to lash out."

"We need a campaign," Helios said. "Hey, don't look at me like that; this isn't any different than when we were out there drumming up votes and funds. We know Stamper's ideas, his general philosophy about Wiccans. Making those ideas look bad will be easy compared to what we went through just a couple of months ago"

"Speaking of funds, how are we going to afford this, whatever 'this' might be?" Barnstead, among his other talents, had been an accountant and was most helpful when it came to financial matters in Starr's campaign. "If we use Party funds, we're going to have to justify it to everyone else in the Party. And I'm sure there'll be an uproar about it. Using money for promoting a bill or a candidate is okay; using it to fight another Wiccan's free speech is another. We'll have problems on top of troubles if we try."

Both Helios and Starr began talking at once so that Lady McGuire's remarks were drowned out. A three-way argument was waged for the next minute until she found a break in the conversation. "I'll pay for it," she managed to slip into the brief silence. Everyone immediately turned their attention. Starr was the first to speak.

"I beg your pardon? *You'll* pay for it? Do you have any idea how much money we might have to spend?"

The older woman smiled. "Why, yes, I probably know better than you do since I've done this sort of thing before."

"Excuse me, Lady McGuire..."

"Oh come off it; let's just use real names here, please."

"Fine. Now, just how much of this do you think you can fund?"

"All of it."

That made the president blink, and her brow shot up in question.

"You don't think I run that rundown shack of mine with gifts from grateful clients, do you? Believe me: I've made gobs of money investing in my visions. I haven't always been right but I'm so far ahead of the curve it's embarrassing. I'm not a pauper by any stretch."

Everyone paused to consider the situation. Everyone except Maggie kept blinking at one another a few more moments until Helios spoke up with a grin a mile wide. "I move we have Lady McGuire pay all our bills from here on in."

"Second."

"Second."

They all laughed. It was one less problem they had to solve. What followed was a brainstorming session that lasted for a couple of hours. When they were done, there was a clear plan of how they'd handle the 'war of words' that seemed to have been such a big problem when they'd first come into the room. Eric Stamper was going to have a problem promoting his ideas without some heavy competition.

Starr felt like a late night snack before going to sleep, so she found her way to the White House kitchen. There was plenty of activity even at that late hour. Bakers were baking the next day's bread, cakes, pies, and fancy bad-for-the-waistline treats that would be fed to the hundreds of people who would come and go over the next day's business. And butchers were... well, *butching*. She had no idea if there was a section making candlesticks but she wouldn't have been surprised.

Poking her nose into one of the many sections emitting wonderful smells, Starr saw a woman she recognized and walked in. "Good evening, Clara," she said to the oversized woman dressed in sparkling white. "Do you think I could get a roast beef sandwich?"

The woman's smile was almost as white teethed and genuine as Dr. Hunk's, thought the president. *WATSON... DR. WATSON! Stop with the 'Hunk" business!* She just *had* to keep from thinking that!

"Yes ma'am, coming right up." In seconds, the woman had cut slices of fresh, warm bread and put them around a mound of thinly sliced roast beef with lettuce, red onion, and mustard for the president. She cut the sandwich diagonally, slid it onto a plate with the presidential seal, and proudly handed it to the president. "Would you like something to drink with that?"

"Decaf if it's fresh, please. If not, I'll take a half a cup of regular."

A cup of hot and fresh decaf appeared in about twenty seconds. Starr was always impressed by the staff at the White House. She was tempted to see if she could stump them with a weird request but she didn't have the heart. Nor did she really have a taste for platypus tongue pâté on rice crackers at the moment. *Still*, she thought wickedly... She thanked the cook, wished her a good evening, and left the kitchen area feeling very pampered.

❧ 21 ❧

The next few days were filled with thousands of small details that needed attention and the week blew past quickly. The president met either electronically or in person with several minor and not-so-minor foreign officials and was so tired by the end of Saturday, she was tempted to sneak out to New Camp David for a day alone with the tall trees of Olympic National Forest in the 'other Washington'. Like most Wiccans, she took psychic and spiritual nourishment from Nature's wild places and she felt the need to recharge. But her Sunday schedule was just as full as the days of the previous week and she knew she'd not make it to the rain forest on the other side of the country any time soon.

Just before retiring that night, she sent a message to her father. Thinking he was probably asleep, she just recorded a short message and sent it to his in-box for later viewing. To her surprise, five minutes later her PerCom notified her of a call from him. Switching it to her wall screen, she answered it in her pajamas.

"Hi, Dad. I thought you'd be asleep by now. It's 11:45."

"Ha! You forget we're in a different time zone up here. The sun won't be setting on us for another hour."

She did feel foolish forgetting that the orbiting station at the end of the long elevator was considered a different time zone. The joke was that since you were going 'earlier' as you rose up to the station, it took almost 'no time' to get there but 'ages' to go down. "You're right, I forgot. It's been a busy week and I'm a little fuzzy headed right now. I was thinking of when we last went to the Olympic National Park, you and me. I'm hoping to get to New Camp David soon. Would you like an official presidential invitation?"

"That'd be nice, but it would only get framed and hung on the wall for now. We're up to our necks installing some new test gear. And they've managed to crowd another three people up here to speed up our work. I'm not sure if we're getting things done faster or just making it all more complicated."

She heard him griping, but she also saw the spark in his eye that told her he was charged up with the research and the promise of new knowledge. And she also knew he was probably working himself at a feverish pace while whipping his workers to do the same. Nothing she could say would slow him down, even if it meant less pain and a greater chance to survive the very disease he was studying. MPN, Morphing Pathology Necrosis, would eventually be conquered; everyone was confident of that. But as much as she wanted her father to be the leader in that cure, she didn't want him to sacrifice his own life for it.

Since the start of the call, Starr had been trying to sneak a look at her father's hand but he'd managed to keep it out of sight. Finally, she decided to be blunt. "Show me your hand, Dad."

He gave her an exasperated look and stalled. "Now, honey…"

"SHOW IT TO ME! Please, for the love of the gods, Dad, do you think I don't know it's gotten worse? Don't you think it's the nine-hundred pound Gorilla in this conversation?"

His eyebrows rose and his jaw became set, but he just nodded grimly and put his hand in front of the lens. Holding it there a moment, he spoke gently, knowing his daughter would be afraid of what she saw. "Strange you should mention Gorillas. You remember Carl Eng? He and Dr. Douglas Whitworth from Oxford have been conducting tests on some monkeys and such to see why they don't get MPN. Guess what? It seems the same gene that we think caused the opposable thumb has a little hook on it that…"

"Dad. DAD! Would you stop trying to distract me?" What had happened in just over a week to her father's hand was terrifying to her. There was a big difference and she knew that the MPN was progressing faster than normal… *much* faster. "What's going on? Why is it happening so fast?"

He pulled it away from the camera and looked at it as if he hadn't noticed. Of course he had; he was aware of it every moment.

"This? Well, you know cells work a little different in low G, right? Well, we figure that's the reason it seems to be going faster than normal. But don't you worry, kiddo, we're going faster than this stuff. I'll beat it to the finish line; you just wait and see."

She knew her father well and she could read him like a book. From what she saw on his face and heard in his voice she knew he believed what he'd just told her as 100% truth. But as much as she wanted to believe it as completely as he, she couldn't be convinced. The memory of her mother dying from MPN was too strong, too vivid simply to trust that her father would 'beat this thing'. But she also knew that the last thing he needed right now was for his own daughter putting negative energy into his efforts. So she buried her thoughts and emotions and smiled at him. "I know you will, Dad. And I can't tell you how proud I am of you. The day you can announce to the world that you've found the cure, I'll be so happy to stand in the crowd and know it was my dad, Dr. Martin Draper, who headed the team that made it happen."

"Ha! Stand in the crowd? I expect you to give me a medal or something, honey. Not for finding a cure; that's a team effort. But for putting up with the cooking up here. Dr. Mendoza does most of it and I gotta tell you, the stuff is mostly horrible." He gave a sour look and shook his head to emphasize his words. "And Rosie's beans? Oh brother, the methane up here is denser than in a cattle barn! The air scrubbers are working overtime, but it doesn't help much."

She knew he was trying to cheer her up and just the idea that he was worried about *her* feelings nearly broke her façade of control. Nevertheless, she managed a smile and a chuckle. "I'll ask Congress to make a special award for methane tolerance above and beyond. Just for you, Dad." She had to break the call off before she lost control in front of him. "Look, Dad, I've got to get to bed. I need to be at my best when President Zorlaninsky comes calling tomorrow. He's a sly old dog and I know he's going to want something I won't want to give him. So I need my beauty sleep."

"Tell him to go..."

"Daaaad?" She wagged a finger at him. "Be nice."

"Yeah, well I'm old enough to remember when Russia couldn't put two rubles together but was plenty willing to blow us off the face of the planet."

"Different time; different country, Dad."

"Oh, really? You think so? Then why is Nitchy's new novel so gloomy, so dark, so, so... *Russian*? It's their *nature*, Starr. Russians are always gloomy and pessimistic. It's in their genes. Rasputin genes is what they have, mark my words."

Now she could chuckle for real. Sometimes her father just cracked her up. "And on that note, Dad, I'm going to shut down and go to sleep. You get your rest, too, please?"

"You bet, honey. I'm sacking out here in the lab tonight because I have to be up at two to change the filtration on an experiment. But at least I don't have to sleep in the methane factory." He put his splayed hand up to the lens and said, "Blessed be, sweetie."

She put her own hand up and smiled. Her dad hadn't called her 'sweetie' in years; not since her mother died. "Blessed be, Dad. I'll work on that medal for you tomorrow." She knew a woman who did marvelous artwork in enameled metals. She'd contact her about designing a 'medal' for her father and find a way of presenting it to him at a suitably embarrassing moment. The thought buoyed her up until she told the lights to dim and snuggled into her bed.

Then images of her father's morphed hand came back to fill her thoughts and the president of the United States cried herself to sleep.

✑ 22 ✑

As expected, the following day was dominated by the meeting with the president of Russia. Allinov Kordia Zorlaninsky, unlike his predecessor, was young, only fifty-four. He also was from money, a rarity in Russia. Starr's people had informed her of his family's history and it sounded more like an old film video called *The Godfather* than anything else. Zorlaninsky's father, grandfather, and grand-uncles were high up in the *Mafia* that had gained so much power by the turn of the century. But it seemed that since the two brothers had gained control of the purse strings, things had changed quite a bit. Or so it appeared. Allinov had gotten into politics during his college days and had used his money and influence to climb the complex political ladder of Russian politics.

But money and influence alone weren't enough to get to the top of that mountain; in today's Russia, you also needed the same kind of political smarts and public charm that politicians in the USA had to have. And Allinov Kordia Zorlaninsky had plenty of charm. The NSA had warned President Draper that Zorlaninsky would probably be wearing pheromones designed to turn on most western women. It wasn't illegal and there wasn't anything that could be done to prevent it. But it was likely to make Starr more charmed with the Russian president than she would otherwise be and that could complicate things. To date, no preventative measures had been found suitable for resistance to the pheromones other than a bio-suit. Like most pheromones, absorption through the skin was almost as effective as inhalation.

The usual media circus occupied the first hour of their meeting but then they got down to business. 'Allin' (pronounced, 'All-leen'), as the Russian President insisted she call him, spoke excellent English and there was no need for translators. Starr had been right when she told her father Zorlaninsky would be asking for something she didn't wish to give. The trade conditions between Russia and China were not favorable to the Russians. This was primarily because of the poor condition of the Russian money at the turn of the century when the current applicable trade agreements had been worked out.

Now that Russia had a stronger economy, they wanted China to change the rules more in favor to their neighboring country. Of course, the largest economy on the planet wasn't inclined to do this. So Zorlaninsky wanted America, the second biggest economic power in the world, to intervene.

It wasn't anything new or unexpected. Russia had been chafing against China's policies for decades and nothing substantial had been accomplished. Starr listened politely to the man's proposals and persuading arguments and then told him that there wasn't anything that America could do or say to make China any friendlier to her neighbor. The centuries old animosity between the two countries had never gone away, even during the twentieth century when they both were deemed Communist countries. The two countries, China and the then much stronger USSR, had always kept a wary eye on one another and now wasn't any different. Trade was indispensable to both countries but distrust and dislike between them was not lessened by that necessity.

At the end of their mostly ceremonial visit, they emerged from their private meeting and provided the usual polite words to the media, shook hands (much of the world still used the custom), and parted ways. It frustrated Starr that nothing had really happened other than perhaps both of them had been able to size up the other a little better. But that was the way of politics sometimes. She was sure the political pundits of the media would take another two days to tell the public in a million words that nothing really had changed. The thought made her smile as she walked back into the business section of the White House.

A stray thought ran through her mind: The West Wing was the operational hub of the administrative branch of the government. And it was Water, the Element in the west that gave meaning to everything in the Wiccan traditions. How appropriate. Or was that once again something the Masons, who had designed most of the government's main buildings in D.C., including the White House, had done intentionally? Perhaps the answer would never be known, but it was something else that gave her pause now and then. Over the last three centuries and more, a great deal had been made of the influence of the Masons on American culture. And, in his interview, Stamper had argued that Wiccan ideals had been 'kept pure' during the American Revolution and the formation of its government by 'hiding' within the Masonic lodges of the colonies. As laughable as it might seem, there could be some truth to the notion. Another explanation was that Masonic concepts had made their way into modern Wiccan thinking. In the long run, she wondered if it mattered which was true.

✍ 23 ✎

The twentieth century had been a remarkable time of technological change. Just as the Industrial Age had transformed Europe and its rebellious colonies, making everyday life into a completely changed social and political scene, so too did the Information Age impress a whole new paradigm on the world. As hard as any political system tried to suppress its effect, the free exchange of ideas and the ability to broadcast them to the entire world's population had made significant changes in the way people worked, thought, and conducted their lives. No part of the planet was unaffected by the ability to communicate virtually instantaneously from anywhere to anywhere else. One scholarly study from France, completed in the early sixties, reported that the average human (even when including the purposely technology-shunning communes still functioning in South America and some Pacific islands) averaged sixty-three technology assisted communications a day and had an average 'friends' list of over three hundred people with whom they communicated at least once a month. Every PerCom sold had a feature to take 'instant notes' directly from the voice input of its owner or those who called. If it weren't for this one feature, most of the communicated information would have been lost or simply delayed until it was worthless. The amount of time spent on PerComs by most humans had risen to nearly twenty percent of their day. For any in a position of directing or managing any commercial or political entity, that was probably doubled.

However, there was a demographic group that saw a dramatic drop in PerCom use. Some, actually a very small group, used their units considerably *less* than average. These people were so important that access to them was nearly impossible for the average human. The president of the United States was one of this group, as were the heads of state for nearly every other country on the planet. The president's PerCom address was not only kept secret; it was shielded and filtered by some of the most sophisticated software and hardware known. If you didn't have any business calling the president, your call was shunted off to one of several people or programs that simulated secretaries or underlings of various sorts. The group President Draper had formed right after her inauguration to take the calls from Mr. or Ms. Average Citizen was inundated from the start (the first day saw only twelve thousand calls but the number had grown every day after that). It would have been impossible to manage if it weren't for the software that had been set up. The ability to make synoptic notes from the voice or written calls was similar to the programs of the PerCom and, combined with even more sophisticated AI response programming, few people knew that they weren't actually talking or messaging a real person. The filtering processes allowed most of the really important information to reach human eyes and ears more quickly.

The person in charge of the Public Input unit was Arlenna Nguyen, a young Social Systems expert who had come to the attention of Helios two years back. Having reached the age of just thirty-one, Nguyen's appointment to such an important job was questioned by many. But Helios had faith she could fill the required boots and wanted to give her a try. His estimation of her abilities was almost certainly influenced by the fact that he also found her extremely attractive but their relationship was hardly what would be considered close. He was twenty years her senior and both of their jobs demanded a 24/7 dedication. Anything more intimate than a smile as they passed each other in hallways was on hold for the time being. However, her visit to his office was a welcome surprise.

"Got something nice and juicy, Arlenna?" He leaned back in his chair and jokingly wiggled his eyebrows. "It must be good to make you come all this way to hand it to me personally. Or are you just in need of some good, old fashioned ogling?"

She gave the remark a small but encouraging smile. She was attracted to the handsome man but wasn't about to follow up on it while on duty... which was all the time. "This stuff really *is* important so I decided to bypass the usual twenty intermediaries and get it to you now." She handed over a folder marked 'Confidential'.

He took it and keyed open the seal. "Run it down for me."

"At first I thought it was just another crank invention, another 'magic bullet' for dead water. But this guy isn't fooling. Or maybe he is a crank and the test results he says he's gotten are just wishful thinking. But I ran this by 3F in the lunchroom an hour ago and he says it looks like the real deal. Oh, did you know he and Agent Morgan are engaged? You should see 3F; he's grinning like a schoolboy and, believe it or not, even less coordinated than his usual self. Downright goofy."

"Yeah, I know. I think it came as a surprise to most everyone." He waved the envelope. "So why send this information to us? I mean, if he's got a real cure to the problem, it's worth a fortune. Why not keep quiet about it until he gets everything in order to put it on the market?"

"Read what he says in the second paragraph of the synopsis. He wants government protection. He's afraid somebody, and I think he means Stamper and friends, will try to rob or maybe even kill him to suppress the information. I don't know, but it might not be completely groundless. Back in the twentieth century, carmakers and oil companies suppressed ways to increase engine efficiency and prevent some good mass transit schemes from being implemented. Rumor had it that sometimes they got 'enthusiastic' with their methods for suppressing stuff."

"Okay, we can talk with the Secret Service if need be. I presume you've got a dossier on him?" She nodded. "Who is he; what does he do when he's not inventing magic bullets?"

"He's Dr. David Jones." Helios gave her a raised eyebrow. "Hey, I didn't name him; talk with his parents. He's a microbiologist with the University of Utah on a grant from the NSF for work on MPN. He says he invented this thing in his off time and it doesn't fall under work-for-hire rules. That needs to be sorted out, of course. He's got something like four PhD's and speaks about a dozen languages.

Never married and if you look at his picture, which is in there somewhere, you'll see one of the reasons why. He looks exactly like an actor made up for a mad scientist holo-vid."

Helios looked through the material and found the picture. Arlenna was right; the guy really did look the part. Wild, flyaway white hair, buck toothed, hooked nose, bulging eyes... and those were his *good* features! But he didn't care what the man looked like if he really had something to take care of the water problem. Statues would be erected to him if his invention worked.

But Helios wasn't a scientist and skeptical that some relatively obscure academic had discovered a cure for the biggest threat to civilization since the fusion bomb but was handing it over to the government because he was paranoid. He gave the material a cursory look through and then handed it all back to her. "Take this back to 3F and tell him to give us a recommendation by tonight. If he thinks it's got potential, we'll set it up for Dr. David Jones..." He paused to smile at the name again, "... for Dr. Jones to come to Washington and meet with some of our people. And we'll all keep our fingers crossed that this," he tapped the folder with his finger, "is the real deal. Good lord, I can see the headlines if it is: 'Davie Jones Solves Water Problem'." He chuckled again and shook his head. "In the meantime, treat it as high security, okay?"

She nodded and turned to leave but stopped at the door to look back. "You know, I find it encouraging that 3F and Morgan found time for their romance. Kind of gives you hope, right?"

By the time her remark and its implications had processed through his brain enough for him to glance up, she was through the door. But before it had completely closed, he noticed that her receding backside had possibly a bit more sexy movement than usual. Yes indeed, he thought, there was always reason for hope.

❧ 24 ❧

Since the invention of radio, individuals, businesses, and governments had been engaged in a two-way struggle to develop ways to keep wireless transmissions secret and to listen in on other transmissions which were supposed to be secret. Security of information was an arms battle of sorts with continuing escalation on all fronts. With the advent of personal computers and worldwide wireless information, this battle was even more complex. It became an accepted rule that no matter how 'secure' a transmission of any kind was, a way to intercept it would eventually be discovered. And so codes became an important part of everyday life, not only for governments and business interests, but for individuals as well. Code making and code breaking was a growth industry even in bad economic times.

In the early part of the twenty-first century, a young computer genius developed what became an important breakthrough in code systems. It was based on two components of the humans involved in the information to be transmitted: their DNA and their thumbprint. The individual algorithm produced by this key was said to be more unique than a single atom in the sun. For over thirty years, no means of breaking this code had been found. Then, in 2043, a child of fourteen figured out a way to circumvent the whole system with a simple circuit made, in part, from one of her toys. The world groaned while the code makers clamored to set things right again and everybody could rest easy that everything was being made secret once more. For two days, all banks were shut down and nothing happened in the world of business. The total cost was estimated at over ninety-three billion 'Yoons' (UN$), or about two-point-two trillion US Dollars. The politicians and media decried the financial disaster and made a great deal out of it until it was pointed out by the same young lady who had broken the DNA-Print system that the so-called 'cost' was in money that had *not* been spent. And, she said innocently, if you wanted to say that money that wasn't spent was money lost then the total 'loss' on any day would be infinite.

Everyone blinked, dropped their jaws, blinked again, closed their jaws, blinked again, and uttered the only comment that made any sense: "Duh." That child, the girl who had shown how complex things could be made simple and how simple things could be made to seem complex, was the same genius who later had made the production of Bucky Ball chains economical so orbiting satellites on the ends of elevators to the sky could be built. She was also the youngest double doctorate in the history of Cal Tech and now was in charge of the National Science Foundation. Her name was Fiona Houghton and at the tender age of 'forty-ish' she was in charge of the largest and best-funded science research and technology center in the world. Even the UN didn't have as great a collection of powerful and educated minds as the NSF. And nobody else had the genius of Fiona Houghton. It was said that she could see into dimensions beyond existence. Whatever made her mind work, it was beyond nearly everyone's understanding. Once, in an introduction speech to an international science symposium, Dr. Houghton was called 'the goddess of science.' Around the halls of the NSF, she was referred to simply as, 'The Goddess.'

Twice in less than a week, 3F had come to see Dr. Houghton. As it happened, when he came calling a second time she was in her office with two other physicists working on the first problem he had presented to her, the existence of magnetic spheres. This time, he wanted her opinion about the invention and theories presented by Dr. Jones. She introduced him to her two colleges and then asked Conner Hollander, a man with pure white hair slicked into an old fashioned pompadour, to explain what they had been discussing.

"Yes, well... ahem... if, uh... if you could build such a device, that is... if you could... well it would exist... in a stable state, that is... for as long as it didn't fall close to a magnetic force stronger... locally, that is... stronger than the surface of the sphere. Of course, the amount of area... of the sphere, that is... the outside magnetic force would have to affect would depend on the size... of the sphere, of course. I figure... just hypothetically, mind you... I figure the ratio would be approximately... just in theory, mind you... the diameter divided by $2\pi^2$."

"The 'trigger,' Conner. Tell him what could trigger it."

"Oh, yes. Yes, of course. Well... yes, the trigger. You see... if you wanted to destabilize it... the sphere, that is... if you wanted to destabilize it, all you would need is another magnetic source. Any kind of magnetic source... that is. I understand you found such a magnetic... electromagnets, that is... you found them attached to pieces of furniture... in Mexico City, that is. That would do it... trigger the destabilization of the sphere, of course. But all you would need... to destabilize it... the magnetic sphere, you understand... would be a simple device like this." The man held up his PerCom. "Like the one in this... the speaker in it, that is... or some other electromagnetic generator."

The fellow appeared to have exhausted himself by simply speaking. Apparently communicating in words wasn't his strong suit. But it gave 3F pause to think of the implications of what he had proposed. If true, a magnetic sphere could be triggered by any device used to produce an electronic signal. It could be 'aimed' and maybe detonated by nothing more than a call to a person's PerCom! He was chilled by the thought but he was there to get Dr. Houghton's opinion on the information Dr. Jones had sent.

He asked to see her privately and instead of asking the others to leave, she escorted him through a door and down a short hall. It opened to a bathroom and she led him inside and closed the door. "What's so urgent, Franklyn? You look all worked up."

He handed her the security portfolio with the materials Dr. Jones had sent and outlined what the Chief of Staff wanted to know before offering it to the president. "Helios needs a quick opinion on this. I'd like you to take ten minutes and see what you think."

She started turning pages, scanning each one quickly and absorbing the information as fast as she could move her eyes over the text and equations. 3F remained quiet while she studied the material. Fiona's ability to read a page as quickly as most people took to read a sentence was legendary in the halls of the NSF and in less than two minutes, she looked back up and nodded. "It's possible. I'd like to confirm his test results, of course, but he might be on to something. Goddess knows it would certainly be wonderful if true. To be honest, though, I'm a little doubtful. It all seems a little too good that we could replace the IC with this fellow's synthetic crystal and, poof, no more dead water. I'd like to run some experiments; could you give me a copy of these last five pages?"

"Sorry," he shook his head as he took the papers back, "D'Amico wants this all hush-hush for now. I'm sure you'll get a chance at it all later, but it's all classified at the moment."

"Well, I'm going to run a few tests on some of the things I remember. Can't stop wondering about that sodium and sulfur combination." She got a faraway look for a couple of seconds but then smiled at him conspiratorially. "C'mon, they'll think we're messing around in here if we don't go back." She put a hand on his shoulder and gave him a push back toward the hallway. Moments later, as he walked out of the building, he was shaking his head in envy at how the woman could absorb the information so fast.

Franklyn had been raised a nominal Quaker but had drifted towards Wicca in his teens. Sometimes he wondered about the religion's emphasis on the feminine aspect, and at times it seemed to him that women *had* gotten the best break from the gods. But as he got on the auto-tram back to the White House he chuckled to himself as he recalled what he'd been told years back by an elderly fellow at a May-faire. The man might have been getting on in years, but he'd obviously not lost his taste for beautiful young ladies since he was escorting two of them to the Aphrodite shrine at the time. With a waggle of his bushy eyebrows, he'd told 3F, "The best part of being a Wiccan *man*, my young bucko, is Wiccan *women*." Maybe the gods hadn't favored the females any more than the males after all, he thought with a smile.

✎ 25 ✐

"It's *imperative!*"

"I know! I just can't seem to make it as large as I want. Nothing I do seems to work. I've been at it night and day, father. I'll *do* it; I just need a little more time, that's all." He had a way of making her feel as if she was a failure and she hated herself for not being able to live up to his demands. But she had been able to form the first stable magnetic sphere ever made, damn it. Why couldn't he recognize her abilities and at least offer some appreciation?

He reached across the table and touched her. "Then try again, Cassie. You know the longer this situation goes on, the stronger she'll become. We've managed to lull them into thinking these things are basically harmless, so we must hit her soon, before they return to a higher state of caution."

"I understand that, but you were the one that wanted to start the attacks this early. I *told* you the spheres were problematic. We shouldn't have begun until I'd worked it out better."

"And let her highness prance around as if she were a real witch? She's the one who has caused us to act quickly." His argument played to her fanaticism about Wiccan purity, of course, but he didn't care what motivated her. He just wanted Draper out! He hadn't spent most of his fortune just to see somebody else get to the pinnacle of power in his place. It galled him to play second fiddle to her but at least he'd seen early on that he couldn't win against the machinations within his own party. When he assumed the presidency he was going to make sure there would be an 'accident' that would rid the world of the Lady McGuire once and for all. And maybe those twin jerks, Hartford and Barnstead. He hated Barnstead almost as much as McGuire. Their psychic powers were formidable and a threat to him.

She pulled away and stood up. The bar and game room of his 'hunting cabin' might have been luxurious and large, but right now it pressed in on her and she needed to move about. Her head hurt and, since arriving at the VP's retreat, her anxiety to destroy the president had grown to nearly an explosive force inside of her. She fixed herself another drink and was turning back to her father when she suddenly stopped moving. One hand was out, frozen at the beginning of some gesture, and her mouth seemed to be about to form a word. The Vice-President, alarmed by her sudden 'freezing,' was about to ask her if she was all right when she just as suddenly began to move again. With a look of triumph starting to spread on her face, she spoke almost in a whisper. "If I can't make one large sphere, why not two smaller ones?" Then she almost giggled, so pleased was she at the simple but elegant solution. "Great Goddess, it was so obvious... I feel so... *lame!*"

Hunt was about to speak again but she moved quickly, making ready to leave. "I've got to check out a couple of things, but I'm sure this will work. Give me a few days and we'll be able to strike." She gave him a quick hug and an air kiss and flew out the side door. As she drove away, he smiled to himself and picked up the drink she'd left untouched. He silently congratulated himself at being able to keep her under his control. It had not always been an easy matter to do so when she was younger. She was much like her mother in that respect.

Lillian Whatcom had been only twenty-four when she'd met T. J. Hunt. The dashing and influential politician had entranced her from the start and it took only minutes before she'd gone with him back to his hotel room near the state convention center. That night, she had done things with him that she had never thought of doing with any other lover and by morning she was exhausted. She had been used only for his pleasure and she'd had little of her own. But for reasons she didn't understand, she didn't resent their liaison.

Two months later, she knew she was pregnant and there wasn't any room for doubt that Hunt was the father. She'd come armed with the DNA tests in the hope that he would honor the conception. To her surprise, he never bothered to question the paternity. But she was never able to explain how she had agreed to raise the child and allow him to remain quietly in the background, providing the financial support necessary to see to their needs. For the first fifteen years, the arrangement had seemed to work quite well. Whenever the subject of her father came up, Lillian had simply told Cassie he was an important man who was providing for them both and she shouldn't rock the boat.

But that arrangement didn't always suit the young and extremely inquisitive teenager. She had run away from the special school where she was being boarded and had, in less than four days, found out that it was Senator T. J. Hunt who was her father. On the fifth day, while both her mother and Hunt had private and civil authorities out looking for her, Cassandra appeared at Hunt's DC offices and demanded to see him. Five minutes later she was seated in the shielded room Hunt used only for his most private meetings.

It was in that first face-to-face contact that Hunt had become fully aware of Cassie's surprisingly powerful intellect and her gift of foresight. And it was then she had first fallen under the spell of her father's powerful charisma. Everything he said seemed to become her thoughts and wishes. When she finally left that day, she was convinced that it was to her benefit never to reveal she was his daughter. She also had an overwhelming desire to please him and to dedicate her life to his interests and goals. She returned to her schooling and thereafter was a model student and one of that school's most voracious learners. A dozen years later, Cassandra Whatcom had a BA in Magic Arts, a Masters in Political Science, and a PhD in Integrated Sciences.

Hunt had then told her she should look up his old friend, Eric Stamper and see how she might be of use in his business. Without telling him she was his daughter, T. J. had persuaded Stamper of Cassandra's usefulness and it didn't take long before the rich man and the lovely young genius became a steady pair. Hunt's dream of becoming President of the United States had taken another step forward.

But even his magical abilities of persuasion couldn't guarantee that result. He was able to enchant nearly everyone he made personal contact with but he couldn't physically touch every voter. Even though it galled him, he knew his bid for the nomination would fail when the first primaries had come back showing Draper's popularity. A graceful exit at that point was the smartest thing he could do and he started planning how he would get the nod for the Vice-Presidency. As the saying went, he would be only a heartbeat away.

Winning the VP spot actually had been easy. Draper had been terribly inexperienced concerning the whole presidential bid process and had taken her lead from Trenton and Barnstead entirely. They were the ones who actually had won the election; Draper was just a tool. She had taken their advice about using T. J. and his campaign 'war chest' money. Of course, he had been the one to make that their only recommendation. Five minutes with each of them had been all that was needed. Draper had accepted their advice without him even having to be there to 'persuade' her. But once the election had been won, she had no further use of him and he had been relegated to the face in the background as soon as she had taken office. More than anything else, *that* had made him want her dead and gone quickly. Using is daughter's fanaticism concerning 'spiritual purity' was the easiest way to insure that he would move into the White House quickly.

He could care less whether Draper was a 'real witch' or not; his own spiritual alignment was only a show for the party hacks anyway. But Cassandra's energy was entirely focused on the single issue of a person's religion. If you weren't her brand of Wiccan, she considered you to be not simply lesser, but an *enemy* of her version of the One, True Old Religion. He would have laughed out loud at her ranting if he didn't need her to kill the president. As it was, he had to be careful with his words so he wouldn't alienate her. Powers of persuasion aside, he couldn't make someone a complete puppet. And there were some things his daughter would find abhorrent about his ideas if he spoke about them the wrong way. For now, he found her useful. But after he was sworn in as President he would have to find a way to rid himself of her annoying presence.

❧ 26 ❧

Starr was used to hard work and a busy schedule. She thrived on the challenges of a life of public service and had never involved herself too much with a social life except as necessary to fulfill her work. She had never lacked for friends or companions but had little experience with infatuation or romance. She was far past her teens and the hormonal chaos that usually caused so much confusion. Her parents had somehow managed to keep her focused enough that those times were filled with plenty of good memories and far less of the normal angst that most people experienced during puberty. She had taken a few lovers in her time but it always seemed that after a short while there wasn't anything else to say except a gracious farewell. She'd remained friends with a few over the years and had even become godmother to a set of twins born to one fellow she'd spent time with many years before.

So it shouldn't have escaped her that she was infatuated with Dr. Elliot Watson. However, the schedule of a president is such that it is easy to put personal matters in the back of the mind. Anyone who filled the office had to be able to compartmentalize their time and attention so they could focus completely on the situation at hand and not let their thinking be distracted by anything else. A good number of her staff was there for the sole purpose of maintaining some kind of order to the outrageously complex issues the president faced throughout the day. In part, they were there to act as pressure valves so she could move from one issue to another without missing a step. It had taken a little getting used to, but when Draper decided what course of action needed to be taken on a subject, she had someone who could carry out her directions. Her job was demanding enough and she had to trust that her staff was both competent and dedicated.

Of all the people who surrounded her on a daily basis, Starr Draper was most confident of her Chief of Staff, Helios D'Amico. She'd known him for years and their psychic bond was so complete that she actually felt a little empty when he wasn't near. It wasn't the emotional void two lovers might experience if separated, but it still left her with a feeling of incompleteness if they were too far apart for an extended period of time. Their mental bond wasn't the same as what might be called 'mind reading' but was tremendously useful to both of them.

She hadn't called him to her private office but he showed up only a minute after she had decided she needed to talk to him. She didn't look up as he came in and he hadn't bothered to knock. She just began speaking as soon as he had entered.

"I'm worried over this analysis of the China exports for last quarter. We've got to find a way to reduce our trade imbalance or we'll be back to the same problems we had with them back in the twenties."

"I know; I've put Secretary Irving on it this morning. I told her that you'd need something by next week. She gave me a sour look but promised she'd work on it."

"Well, she's got a lot on her plate but I'm glad she's the one heading up Commerce right now. To be honest, I think President Picossa's Secretary was a twit. We'd be two points *ahead* instead of *behind* China if they'd gone with the UN's basic tax instead of complicating it until every pirate east of the Potomac could mess it up." She smiled up at him. She was glad she could gripe to him and be sure it never got outside her office. Also, it was reassuring to know he'd taken care of her concerns ahead of time... as usual.

Such meetings took place several times a day and they would part company with the same lack of formality as they had when coming together. "Hello" and "good-bye" hardly ever were spoken; it wasn't necessary. So it was surprising to Starr that Helios hadn't simply left the office after their exchange. It took a moment to realize that he was still there. She looked up with a bit of concern; if he had something else to say she couldn't discern what it might be, which was unusual. They had long ago dropped their mental shields to one another. She cocked her head, silently asking what else he wanted to say.

Without any preamble, he came out with it. "You need to take a rest."

Now that he'd spoken his thoughts, she detected something else. "And?"

"And you should take Dr. Watson with you."

"But I feel f... Oh." It had taken a beat for her to catch his meaning. She raised her eyebrow and smiled ruefully. "Are you telling the president that she needs to get laid?"

"Well yes, Madam President, I think that's exactly what I'm suggesting," he said with a small smirk.

She gave it a moment's thought. "Well, uh... that might get complicated, don't you think? Besides, I don't think the good doctor is much interested in my body. For sex, that is."

He gave her a shrug as if to say, why not find out? Again, she sensed he was trying to hide something. "What do you know that I'm not supposed to know? C'mon, this isn't like you, Helios."

He looked at his feet for a second, then back at her. "Ask Lady McGuire," was all he needed to say.

"Maggie? *Maggie* told you to tell me?" She didn't need to see his head nod; she knew what he was saying. The Lady McGuire was playing matchmaker and using D'Amico as her foil. In a way, it was touching but it also seemed sort of intrusive. She could see Helios' discomfort in the matter and decided to let him off the hook. "Well, thank you for passing that on, Helios. I'll deal with it from here." With a lopsided grin, she shooed him out with a flutter of her hand and looked back down at her desk screen until he'd left. Then she changed the screen to the wall unit facing her and had Lady McGuire's personal PerCom unit called.

A moment later, the woman's face appeared on the screen and she began to speak before Starr could say a word. "You can thank me later, Madam President." The irony of the preemptive response was not lost on Starr. "The answer is that your 'Dr. Hunk' *is* attracted to you. And you can always get another doctor if things get too complicated."

Starr sat silently a few moments, purposely clicking her fingernails on her desk so the Lady could see. If it had been almost anybody else, Starr wouldn't have hesitated to threaten them with an audit from the IRS for being so meddlesome and impertinent. At the very least, it would have been political Armageddon. But the relationship between them by now was as friends, not as President and world famous seer. Any pretense of anger from Starr would have been a sham the older woman would have seen through immediately. "By the gods Maggie, you are impossible at times, you know that?"

"Yes, I've been told that a few times before. But think about what it's like on my end: I've got a thousand things going on in my head and I've only got time to take care of a few dozen in each day. I saw this and decided to enlist Helios' aid in bringing it to your attention. Don't be angry with him; he didn't want to say anything to you at all, but I convinced him it was for your own good to at least bring the subject up."

"You could have called me yourself. You know I would take your call any time of day or night."

"Yes, but you wouldn't have had time to process the suggestion before rejecting it as the interference from an old witch. Now, at least, you've decided to look into the possibility before throwing the whole thing away."

"You *are* an interfering old witch and you know it, Maggie," she said with a grin.

The woman tilted her head as if the president had just complimented her. "True."

"And you also know that you're as charming as an enchanted frog and can get away with almost anything because of it."

"Also true."

"So I'm going to get off this subject and ask you about something else."

"Of course, what is it?"

Starr had a fleeting moment of being unsure what to say. But she squared her shoulders and blurted it out. "I want to know about my father, if the MPN is going to kill him. And I don't want it sugar coated; I'm a big girl."

Lady McGuire sat back and sighed. "The short answer is I don't know. I've been expecting that question for a while and I'm not saying this to spare you pain; I'm well aware that not knowing is a horror in itself. I wish I *could* tell you, even if it were that he would be taken by this curse. But I really can't see it one way or the other. There simply are too many unknown factors involved. I'm sorry; I'd really like to help settle your mind, but in this I can't."

Starr trusted the woman was telling her the truth but it frustrated her terribly. She had argued with herself about even asking Maggie and considered how she would feel if the woman told her that her father would suffer the slow and painful death she had witnessed in her mother. She had also considered how she would feel if the opposite was true. What she hadn't considered was the possibility that Maggie would say she didn't know. It simply hadn't occurred to her and it left her feeling numb.

"You have to understand," the woman continued, "I'm a seer... and a damn good one if I do say so. But I simply can't be aware of everything that's going to happen, not by a long shot. And, most of the time, I just choose not to look into a future path. But when I do, it's like trying to see around all the corners in a maze. Some corners *split*. I can't say it more clearly, sorry. But what that means is that a path has somewhat equal possibilities to go in more than one direction. I'm afraid that's the case with your father. But at least that means there's a chance for the best to happen. And we both know that the vision we keep in our mind is a strong magical force in shaping our future." Starr nodded in agreement but she still wished the woman had some information that would help settle her mind one way or the other.

Rather than beat the subject to death, she decided to return to the original subject of her call. Starr smirked as a thought hit her. "You know, of course, that if the media knew about this conversation, they'd have a field day. I mean, 'President Seeks Services of Soothsayer About Sex' makes a great headline, doesn't it?"

"It sounds more like a child's tongue twister. But neither of us is going to talk about this to anyone who would create such a horrid headline as that, right?"

"Ha! Not likely. I would hope my press coverage doesn't include anyone with such rotten writing abilities." Wanting to end the conversation on that lighter note, Starr thanked her friend and quickly said goodbye. Turning to look out on the vast lawn and gardens in back of the White House, she mulled over the Lady McGuire's words. As every witch knew, thoughts had power. Yes, if she could keep a positive vision of her father being in good health, it *would* make a difference. But her fears kept trying to erase the image. It troubled her that she couldn't be more disciplined, especially when it mattered so much.

❧ 27 ❧

She had wrestled with thousands of perplexing problems before, of course. And, once again, it only now occurred to her that to be distracted with how difficult it was to control her thinking about things was nothing more than a way of avoiding doing something about them. Her spiritual and magical training was for nothing if she didn't use it in such times. So quietly, confidently, she started to concentrate on her breathing. Then, as she descended into a calmer and more focused state, she sent her consciousness inward to her chakras. It came as no surprise that they were out of balance. That was what happened when one was so caught up with the outer world and agitated. It always seemed she waited until her world was a chaotic mess before she used this technique and, as always, she mentally chastised herself for waiting so long.

She gave her attention first to her heart chakra. What a mess, she thought. It pulsed in dozens of colors and shades and was totally out of sync with her mind. She mentally built a soft vision of love and light and 'fed' it to her heart. It was like feeding a baby; it would sometimes take the nourishment and then turn away and watch everything else except the spoon she held in front of it. Then it would unexpectedly reach out and try to grasp the spoon, sometimes dumping a little in its need. But she knew to be patient and keep giving it the light it needed until it 'burped' and seemed satisfied.

Next, she focused on the base of her torso. Though this part dealt with a great number of things, she knew it was most influential in her creativity. Most people thought that meant only sex but it was much more inclusive than physical lust or procreation. The need to create, to express one's life in meaningful and original ways was so basic to humans it was possibly the most powerful force available to every person. Even when the body was dying, it motivated nearly every thought and action.

The chakra was dim and fragmented with only threads holding some parts together! No wonder Lady McGuire had told her to take some time off and have sex. It was probably the surest way to repair the damaged magical organ. Once again, she tried feeding it light but this time with very limited success. She made a mental note to see to it that a more permanent solution was found and implemented soon.

Her last 'stop' was the mentality. The mind was always the most difficult to access consciously. It had to be approached as if it wasn't really there, much like a skittish animal. Finally, she caught a quick glimpse. Not as bad as she'd thought. It was at least in one piece. The difficulty she'd had trying to find it wasn't unusual, especially when it was working well, which seemed to be the case this time. She left behind some light for it to find later; she didn't want to go to the trouble of trying to confront it directly. Such effort was usually not necessary and she was confident that it would find her gift at the most appropriate time.

Though her meditations took only minutes from her schedule, she was still the president and she had a nation to take care of. Her timeout was necessary for her own well-being but her internal 'efficiency expert' was beginning to tap its toe and was about to nag her if she didn't get back to work. Her usual return-to-the-mundane routine had just begun when she was interrupted by a sound. It took a moment for her to recognize the bell-like tone of her childhood giant pipe, the sound she'd experienced in her dream in Mexico. Once again, for no reason she could discern, it seemed threatening. She instinctively wanted to run away from it or make it stop. And, the moment she thought about it, it did stop. Her consciousness returned to the outer reality just as a soft tone indicated a call on her personal PerCom line. That tone was limited to one person: her father and the timing of it coinciding with the tone in her dream made her afraid to answer. She put the rest of her office on hold and activated his call on her wall screen. What terrible news would she learn now?

At first, she didn't recognize the image on her screen; what *was* that? But before she was able to voice the question, her father's voice came through, and the image pulled back enough for her to identify the image as a small drinking glass that had at first been put too close to the lens. As it receded, her father spoke.

"That, Madam President, is the sorry excuse for champagne they shipped us for this occasion. On behalf of the L5-B Gates Lab team, I'm proud to announce the beginning of the end of Morphing Pathology Necrosis as of twenty-twenty-three p.m., GMT."

The picture swung to show her father standing with about a dozen other people in white coats raising their glasses. "And you," her dad said from the middle of the group, "other than some nano-facturers dirt side, you are the first to hear the good news." They all took a synchronized drink from their not very elegant glasses. Some, like her father, took only a small sip while others seemed to guzzle the pale liquid. By the look of it, she estimated some had been more than just sipping their drink for quite a while before her father's call. The party-like atmosphere at the Gates Lab, even though thousands of miles away, was almost palatable through the PerCom's screen.

He stepped slightly closer to the screen and continued. "We've managed to isolate the DNA portion that causes *this*," he defiantly held up his affected hand. To her horror, the diseased outgrowth was unquestionably more advanced and now she could see it was almost like a sixth finger, only springing from the *back* of his hand. Even with the wonderful news her father was telling her, the sight of that unnatural appendage struck fear into her heart.

"I know," he said more gently, "it's still there. We're working on the second nano batch right now. I figure it'll take another two weeks to get enough of them made for the trials. But *then*," he clenched the fist in defiance of the pain it must have given him, "we'll show this bugger who's the better." Shouts of joy and triumph from the scientists behind him confirmed the confidence they all had in her father's words. He now stepped even closer and spoke quietly to her. "I know how you've worried, sweetie, and I'm sorry for that. But *this*," he held up his deformed hand again, still clenched, "is going to be *gone* in short order. I'm taking the treatment already. We'll see how long it takes for something this small and then we'll know better how much it will take for us to wipe this monster from the face of the earth!"

Starr stood, fighting the waves of emotion that were running through her at the moment. She was elated, proud, relieved, surprised, and probably a little in shock. What her father and his team had accomplished was barely short of a miracle, both for himself as well every other victim of MPN. It wouldn't bring back any of those who had suffered and died, but it would be the end of the terrible disease that had taken her mother and over five and a half million others.

She let the tears flow without shame as she sobbed her thanks to them all. Then, on a more sober note, she said, "We'll have to hold off letting the world know until we can get the cure out to everyone. As wrong as it may seem, to announce it now, when we can't make it available for all, would only make the deaths and misery of the untreated all the more bitter. You'll wait until then, I take it?"

"Yes, of course. But we've already let Moser/Gainer in North America and VonSteigen in Europe start production of the nanos for injection to our design."

"You're that sure, then?"

"Positive! Not a shred of doubt. NEWTON says 99.9%, which is as sure as any computer can be. And our trials on the pigs cured every last one of them. I *told* you we'd beat this damn thing, didn't I?"

"Yes. Yes you did, Dad. And both as your daughter and as President, I can't say thank you enough." She stepped back to her desk. "And now, people, both you and I have much to accomplish. And all that," she motioned at the party behind her father, "is, I'm sure, just the beginning of the revelry that will happen when you can announce this great magic to the world.

"Once again, ladies and gentlemen, you have the gratitude of this nation, the entire world, and my own personal thanks. I, like you, look forward to the day when MPN will be nothing more than a forgotten set of initials in some history book. Blessed be to you all." She switched off her PerCom and sat down with a big sigh. She knew that the news would eventually leak somehow, but, for the moment, she had to be very careful whom she told and how her office – no, her *nation* – would prepare for the wondrous announcement.

She switched off the privacy hold to her office and... no surprise... Helios buzzed her seconds later. "Come to my office," she told him. "We have great plans to make." He would know the details in a minute and the world would know in less than a month. But she wanted to start plans for the party early because it deserved to be one hell of a bash. Starr Draper wasn't about to let the rest of the world outshine the celebration they would be throwing to honor her father and the rest of his team!

❧ 28 ☙

"I'm disappointed you felt it necessary to hide all this from me. Did you really think I don't know what's going on in my own house?"

She didn't know yet what or how much he knew. He'd simply materialized at the locked door to her basement lab and knocked. Of course she'd closed the door to the space where she was working on the magnetic spheres before answering but Stamper didn't even step in. He simply took her hand and led her upstairs to his study. There, he told her that he knew she was working on *something* that was important to her and he was sure she thought he'd disapprove if told. But he wanted to know anyway. With only a hint of disappointment in his voice, he asked her what was so important that she had sequestered herself so long.

To be confronted by him was perhaps inevitable. All the equipment had been purchased by him in one way or another and, though he usually didn't bother with the finances of his many companies, he did have access to the books at any time. But to have to explain her work to him now was quite possibly the least favorable. She had spent a great deal of time away from him since their visit to the conference in Mexico and, in her fever to refine the process for making the spheres better, she'd forgotten how much he craved their relationship. She shouldn't have been so distant but she had easily put him aside in her desire to see the president brought down.

Her mind raced to find the right words and tone to control the situation. To be thwarted in her plans now would be unthinkable. Not when she was so close.

"Eric," she began in as calm a manner as she could muster, "you have worked for years to insure that the Craft remains not only alive but well. You've poured your resources and your time into getting others to recognize the importance of maintaining a true heritage and line of lineage from Gerald Gardner. It's been an honor to stand alongside you as you've fought to keep the Craft pure and whole. It was one of the things that first attracted me to you many years ago."

He smiled ruefully. "Well," he said, "I knew it couldn't have been my pretty face."

She smiled back. It wasn't just flattery; she really did admire and, in her own way, love the man. Right now, though, she needed to sway him so he would let her continue what was even more important to her... and what was important to her father as well.

"What would you say if I told you that I'm working on something that would help your plans take a giant leap? What if you could stand proudly next to the president of the United States and confidently say you knew that person to be a true witch?"

"Well, I guess I'd jump at the chance, Cassie. But I don't believe you're cooking up a Frankenstein's monster down there. And, even if you were, I sort of doubt we could sell it to the citizens of America to vote for a monster with door handles in his neck."

"No stitched together monster from a lab, no crackling wires or parts from graveyards. You're absolutely right when you say the American people wouldn't elect somebody like that. But they have elected a monster, Eric. She's in the White House right now. You said it yourself: she's a sham of a witch, a prancing pretender, a *showgirl* with robes! And she got into office because of some very shady magic perpetrated by McGuire and her cronies."

"Yes, but don't forget that your father got in on the same ticket, Cass."

His words made her pause. She wondered how long he'd known of her relationship to T J. But it made her task of convincing him easier in a way. Her surprise at his revelation must have shown on her face, because he went on to say, "Oh, yes. I've known about his clandestine parenting of you since before he ever pushed you at me. I might seem blasé about folks and take them at face value sometimes, but I've got an army of snoops making sure I know all there is to know about the people I do business with. I'm not the fool some think I am; please don't insult me with that estimate, my dear."

She was well aware of his 'army of snoops' and had used them herself on several occasions. It wasn't that he knew about her being TJ's daughter that surprised her; it was the fact that for years he hadn't let on. But his reasons didn't concern her now. The most important thing now was to make the spheres so she could eliminate Draper. She would be the one to do it; she'd seen it in the cards as well as her dreams. The current president had to die. Then her father would sit in the Oval Office and she would finally be able to claim him as her father. They would stand together against the treachery and duplicity of those who sneered at the power of the Goddess and Her chosen children!

Her thoughts seemed to burn her and she couldn't sit still because of the energy she felt rushing around and through her. She shot up and paced nervously, furtively looking between Stamper and the doorway that would take her back to her laboratory. She *had* to get back; every minute counted. Why couldn't he just leave her be? She felt caged and had to fight the urge to scream and run back to the sanctuary of her lab. It was like Stamper was purposely trying to torture her, hold her back and keep her from doing the will of the gods!

Something pulsed through her: her father's words resonating in her brain and she rounded on Eric with a look so fierce he actually flinched. "You're like all the rest," she screamed. "You want to have everyone bow down to you because you're such a true believer. But you don't want to *do* anything! You're no better than *she* is! By the gods, Eric, I thought you really cared. I thought you of all people would know how important it is to put my father in the White House, to give him the reins of power before Mother Earth decides to give up on us all! How much time do you think we've got? How much longer can we go on using Her as our garbage bin and just take, take, take?"

Her sudden outburst transformed his concern into something close to panic. She was flailing about and moving around the room as if she were drunk. She'd tipped over a chair and stumbled but hardly seemed to notice. Her face was so red it looked like she would explode. He reached out to her but she shied away like a child trying to escape a scolding. Eric turned to the wall screen and shouted, "Computer! Medical emergency! Send the medical team to my study NOW!"

In an annoyingly calm voice, the computer said, "Medical team alerted. ETA, forty-seven seconds. Is emergency transportation required?"

"What? Yes, yes, summon the LandVan to wait outside the East door."

"Done. Will you take a call from Max Snider in Germany, Mr. Stamper? He says you were expecting his call."

The computer's calm and efficient tone was really beginning to get to him. Damn the machine, couldn't it understand the word, 'emergency'? He'd tell it to shut off if he didn't think he might need it to communicate something else. At the moment, however, he was much more concerned with trying to get Cassie to calm down before the medical team arrived. Knowing it was fruitless to reason with the computer, he shouted, "Tell him I'm dealing with something else and I'll get back to him later. Now, when is that damn med team..."

Just then, the door was thrown open and three members of the medical unit Stamper kept with him at all times rushed in. The one in the lead, Doctor Fetini..., Felini? Stamper couldn't remember the man's name at the moment, but it didn't matter; Cassandra obviously saw the man as a threat because she was backing away from him with a wild look. It didn't take a psychic to see she was ready to bolt. But there wasn't anywhere she could go that wasn't blocked. The room had only one door and the other two members of the team were right in front of it at the moment. She was frantically looking around and making a low, almost feline growl. Her movements were becoming more and more furtive as she slowly backed toward windows that overlooked the terrace twenty feet below. Just before she turned, Stamper knew what she was about to do and he leaped to catch her before she reached the window. But he was too late. She leaped like an Olympic runner jumping a hurdle.

Stamper was old enough to remember when every window was made of glass. He momentarily expected there to be a crash with lethal shards raining down on Cassandra as she fell to what would undoubtedly be her death. However, the builders of his house had used nothing but the best materials and that meant every window was made of quarter inch thick Zellan, commonly known as spider glass. Not only was it a very good insulating material, it also was nearly unbreakable. It could take a high powered 80 mm round and barely show a mark. Cassandra would certainly have bruises but she bounced off the window like a tennis ball. The moment would have been comical if it weren't for the fact that she had been serious about jumping through the window. As it was, her desperate lunge had left her a stunned tangle on the floor of his study.

Stamper reached her only a heartbeat before the doctor. He held her close and she blinked up at him uncertainly. As the doctor checked on her, understanding came back into her eyes and she began to sob quietly. The doctor pulled out a derma-ject and pushed it against her shoulder to let it press a sedative into her. It took only a few seconds before she began to respond.

She stopped crying and slowly detached herself from Stamper's shoulder. She started to push herself up and winced. The doctor told her she'd probably cracked a rib and wanted to scan her. She nodded her compliance silently and Eric saw she was becoming more lethargic by the moment. A few seconds later, she leaned back on him and her head lolled as she fell asleep.

"She should stay asleep for a few hours, sir," the doctor said.

"Good, I think she could use a bit of rest. Completely check her out and then take her up to my bedroom when you're done."

"Certainly sir. Is there anything you can tell me about what brought on this... uh, *event*?"

He didn't want to have to explain anything to the doctor at the moment, so he just shook his head and then carefully shifted Cassandra's limp body over and into the doctor's arms. He was sure that whatever she had been doing in her 'hobby lab' was connected somehow to the wild rant he'd seen moments before. He had to see what was in that lab.

❧ 29 ❧

It had taken slightly less than forty-eight hours before the news leaked. MPN, the scourge of the twenty-first century, was going to be brought down. The leak apparently came from Italy but it was being broadcast to every PerCom and computer in the world minutes afterwards. Starr knew it eventually would leak but she had hoped for longer than two days. Nevertheless, she'd been able to secure an open date reservation at the L-10 platform for the celebration when her father's team was ready to declare it officially. The platform was the largest and newest, boasting a capacity of over five thousand people. Finished in 2073, it had been the first privately funded elevator station and it was open to anyone for six hours if they had a *lot* of loose change in their pocket.

Starr had used her office to persuade Theodore Turner II, the CEO of S/T (Space Tours), the largest interest in L-10, to clear the second week in September and to keep it open for the celebration. The lab team had told her that was when they expected the official announcement could be made. She had preempted everyone else in making plans and she had used that lead time to put out invitations to every national leader and some very notable scientists to 'join her' in celebrating the announcement from the team led by her father. It had taken some scrambling to get it all set in stone before other countries had begun their plans but the prestige factor had spurred her people into moving at light speed to make all the arrangements.

There were also ninety-four 'suites' that rented for five grand a night (complimentary breakfast included). Starr had seen holos of the suites and wasn't terribly impressed. The bedrooms were five by ten meters, barely large enough for a queen sized bed, and the 'entertainment rooms' next to the bedrooms were not any bigger. Still, being able to impress your friends with pictures of you looking down on everyone else on the planet was obviously worth it because the 'hotel' was always booked months ahead. And, although she hadn't experienced it herself, she knew that sex at 1/10th Earth gravity was supposed to be... well, *erotic* was how the hotel's information site had put it.

With that thought, Starr shifted to ideas about 'Dr. Hunk'. Maybe she would book the presidential suite, which was supposed to be three times the size of the regular ones, and have a private party of her own. Hmmm...

❧ 30 ❧

"I have no idea what she's been up to down there, Tom. I've got one of my people working on hacking her lock, but he says it might not happen until tomorrow. Do *you* have any knowledge about what she's been doing?" Stamper suspected the Vice President had more than a hint about what his daughter had been up to in her lab but he wanted to see how forthcoming the man would be with him and this was the test. When he said he was trying to break into her inner lab, he'd seen Hunt's face tighten. Stamper had come to read Hunt very well. Playing poker with him for years did that.

"I know she's been working on something involving magnetism. She's seemed... how should I say this... unusually devoted to whatever it is. You don't think that her hobby has somehow affected her brain, do you? I mean, maybe some chemicals she's been using? Or perhaps magnetism itself? What does the doctor say?"

Stamper had known Hunt for many years. He'd seen the man convince others that black was white and had suspected for a long time that the Vice President had some sort of unusual mental abilities. However, he was also fairly sure that T.J. wasn't able to persuade people at long distances. And not over a PerCom unit. What he was able to do, however, was convincingly lie or distract. And Stamper was sure that was what he was trying at that moment. But rather than confront him, Stamper decided to simply ignore what he was saying.

"She's getting the best of care and if she needs anything outside of the house, we'll of course get it. But if you can think of anything... *anything* that might help her, contact me immediately."

"Of course, Eric. You know how deeply concerned I am, just as you. And you'll keep me informed about her condition?"

"I'll be in touch." He switched off before Hunt could say anything else. Even if the man was the Vice President of the United States, Stamper wasn't going to scrape and bow to him. He'd known Hunt too long. And, although he knew the VP could wield considerable power, Stamper wasn't intimidated. He was a citizen of the UN and Hunt wasn't *his* vice president.

He was now sure that Cassandra and Hunt were connected by more than blood. Hunt might be able to magically convince people to do what he wanted when he was close to them, but Stamper thought he relied on it too much. It made him an unconvincing liar, at least to those who knew him well. He was positive that Hunt knew a lot more than he was telling. And whatever it was Cassie was so compelled to work on day and night was something neither she nor Hunt wanted him to know about it.

Which meant he wouldn't approve.

And that meant he *had* to know what was going on.

His relationship with Cassandra was less than a marriage but more than casual sex. Much more. He'd always thought she had his best interests to heart and was saddened to know she was engaged in something that she knew he wouldn't sanction... whatever it was.

Cassie wasn't going to wake up for another few hours, but when she did he was going to get some answers. Their relationship had always been based on mutual love and trust and he would have liked to think it still was. But it looked like he'd been played the fool and it didn't sit well with him. He decided to go back down to her 'lab' and see why his damn techie wasn't able to break the code on that inner area she'd locked up. If he had to, he'd blast it; he *had* to find out what she was working on.

ᨘ 31 ᨘ

T.J. was worried. If Stamper broke into his daughter's work space, would he understand what she was working on? She undoubtedly had left some kind of notes; she was too careful, too methodical to leave everything to memory. Of course he didn't understand how she'd managed to accomplish the magic that had eluded others concerning the magnetic spheres she'd developed, but he knew she was just as disciplined a scientist as any who worked for GE or Dow-Sony. He was sure she would have recorded everything she'd done up to the moment she'd walked out of the lab that day. Would she also have implicated him in her notes?

If she had, he'd have to deal with it. She couldn't be allowed to testify against him. As much as he'd found her useful, he wasn't about to be brought down because of her carelessness. He'd made a mistake with her mother by not making her have an abortion. And he had found Cassie's genius useful but he didn't have any paternal feelings for her; she was a tool for him to use and that was all.

Just like everybody else in his life, he thought, she'd let him down. He wasn't really responsible for her taking his wish to be in the president's chair and making it into some mad compulsion. She'd done this to herself. His powers of suggestion had only given her a little nudge, not this madness, this insane impulse. He had to eliminate her and find some other way to have the president assassinated. It was fortunate he'd prepared for such contingencies long ago by enlisting someone on Stamper's staff. It might be time, he thought, to make his wishes known and prove he hadn't wasted his money.

↠ 32 ↞

"Yeah, but look at her eyes. See? She sees it the moment it passes Maxwell and drifts into the room. It heads straight for them and she doesn't even seem to react until the last two and a half seconds. Already Stamper's eyes are big and his mouth's open in surprise, but she's still calm. And then… there, right there! She makes that 'I'm frightened' look and shields Stamper right then, a heartbeat away before the thing 'explodes' and fills the place with a giant fart."

She smiled. "You have such a colorful way of describing it, Frankie. Maybe we should reword the official report to include your characterization." All jokes aside, 3F had found something they'd missed before. She too had many times gone over the various videos showing how the strange sphere had first appeared and ultimately attacked Stamper at the conference. But she hadn't noticed what 3F had seen. It looked suspiciously like Stamper's girlfriend had *not* been as surprised as everyone else when the 'giant fart' had made its appearance.

Once again, she wondered at the comparatively non-threatening aspect of the 'bomb'. It had been barely more than a schoolboy's prank. She shuddered to think of what the sphere *could* have released. Why indeed did it only hold a bad smelling gas? In truth, the only injuries it had produced were the result of people rushing around to escape it. Two delegates had been treated for bruises and one had a sprained ankle; that was the worst of it except for the cleaning bill of the dining hall and Stamper's wardrobe. And Cassandra's. And El Presidente's. If Whatcom had had something to do with it, and it now appeared she definitely had foreknowledge of some kind, then the question still remained as to why it had been perpetrated in the first place. Whatcom could have staged the entire thing as some sort of demonstration, implicating somebody other than Stamper or herself since they had been the 'targets' and throwing them off the scent. That made sense in an odd way. But why just a demonstration?

"Why wasn't this thing lethal?" She wanted 3F's perspective; she didn't really have any idea how his mind worked but she knew it was different from hers and she valued his thinking.

He squinted his eyes at the screen and pursed his lips in contemplation. It was all she could do not to laugh; he looked so cute, she thought. Just like a husky pup she once had, he then tilted his head and stared. After almost a half a minute, he finally spoke.

"The simplest answer is that the bad guy didn't want to hurt anybody." He looked at her and saw she wasn't impressed. "All right. The not-so-simple answer is that somebody might have been making a trial run with this. If I'd invented a magnetic sphere and was using a delivery system like they did with this one, I'd want to make sure it was workable. Also, let's say the bad guy, or maybe girl, wanted to throw us off from looking at them. Why not make Stamper the target? Everybody at the conference blames him for the dead water situation, right?"

"The problem with that is this magnetic sphere thingy obviously took some timing and a whole lot of preparation. Nobody knew Stamper was going to the conference until just a couple of days beforehand." She turned back to the screen showing a frozen picture of Whatcom sitting next to her boss/boyfriend. Pointing to it, she said, "But it's a good guess *she* knew he was going before anybody else did. If she'd made magnetic spheres before this..." Her voice trailed off as she thought about it. But 3F got there before her.

"...then all that remained was to pack one up with the luggage, right?" He finished her thought, even though it didn't make a lot of sense. They were both looking at the screen, wondering when, where, and how the sphere had actually been produced. And then, though neither of them noticed, they both tilted their heads to the left in contemplation. Then, to the right. It looked almost like a dance.

❧ 33 ❧

Julio Akisawa awoke at five-thirty every day whether he had to work or not. It wasn't always to his liking but he had grown to accept it as the way things were and there wasn't anything to be done about it. He would rise, shower, don his running suit and shoes and drag his lazy dog out the door to go their usual three and a half miles down to the shopping mall and back. Somewhere around the tenth block, Hulk, his miniature Dobie-doodle, usually got up to actually running. Before that he would keep up, but whine and insist on stopping at every patch of grass or fire hydrant to read the P-mail and leave a little of his own. On the return trip, Hulk would most often be ahead of his master and barking as if he was Julio's coach, chastising him for being so lazy. By the time they returned home, Alicia, his wife of twenty years would have breakfast ready for both 'her boys'. Then, if it was a work day for him, he would go and start his ancient pickup that took all night to recharge and make his way to the White House grounds where he was chief caretaker of everything green and growing. Over the years, Julio had become somewhat jaded about the occasional sighting of the president or other high official and had almost become blind to the ever-present Secret Service people that occupied every corner of the property both inside and out of the most famous home in the country.

The previous administration's First Lady had taken a great deal of interest in the flower gardens, which were Julio's pride and joy. With the large greenhouse next to the quarter acre of land that grew decorative flowers and foliage, Julio was able to hand over a large bunch of gloriously flagrant blooms any time the quiet woman visited his domain. He had not yet met the new president but had seen her from afar as she boarded the 'chopper' from the back lawn or when she was taking a meal on the Rose Garden's patio.

He had stopped trying to see the 'important people' a long time back. He was a simple gardener and more than happy to have the well-paying job that kept him and his Alicia comfortable and happy. At a little after eight in the morning, the sun was already hot and Julio expected it to be another sticky day. That was okay with him; he didn't mind the heat. It was the bitterly cold days of winter that made every joint ache that he didn't like. But as he was pushing a cart along the path in back of the House, he was smiling and thinking of the sushi cakes his wife had made for his lunch. He wasn't hungry this soon after his breakfast, but his wife's cooking was tempting even on a full stomach. His eyes were down, watching the thin pathway between some trees when he made a turn and came to a sudden stop. There, by the sycamore that was at least two hundred years old, sat the president herself. Her back was to him and he doubted she knew he was there.

Deciding that it wasn't his place to speak or disturb her, Julio carefully turned his cart to leave. But, just as he was about to take a step away, she spoke.

"Please don't go. I'm just enjoying the morning sun. I'd appreciate the company if it isn't a bother."

He turned again and smiled. He never expected a president to be concerned about 'bothering' him. The idea was more than amusing to him. "I'm just the gardener, Madam President. I work for *you*, so if you wish to have me take a break, who am I to commit treason and refuse?"

Her laugh sounded almost like a small girl's to Julio, which itself was surprising to him. She patted the ground next to her, indicating she wanted him to sit there. He was a little nervous sitting that close to the president and wondered if he was committing some social faux pas that would look bad on his record.

She must have seen his hesitation or read his face because she laughed again and patted the ground more firmly. "Oh, for heaven's sake, come on. I won't bite." Then she turned slightly more serious and, he thought, maybe there was a note of pleading in her voice when she said, "Please."

So he sat and was happy that no Service people jumped out from behind the bushes to put him in restraints, but he still felt it a little strange. The president appeared relaxed and was picking absently at a huge clover bloom, pulling the light blue-purple tubes out and sucking the honey from the tip of each before discarding them. Her eyes twinkled a little at him as if she was committing some kind of forbidden foolishness.

"My mother used to tell me that I'd get sick doing this; she'd say the dog had piddled on the ones in our back yard not more than ten minutes before I'd pick one. I never believed her, of course. I remember telling her one time that the dog must have been diabetic because his pee was sweet." She grinned at him. "I'm playing hooky from my work right now. So you're the one who keeps this wonderful place so beautiful?"

He nodded his head, still shy to speak to the president.

"Well, thank you. I'm afraid I'm terrible when it comes to gardening. The best I ever could do was mow the grass when I was a girl. And that was just a matter of getting the mow-bot out of the shed and switching it on." She sighed and leaned back on her elbows, turning her face to the sun for a moment. Then she looked over at him with a more intense gaze. "Could I ask you a question, friend gardener?"

"Of course, Madam President. Anything you like."

She sighed again and picked another clover bloom. "'Madam President... I still can't quite get used to that. I'm just Starr Draper to me. Just another human being trying to figure it all out before it's my time to make the next step." She plucked at the flower in her hand and sucked thoughtfully for a second. "Tell me, friend gardener, are you married?"

Now he felt a little more confident. His wife Alicia was always a comfortable subject for him. "Oh, yes, Madam President. My wife and I have been married for more than twenty years. Twenty-three to be exact."

"Any children?"

He glanced down a moment but then met her eyes again. "No. My Alicia was a victim of MPN but was one of the lucky ones who got better. The doctors still have no idea why anybody does.

They said it was a one in a million chance. But we prayed and she got better. But we can have no children. Still, I have my Alicia and we are happy."

It was the president's turn to be silent for a moment. She remembered her mother and the terrible time she and her dad had with the pain and heartbreak MPN had put her through before finally killing her. She looked back at the man sitting across from her and said, "I'm so very glad to know you and your wife had the good fortune of beating the high odds." She paused again. "But tell me, what do you fear the most, friend? Of all the things that could distress you, what is it that makes your heart the heaviest? If you could wave a magic wand and make one thing different, what would you choose?"

Julio had never really considered his world in that way, but he didn't hesitate in his answer. "Water. We must have good water, Madam President. MPN is terrible and everybody lives in fear of it, but if we can't keep the water alive, everybody will die." He swept a hand out to indicate all the plants surrounding them. "And all this will die. We will become nothing. The Great Mother will not even be. We *must* cure the water or nothing else will matter."

She silently nodded her agreement and continued sucking the clover. "I wonder if there really was life on Mars and maybe the water was killed there. Maybe we will suffer the same fate."

He looked at her and saw a woman weighed down by great problems. His instinct was to help however he could, so he said, "I hope that is not possible here. Even though people are often not wise, the gods are in us... just like they are in the flowers and the trees. I have seen trees grow from fallen logs and I have seen flowers bloom from crushed plants." He paused, and then continued almost in a whisper, "I have seen my Alicia live when all the doctors said she would die." He stopped, embarrassed by perhaps being too bold in his words. He was only a gardener and she was the president.

She studied him for a moment. Then she smiled and spoke as she stood up and brushed off her pants, "You have been my priest, friend gardener. Thank you. In my job, it is all too easy to forget how truly blessed we are."

He also stood and once again felt self-conscious talking to the president. She held up her hand with the fingers splayed and he automatically held his up but was suddenly shy about touching fingers with her. She laughed again and stepped forward to touch his hand. "Love, laugh, and live well, friend. My thanks to you for sharing your wisdom."

He bowed slightly to her and responded, "I wish you well too, Madam President. It has been my pleasure to meet you. Blessed be."

"What is your name, friend gardener? I know your wife's but not yours."

"It is Julio... Julio Akisawa."

"What does your wife do, Julio... besides give you obvious great joy?"

"She does not work outside our home, Madam President. The terrible MPN has gone but she is not strong."

Starr tilted her head and thought a moment. "Have you been to the western camp, Julio, the one in the Olympic Park?"

"No, Madam President. I have tended these grounds for many years and know every tree here. But the other white houses I have not seen."

"Ah," she said and began to turn away but then looked back, "You would love the trees there. They speak to you with many voices." Then she started walking back along the pathway. Julio was startled by movement all around him as Service agents seemingly appeared from behind every bush and tree to follow the president back to the White House. How lucky he was, he thought, to live so free. He would never have to be in a cage of guards. He had his trees and flowers.

And he had his wonderful Alicia.

✎ 34 ✐

When she opened her eyes, she was sure she knew where she was but not how she'd gotten there. She felt strange and her eyes didn't want to stay in focus. Trying to move made several parts of her body object with sharp pains telling her to stop. A soft moan escaped her lips and something touched her hand. She glanced to her right and saw Eric looking down at her. His mouth was moving and she heard sound but it took a few seconds for it to make sense. A small stab of fear pushed her further towards full consciousness and the sounds began to become words.

"... still and just rest. He says you've got a cracked rib, some bruises on the left arm and shoulder, and you're dehydrated." He pointed to a clear bag with a line going into her arm. "That's what the IV drip is for." She probably should have been alarmed but for some reason she just couldn't muster up any energy to power such an emotion. She tried to ask him something but, once again, she had trouble making words. It seemed she was only capable of primal sounds for the moment. That too was troubling but still not enough to make her panic.

He seemed to sense a little of what she was trying to communicate and gave her a genuinely warm smile. "The doc had to tranc you. You were pretty wild there for a while. You tried to jump out the window. Whatever the problem is, Cassie, we'll settle it and make it right." He patted her hand and looked away. Then he stood up and ran a hand over his face. Were those actual tears she'd seen just before he stood?

"I suppose I haven't actually said it before, but..." He paused and then blurted out, "... I *care very deeply* for you." He quickly turned toward the door as if to leave but came back and his face was taught and red as he sat again on the edge of the bed. "I don't expect you to... well ... it doesn't mean..." He stood up yet again and stiffly walked to the door. He reached for the handle but stopped and spoke from where he stood.

"I'm... uh, going to get the doctor to look in on you later. You... you just rest for now. When you feel better, we'll talk, okay?" He quietly closed the door behind him and, though she tried hard to make sense out of what had just happened, she simply couldn't concentrate and was soon asleep again.

When next she opened her eyes, the doctor was fingering her IV line. She turned her head and he quickly took a step back as if she'd caught him doing something wrong.

He smiled to cover his look of surprise. "How are you feeling Ms. Whatcom?"

"Groggy." *Well*, she thought, *at least I can talk now.*

"I expect that will wear off soon. You must have been missing a lot of sleep because the sedative I gave you, though fast acting, wasn't supposed to put you out for ten hours." He said everything with a courteous smile, but she sensed an underlying tension in his voice.

"Ten hours?"

"Yes. Mr. Stamper said you awoke a few hours ago. But you fell asleep again and he didn't want me to disturb you." He paused and glanced at some readings on his PerCom screen a few seconds before asking her, "Do you remember being in Mr. Stamper's library earlier?"

Warning signals were going off in her head and she chose her words carefully. "Yes... We were arguing. It's personal, doctor. I'm afraid I got too angry and, as you say, I've been burning the candle at both ends lately. I... I lost it. Eric called for you and I panicked, thought the window was a door and bolted." A broken rib and some bruises was what Eric had told her was the extent of her injuries. She didn't want or need the doctor's attentions. She tried to make her next words sound light and casual. "I really feel stupid, running like that. My mother used to always tell me to look before I leaped. Guess I forgot that this time, huh?"

The doctor was still smiling but she got the distinct feeling she was being studied like a bug under glass. A feeling of urgency to be away from the man and back in her lab was growing stronger by the second. "Is it all right for me to get up? I mean, get this thing out of my arm so I can go pee?" She really did need to use the bathroom and if she could get rid of this doctor maybe she could make it right with Eric and then get back to her lab. She had to try.

"I'm afraid that's up to Mr. Stamper. We're all very concerned for your state of mind, you see. Can you explain what has gotten you so... how shall I put this... so *fixated* these past few days?"

She wasn't going to explain anything to this two-bit pill pusher. She doubted if he knew what real dedication was. She thought she remembered he was a Methodist or Lutheran or maybe one of those pencil-neck Unitarians!

"My state of mind?" She tried crossing her arms but the I.V. line got in the way. "I take a few days off for my own projects so I'm 'fixated'. That's great. I don't need to explain anything to you, *doctor*. Not a thing! What I do on my own time is none of your business."

In the back of her mind she knew it wasn't the best strategy to get angry at the man but all she could think of was destroying Draper. She didn't think it strange that her world had narrowed to this single focus and the only thing that mattered was seeing her father take the president's place. It was more than important; it was the *only* thing in the world. And this smug jerk was in her way. She had more urgent things to do than lay around answering his nosey questions.

Besides, from the moment she'd opened her eyes, alarm bells had been going off about the way the doctor was acting. She had a sense she was in danger and she'd learned a long time ago not to second-guess such feelings. The compulsion to get back to her lab merged with her fight-or-flight reactions and she was moving before she even knew what she was going to do. Somewhere in the recesses of her mind a plan of action had formed and she was acting on it before her conscious mind knew any of its details.

"To hell with you," she said and reached over to pull out the I.V. line.

Out of the corner of her eye she saw him reaching to stop her and she was ready for him. He was so focused on the I.V. line he never saw the roundhouse left to his jaw. It felt like she'd hit a rock but the result was worth the pain. He dropped without a sound and was out cold. Just to get out of bed hurt like hell but she gritted her teeth and moved carefully but as fast as she could. Then she ripped the I.V. line out. That hurt plenty but nothing was going to stop her.

For some reason, a phrase came to mind, one that she remembered from talking with a proselytizing Christian years back. It was supposed to have been said by their messiah in answer to some question put to him. She looked down at the unconscious doctor and smirked. "I'm doing my father's work." It was such satisfying irony to use the words from his precious book. She couldn't resist the urge to give him a spiteful kick to the ribs. His arm jerked and an old fashioned hypodermic syringe and needle fell to the floor. She didn't know what medicine he might have been ready to give her, she figured it was another elephant-stopper like he'd used before, but she wasn't going to be taken twice in the same way.

She quickly got dressed and opened the door a crack to see if anybody had been set to guard her. The hallway was empty. Even though every part of her body hurt, she sprinted to the stairs. This time, she wouldn't open the door for Eric or anybody else.

She *was* doing her father's work and it *was* holy!

❧ 35 ❧

Stumping idiots! He was surrounded by fools. All that needed was one shot. What was the problem? First it was his daughter going bananas and putting him in jeopardy. He shouldn't have counted on her in the first place; he knew that now. So the simplest solution to the problem was to eliminate her. But could anybody seem to do that? Could his man on Stamper's staff do just one easy thing? He'd been paying the guy for nearly ten years and never asked for anything more than information. Now, when it really counted, he asked for one uncomplicated thing and it should have been done by now.

If Cassandra was dead, he would have heard by now. A single injection and, poof, the problem would be gone. Why hadn't the doctor just gone and done it? It wasn't like unexplained deaths didn't happen every day. And the doctor had assured him that DNA specific nanos were foolproof. When they'd done their job, they'd dissolve and become undetectable. The patient would be dead for unknown reasons. The brain had stopped sending signals to the heart and lungs and the patient had died; so sorry, Eric Stamper.

He'd known Cassie was a loose cannon and made some preparations just in case. When he'd gotten the call from Stamper, he knew exactly what to do and rushed the tiny black capsule filled with the nanomachines to the doctor. A simple shot would have taken care of the matter and he should have been notified hours ago. T.J. gulped down his fourth whisky and paced the length of his office like a caged tiger, silently cursing the incompetent fool. Every time he passed his desk, he'd glance at his PerCom unit and give a disgusted sigh. It was after ten o'clock and still nothing. He couldn't stand it; he needed to get busy on some other way to eliminate the president.

He sat down heavily at the big desk and reached for the PerCom control. But before he could touch it, the soft tone of the unit, a sound much like a large bell or gong, signaled he had an incoming call. When he saw it was his daughter calling, he paused. But Hunt hadn't risen to power by hesitating; he put on his best smile and touched the controls that sent her call to his desk screen.

"Cassie! I've been worried sick about you. It's so good to see you up and about. How are you feeling?"

"Pissed. I'm going back to my lab to finish up my work. Eric barged in a while back and I guess he told some sort of story about me. His doctor gave me something that knocked me out for a while, but I got my revenge a minute ago." He saw her eyes flash when she spoke about the doctor.

"What did you do? What do you mean, you 'got your revenge'?" Hunt had spent a lot of money making the doctor his eyes and ears into Stamper's private life. He was supposed to have eliminated Cassandra but apparently she'd turned the tables.

"I coldcocked him. A well placed left hook. Hah! All that college athletics finally came in handy. Anyway, I'm going to finish my work here and then I'll bring the, uh... *equipment* to the cabin. I want to hide out there, all right? I think Eric is..."

Hunt's mind was racing and he interrupted. "Wait. Let me set up some place safer for you. I'll get back to you with the location when I've made the arrangements. In the meantime, make sure you don't do anything more to alarm Eric. Knocking out his doctor can be explained away; tell him you panicked. He'll be indulgent, I'm sure."

Hunt had to weigh his options yet again and come up with a plan. His daughter was setting a record for wild and unexpected actions. If he could get her to eliminate the president, then it would be worth all the trouble, but he still had to think ahead to when he was sitting in the Oval Office and Cassie was still walking around. She was simply too erratic and his control over her wasn't sufficient to make him feel safe. He had made many connections over the years and now was the time to use them. He reached for the PerCom once again.

❧ 36 ❧

"... and I want our White House gardener, Mr. Akisawa and his wife invited to come along as my personal guests on a paid vacation. They're to be given VIP service all the way. I checked and he hasn't taken more than two days off in a row for years."

The president had decided to take a working vacation at the western Camp David, also sometimes referred to as 'Camp *Other*' because it was in 'the *other Washington*'... the state. She'd been working sixteen to eighteen hour days steadily for months. In fact, even before she'd won the election. She needed to refresh and recharge or she would begin making mistakes aplenty. She had given directions to her staff and made preparations to leave as soon as possible.

Her father had called again and given her the best news yet: The MPN on his hand was responding at a faster rate than they'd anticipated. He proudly held it up for her to see. And though it still made her gut tighten to look at, she could see for herself that the growth was obviously shrinking.

Moving the president and all the equipment, personnel, and technology necessary for her to run the Executive Branch of the government was surprisingly easy. All of the required logistics were always in place to whisk her away on a moment's notice. It might require an immense amount of energy to do it, but it was part of the job for everyone involved in assisting the president to make sure everything was always ready. All the president needed to do was say the word and it was possible to leave in less than thirty minutes. There was even a contingency plan to make it possible for her to be boosted to Station Three, the non-tethered orbiting space station at the LaGrange point between the earth and moon. She had learned that there was also a bunker on the moon with life support for one year for twenty-five people if needed. It had been built in complete secrecy back around 2020 at the time NASA had been showing off to the world its new ion drive rocket it planned to use for the first manned trip to Mars.

Of course, now the ion drive was old technology; the new DE engines used less than 1% the energy and made the trip in weeks. The permanent station on Mars had grown to over a thousand people on a rotating basis. Starr hoped one day to go to the red planet herself before she died.

Keeping in touch with the world wasn't nearly the challenge for the president it had once been. In fact, it was even possible for her to appear to still be in the Oval Office while winging her way to any destination the Boeing i980 was taking her. Her image and the backdrop of the Oval Office could be joined so seamlessly it was virtually impossible to know she wasn't addressing the world from the White House. Conferences with dignitaries, cabinet members, and others that put demands on her time could be made to happen with ease even when she was enjoying the natural wonders of the Camp. In fact, the only real difference between the Oval Office and any of the retreats available to the president were the environmental changes. Starr had always loved the Pacific Northwest but this would be her first time in 'Camp *Other*'. She had finally realized both Helios and the Lady McGuire were right about needing the rest and she'd also given a good deal of thought about Dr. Watson coming along as well. She'd gone over several possibilities, trying to think of a way to bring him along without being too obvious only to be reminded by Helios that he would be part of the staff that would accompany her anyway.

She was in the residential suite when Lisandra called. "Yes, Lisa?"

"Excuse the interruption, Madam President, but we've gotten word of a possible threat that may put a kink in your travel plans."

By now, Starr had gotten used to the reality that the president of the United States was *always* a target of somebody. The fact that Lisa had notified her of this one meant that the Service not only considered the threat to be serious but that they didn't know enough to protect the president without some extreme measures to be put in place. "Okay," she sighed, "what's going to happen?"

"For the media, we're going to paint you leaving on the Boeing. But we'll really put you on the Bullet. It won't take off until twenty minutes after Air Force One but you'll arrive there well before they do."

"But I'll also be as flat as a pancake," she joked. The Bullet was technically a space vehicle. It could reach Mach 6 in less than a minute if needed. The presidential version was possibly the most luxurious space plane in the world. Built only two years before, it was primarily an emergency vehicle to be used only if the president had to be sent into space to be safe. To keep its systems in top order, it was sent up at least once a month to test its reliability.

Lisa smiled at the president's joke. The Bullet was capable of acceleration up to nine time's normal gravity, far beyond most humans' ability to survive. "We'll tell the pilot to keep it a little under six G's just for you, Madam President."

"Oh, *thanks*!" Starr knew she would probably encounter less G force than an old time sports auto for this trip, but it was a running joke that the government had planned the Bullet to pack ten times more people in its space because they would be flattened at takeoff.

The Bullet had two modes of power: an old fashioned ion drive for the boost into space, and a powerful new version of the so called DE or "Dark Energy" drive that was now used universally for interplanetary trips. Of course, the DE drive was forbidden inside a hundred thousand kilometers of any planetary body. There were still fears of it possibly disrupting gravitational forces that held molecules together. Starr wasn't an Integrated Scientist and didn't fully understand how the drive worked. Like most people, she had some qualms about a drive that relied on quantum probability theory. The sticking point was the 'probability' part. But she knew there would be no need to employ the DE drive on this trip. The Bullet would get her to her destination in just over thirty minutes after taking off from LP1, the launch pad directly north of the Washington Monument. She mentally shrugged; it would be her first trip in the Bullet. Maybe she should consider it a precursor to her hoped-for trip to Mars.

She returned to her packing and asked, "Do I need to know the details about this threat or should I just feel inconvenienced?"

Lisa hesitated only a second, but it made Starr look up. "It came from Lady McGuire, ma'am," the Service agent said.

Starr merely raised an eyebrow. "Well then... I guess we'll be riding the Bullet. Thank you, Lisa. I'll be done here in just a few minutes." *Ah, yes,* she thought ruefully, *what a great beginning to a restful week in the woods.* With great power comes great peril.

❧ 37 ❧

Stamper was frustrated at his man's inability to break into Cassandra's inner lab. The fellow had finally told him it was beyond his skills and recommended they blow the door.

"You suggest that I blow up part of my home?" Stamper crossed his arms and glared. "A part of the foundation at that, right?" He told the fool to leave and stood looking at the door a few more seconds before he too started to climb the stairs in frustration.

Usually, when he was this angry he'd turn to Cassie. Her company had an effect that could work wonders with him. But this time she was the *cause* of his frustration and he was at a loss about how to handle his feelings. He wasn't used to being thwarted and his thoughts about the woman were at war with his need to control the situation.

At the top of the stairs he reached for the door, but it opened just before he could touch it. Cassandra and he looked at each other in surprise. He stepped forward, intending to embrace her but she stepped back as he did so. He was confused but he spoke softly to her.

"Cassie. What's going on? The doctor let you up? We've got to talk; what exactly are you doing down there?" He pointed over his shoulder, indicating the area she had been using for her lab.

Part of her wanted to explain, wanted to reach out and just be held by the man. But another part, the one that had been screaming louder and louder inside her for weeks, wanted her to finish her work and see her father take over the presidency. That goal, that overwhelming urge was stronger than everything else, even her feelings about Eric.

"I... I've got to go to my lab, Eric. I can't explain now. I *must* finish my work." She tried to go around him but he stepped sideways to block her again.

"You're not going to... UHH!" She'd forcefully pushed him away and nearly knocked him back down the stairs. He reached out to regain his balance and grabbed her arm. Her broken rib sharply objected and she cried out in pain. He let go and fell back, hitting the door jamb as she took off down the stairs. He'd had the wind knocked out of him and it took a moment to recover and run after her. By the time he got to the bottom of the stairs she'd reached her inner lab and punched the code to open the door that had confounded Stamper's man for hours. He rushed forward to catch her before she could lock him out.

"Stop! This isn't right, Cass. Just talk to me." Again he tried to reach out but once more she ducked out of his reach. She ran to a work bench and grabbed what looked like an oversized tuning fork. Brandishing it one handed, seemingly oblivious of her rib now, she turned and hit him with a solid blow to the side of his head.

He instantly dropped and didn't move. She looked at him with glazed eyes and then, as if she hadn't spent years of her life with the man, as if she hadn't grown to love him and believe he loved her, she stepped over his deathly still body and went to the bank of controls and workbench on the south wall. A feverish drive to complete her mission had taken over and she would do *anything* to satisfy her father's wishes.

In spite of her pains, Cassandra moved quickly and the care she'd taken before to produce the spheres was now replaced with a fierce intensity she'd never known. What would normally have taken hours now was done in minutes. Safety precautions were thrown to the wind and even though she could have blown herself and the entire mansion to atoms, she managed to produce two perfect spheres with the highly explosive FDT35 gas in each. She'd constructed new containment trunks for the spheres two days before and she carefully loaded them onto the magnetic 'cushions' that would keep them safe during transport. Six hours after she'd started, she had completed what would have probably taken a week to accomplish under normal circumstances.

After closing and setting the controls on the second container, she was at a loss about what next to do. All of a sudden her mind hit a wall and she felt as if she'd run a marathon. She reached out to steady herself but missed the workbench and almost fell. Catching her balance, her chest exploded with pain. She'd forgotten about her rib while in the throes of her work on the spheres but all the pain she'd ignored seemed to have been stored up and now came back with a vengeance. Gasping, she stumbled to a chair and held her side.

Through tear filled eyes, she looked for the first time toward the doorway Eric had rushed through hours earlier. She'd completely forgotten about him. Now she saw him lying there on the cold floor and the thought of what she'd done made her feel horrible. Slowly she edged down to the floor and crawled over to him. She was sure he was dead; he hadn't moved since she'd hit him. In spite of the pain, she sat on the floor and raised his bloodied head to her lap, sobbing with guilt and knowing she had cursed herself forever.

But then she stopped. Did she just feel him move? Could it be possible? She looked down and tried to see more clearly but everything was a teary blur. And then she felt it again and she now was sure he was still breathing! Her heart leaped and she tried to lean closer but her ribs once again objected.

"Computer!"

Yes Ms. Whatcom?

"Get medical help down here right away."

Done. Do you wish me to wake Mr. Stamper and alert him that there is a medical emergency?

"Eric IS the medical emergency, you witless pile of chips!" Cassandra had always thought Stamper's house computer was 'helpful' in the most annoying way ever programmed. It never failed to frustrate her with its trivial 'politeness'.

She realized that the medical team would need her to unlock the door to her lab and that meant she'd have to deal with the doctor she'd clobbered earlier. It also meant she had to make the mag-spheres disappear from prying eyes. She gently lowered Stamper's head and made her way over to the door and entered her code. Then she connected the two containers that held the spheres and went over to the wall opposite the door. She touched two spots behind some books on a shelf and the wall opened to a dimly lit tunnel.

When she'd gotten permission to build her research lab in Eric's house, she'd used some of her own money making a secret way in and out of the space. And the absence of any visual security in the lab was no oversight; she wanted it possible to seem to be there even when she was miles away. Having voice communications only allowed her to speak through her PerCom to anyone even when she wasn't in the lab. For her purposes, the arrangement had been very convenient. Now she would escape before the medical team arrived and be able to take the mag-spheres with her just as she'd done before the trip to Mexico City.

The door silently closed as she pulled the containers along. The tunnel ended in the southern section of Eric's property at the land transport building. Cassandra would load the containers and leave the grounds before anyone tried to stop her. She felt bad about leaving Stamper but she couldn't have been any help even if they would have let her near him. And, despite a small twinge of concern, the compulsion to make it possible for her father to assume the presidency was once again taking over her mind. By the time she was halfway through the tunnel, the two mag-sphere containers were trailing along in back of her like cargo cars behind a runaway train.

❧ 38 ❧

Vice President Hunt had been busy making arrangements to insure anything his daughter did wouldn't end up ruining him. He'd written off the idiot doctor who had completely bungled the job of killing Cassandra. The best he could hope for was that nobody would discover she was his daughter. He'd already erased virtually every document and record that could be used to connect them. But Stamper knew, and T.J. was sure his 'old friend' wasn't above using that information to try and control him. Hunt certainly didn't like that and his mind had been racing all night to find a way to eliminate the possibility.

The gong tone of his PerCom sounded and he completed the connection as soon as he saw it was his daughter. Never one to stand on ceremony, and certainly not respectful of his position as VP, Cassandra started speaking as soon as the link was completed.

"I'm ready. I've got two spheres and they're perfect. All I need to know is where they need to be. And," she added with an almost child-like look of adoration, "of course, you need to be far away."

"It's after three in the morning, Cass. What in the hell are you doing? And what's been going on at Eric's house? I've tried several times to reach him since last hearing from you and he isn't answering my calls. Tell me what's happening."

"I'm not at *Storm House* and I think Eric's in a coma. Just tell me where Draper is and I'll eliminate her. You'll be the new president by tomorrow."

Hunt's mind raced, weighing possible outcomes and ramifications of his daughter's actions. Of course he was surprised to hear that Stamper was in a coma, but he couldn't help thinking once again about using the doctor to further his ends. He wondered at his daughter's cavalier pronouncement about the man she had told him she loved. Hunt had used many people over the years to further his agenda, instilling in them a desire to help him. It was a gift that he had and he had no problem using it indiscriminately. But he'd never before found it to make anyone so obsessed they would go as far as Cassandra had. At the moment, his most pressing problem was how his daughter's mania could possibly spill over on him. He finally came up with a plan that might take care of everything.

"Go to Washington State; the president will be at the western Camp David. As soon as you land, give this unit a call. I'll have more information about how to proceed."

"Right. It'll take a few hours. I'll have to rent a skimmer to go from the Whidbey Water Strip to the peninsula and then the rest of the way to CD-2. I'll call you when I'm ready." She ended the call with no more ceremony than it had begun. Hunt was exhausted but he had to move fast. He took a gulp of his drink and then began a series of calls.

❦ 39 ❧

Starr stepped from the Bullet into a heavily shielded bunker deep in the middle of the Olympic National Forest. Still excited from the experience, she turned and looked back at the squat ship now being fueled and prepared for immediate departure should the need arise. Then she smiled like a little girl after her first rollercoaster ride, turning to her security chief.

"*That*," she hooked her thumb toward the ship, "is the most fun I've had since winning the election."

Lisa understood the president's feelings completely. As part of her job, she'd taken a demonstration ride in the ship only a year before and, though she knew what to expect, today's trip had thrilled her just as much as it had the president.

They took a cart from the 'B-Garage' to the residence subbasement and rode up to the main level of the sprawling ranch-style house. The head of the house's permanent staff gave the president a brief tour and then quietly left her alone in the office area. The rest of her people probably wouldn't arrive for a while and she had the unusual luxury of having nothing she *had* to do at the moment.

She went out into the hallway and turned towards the smell of coffee. The kitchen was surprisingly small compared to its White House counterpart, and three cooks were busy preparing a sumptuous selection of sandwiches, snacks, and other menu items that would be fed to all of the other people who would soon be arriving. A short brown man with a chef's hat that looked entirely too tall for him offered her a plate of sandwiches, some fruit, and a huge mug with the presidential Seal enameled on it filled with steaming black coffee. She took the fruit bowl and mug out the door to the small covered patio just beyond the kitchen. Though the sun had been shining brightly only minutes before, the president had just sat at one of the small tables when she heard rain drops hitting hard on the overhang and throughout the lush forest surrounding the retreat.

The air seemed to take on a kind of expectant and muted hush with the background sound of the rain falling all around. And then, just as she began to relax, everything lit up with a brilliant flash followed instantly by a sound like a bomb exploding, making her jump involuntarily. She'd experienced plenty of lightning storms before, many of them right there on the Olympic Peninsula with her father on fishing trips. Still, it had frightened her. She had to admit the last minute change of plans because of the security threat had shaken her. And the ride on the Bullet, though thrilling in a gut-wrenching, amusement park kind of way had left her keyed up. She silently laughed at herself and dabbed at a spot of coffee she'd spilled on her pants. Perhaps she needed this vacation more than she cared to admit.

"Stuff like that can throw even the best shielded equipment out of order."

The noise of the rain and the ear splitting thunder had masked the sound of anyone approaching and Starr was yet again startled when the man had spoken. It was the short fellow from the kitchen. Starr raised an eyebrow and asked, "Does it make cooking difficult? I mean, timing things and electric gadgets and stuff?"

He shook his head and kept looking out at the large grassy area surrounded by huge trees in back of the sprawling house. "No, not usually, but surveillance cameras and ground detectors can be blown or temporarily disabled."

"Don't they have emergency backup power here?"

"Sure, but you can't shield the light receptors of cameras and still have them see, right? And some gadgets, like ground pressure sensors for instance, go nuts when you get thunder and lightning that close."

"Ren, stop trying to scare the president." Lisa's sharp voice came from the other side of the patio area and Starr was yet again startled. When she'd stepped onto the patio, she had believed herself alone. Now it turned out that had been an illusion and she sighed inwardly, realizing... yet again... that the president was never really alone.

"I was just going to ask the president if there was anything else she wanted until the rest of the staff arrives." The fellow seemed defensive and frowned at Lisa as if her command to him was out of order.

Starr decided to nip the conflict in the bud. All she wanted was a little peace. "No, thank you. I've probably already exceeded my calorie budget and we aren't even halfway through the day," she said with a smile.

The fellow gave a slight bow, knowing when he was being dismissed. But as he turned, he paused to throw Lisa a challenging look again and re-entered the building.

Lisa watched him until he was completely out of sight and then turned to Starr. "My apologies, Madam President. Ren sometimes acts like he's the sole owner of CD-2 and forgets this is *your* residence."

"Well, since this is my first visit here, it doesn't really feel much like 'mine.' I assume he's in charge when the president isn't here?"

The security agent shook her head. "No, never. The Service is always in charge. We maintain a 24/7 presence to insure the security even when you're not here. Renfrew just seems to have an unusually high sense of his importance."

"Renfrew?"

Lisa smiled. "Yes, an unfortunate naming by parents who probably had no idea its connection to the Frankenstein story. He bristles at us using the whole name and insists he is to be called Ren."

Starr smiled. The world offered up so many marvelous quirks, didn't it? "And what is his last name?"

"Belvedere."

Starr's smile got even wider. "Ah. It would seem Mr. Belvedere *did* go to Washington... just the '*other*' one this time."

Lisa cocked her head. The president knew she'd finally found a hole in her security chief's knowledge base. At one time, old movies had been a fascination of Starr's and she'd just made a reference that Lisa hadn't understood. "Well, never mind." She picked up her coffee and moved to go inside. "I think I'll take a long hot shower before everybody else arrives."

"Air Force One landed a few minutes ago. They should be here in about five more."

"Oh, well... I'd still like a shower. So far, the day has been much more stressful than I was hoping for. At some point, I'd like this vacation to turn into a vacation."

Lisa caught the implication quickly enough and grinned. "Certainly, Madam President; I'll see to it you're not disturbed."

"Thank you, Lisa." Starr knew she was becoming overly tired and grumpy. It wasn't anyone's fault; it just was. Here in the wildness of the rain forest, her body finally could admit to the weariness of her job.

She needed rest, yes. But she needed something more, something she could not identify but still feel as a hollow spot somewhere within her. Just as she reached for the knob to her private suite, she felt the familiar touch to her mind that she knew was Helios, her friend and confidant. He and the rest of the staff had arrived. It was a welcomed contact and she mentally returned the greeting before entering her rooms and making ready for a steaming shower.

❧ 40 ❧

The president had planned a dinner party the first night to honor her two invited guests, Julio and Alicia Akisawa. The couple had flown with everyone on Air Force One and she'd made sure they had the suite of rooms that was usually reserved for state officials. Starr had inquired about how long Julio had been a gardener at the White House and was startled to find out it had been the same twenty three years he'd been married. He could have taken full retirement by now but still elected to work. His wife was very quiet compared to Julio but both were obviously thrilled to be treated as VIP's.

At one point towards the end of their five course meal, Starr noticed Julio bending forward in his chair, looking closely at one of the decorative bouquets that graced their table. The gardener wore a frown and clearly was tempted to pull the flowers closer to him; she saw his hands twitching but he maintained a polite decorum because he thought it was required. She thought the scene quite amusing and spoke up.

"Do our flowers come up to your standards, Mr. Akisawa?"

He quickly sat back, apparently embarrassed by having called attention to himself. Then he looked at the president and realized she had asked him a question. When he tried to speak, his throat felt suddenly dry, so he stalled and took a sip of water before answering. "Forgive me, Madam President; I was only curious about who keeps the grounds here and grows the flowers.

Starr had no idea who it might be, so she turned to Lisa, who was standing near the door to the kitchen. "Do you happen to know who that is, Lisa?"

"All of the grounds maintenance is done by the Service, ma'am. There is no specific assignment for a grounds keeper."

When the president looked back to Julio, he looked slightly more relaxed. "Well, then, you have your answer, sir: The Secret Service people on duty here take care of the property. And I assume these are mostly the product of Mother Nature, since horticulture is not one of the criteria for becoming part of the agency, I believe."

"Then, forgive me Madam President for being so forward, but I believe the agents who work with the rhododendrons should spray them with peppermint soap solution before winter. These blooms are beautiful, but the stems are not robust, not strong. The plant has mites."

Starr was amused to see several people at the table involuntarily shift further away from the vase of flowers nearest them. "I'm sure Agent Morgan will make note of that and see to it that you are consulted about the exact formula before we leave this vacation home. Thank you. Now, as president, I'm issuing a directive to my favorite gardener: You are on *vacation*, Julio. At least for a while, try to leave the gardening to others and just let Nature be herself for a while." Her gaze shifted to his wife, who was trying to keep from smiling too much. "And I hope you both have a relaxing and pleasurable vacation here this week. But there is a job I'd like for you to do, Ms. Akisawa, if you would?"

The woman was a little surprised but answered quickly enough. "Of course; anything."

"Good," Starr said with just a hint of mischief. "I'd hate to think that the American tax dollars were being ill spent. So I'm appointing you as a watch-dog committee of one to make sure that your husband and you both actually have a *vacation* here. Do you think you can do that for me?"

Both of them smiled but Julio's looked a little sheepish. Alicia answered with a nod and said, "It will be my honor to serve as a committee to watch dogs, Madam President." And the whole room laughed, even her husband.

It was at that moment that the storm that had pestered them for several hours decided to reassert itself with another retina burning flash and thunderous crack. It sounded as if the whole sky had been broken into pieces. Everyone jumped and several ducked low, perhaps thinking the windows would break. Of course they were spider glass and rated to withstand a bomb blast, but that didn't prevent the human nervous system from reacting defensively.

Lisa instantly reached up to the side of her head and Starr figured the miniature PerCom set within the agent's ear had probably sent an amplified version of the thunderclap that had threatened to deafen everybody in the room. She didn't envy her security chief's job one bit, especially at times like this.

The lights in the dining room flickered and then went out. When they came back on a second later, they appeared slightly dimmer. Lisa was moving and talking quietly into a handset PerCom and two other agents had entered the large room. The psychological atmosphere was almost as charged as the one outside their windows. Lisandra approached the president and bent to speak quietly to her.

"We've had to go to emergency power, Madam President. I suggest this dinner be finished soon so we can conserve the fuel cells; we don't know how long it will be before the lines are powered up again. I'm afraid this is a recurring problem we haven't been able to resolve here yet."

Helios sat next to the president and had overheard. He wasn't aware there was any such problem before now and his first concern wasn't about the dinner. "How about communications; are we still connected to DC?"

"Yes, sir. That and Security have priority, of course. But we'd still like to minimize electrical use in case this lasts more than twenty-four hours."

The president nodded her head and then spoke to everyone at the table. "We're going to have our dessert and then shut down the kitchen for the night, people. Mother Nature has decided to put on a light show for us and we're on fuel cells right now. I apologize for hurrying through things, but we never seem to be able to ignore our Mother."

There were a few appreciative chuckles around the room but they were quickly terminated by the next brilliant flash and deafening crash of thunder. The punctuation by Mother Nature caused everyone to finish their main course more quickly. Starr begged off having dessert but stayed until the others were finished. It was ten o'clock before the room was cleared and, though early by normal standards, most everyone's internal clock was still on DC time and they were ready to turn in for the night.

◄§ 41 §►

Starr was restless and paced the living room of her private suite. She'd been watching the storm rage on outside her window for an hour before she arrived at a decision and spoke to the room computer. "Computer, ask Dr. Watson to please come to my quarters."

It took only two minutes before the man appeared at her door. Although he was dressed in his usual shirt, tie, and white jacket, she thought they had perhaps been thrown on hurriedly. There were other signs she'd rousted him from sleep and she felt mildly guilty. But she'd made up her mind.

"Please, doctor, come in. I apologize for the inconvenience."

"None at all, Madam President. Is there a problem?"

Instead of answering him immediately, she went over and sat down on a couch and indicated the chair on the other side of the coffee table for him. He sat and waited patiently for her.

"Yes, there is a problem, doctor, and..." She had to swallow a lump in her throat. "I find myself in an extremely awkward situation at the moment." He started to say something but she held up her hand, silencing him. "What I'm about to say and how this whole thing turns out is going to change your situation completely and I have to tell you that has weighed on my mind for some time now. Before we discuss anything else, I want you to know that I respect you and what you have done for me as well as the rest of the White House staff.

"I expect you'll question that statement in just a few moments, but I'm being completely honest when I tell you that." She paused to take a sip of water because her throat had suddenly gone dry. The doctor had a curious look on his face, but remained silent, so she continued.

"I have an extremely personal... shall we say, 'problem,' that has been making me... hmm... not function at my best." She paused again, trying to gather the courage to go on. The doctor took the opportunity to speak.

"As your doctor, Madam President, I assure you that I would never allow others to know whatever it is that you say is bothering you. You can be assured..."

She interrupted him from going on. "Yes, doctor, I know all that. But you see... it isn't as a doctor that I'm...." Stumps! She hadn't ever had problems speaking her mind with men before; it was maddening that she was so nervous she couldn't simply say what she wanted to say!

She stood abruptly, frustrated with herself. The doctor rose as well and took a few steps towards her, obviously concerned. She turned and walked over to the window to put space between them but she heard him follow her. She turned back and was startled to find him only two feet away. But he didn't come any closer, for which she was grateful at the moment. She forced herself to stay where she was, close... but not *too* close. It was tempting to reach out and touch him, but instead she took a deep breath and grounded her energy as best she could before going on.

"Doctor..." she paused, "no, *Elliot*, this is going to be either a great night or a horrible one. But I'm going to be completely blunt. Pagan women are famous for being blunt sometimes, right?"

"Indeed they are, Madam President. I consider it one of the benefits of being a Pagan man." His smile and the little sparkle in his eyes confirmed his words. Starr felt a slight charge go through her entire midsection

"In that case, sir, I'll ask that we both drop the formalities. I want to be held. Close. And I want you to be the one holding me. I want to take you to my bed and..."

Just then, the storm let loose with another eye-searing flash and thunderclap so close it made Starr do exactly what she had been trying to keep from doing only a moment before. She jumped and wrapped her arms around the doctor before she could stop herself.

But then, feeling his tenderness and warmth, the lingering scent of soap on his skin, she decided that it would be all or nothing from that point on and she melted against him.

She looked up at him and saw he was fighting with himself over the predicament. She decided to not play 'fair,' so she tightened her hold and began to move against him. He looked down and gave her a crooked smile, tightening his own hold on her. She felt his response and knew his decision before he even spoke.

Fire came into his eyes and his voice was rough with passion. "You were saying, Madam President, something about plans you had concerning your bed?"

She reached up and drew his head down to kiss him. Then, when they both needed to come up for air, she broke her hold, took his hand, and led him to the bedroom. She lit a pair of candles on a makeshift altar she'd made on a low dresser and turned as he closed the door.

❧ 42 ❧

Lady McGuire normally rose between six and six-thirty every morning. At her age, a good seven hours of sleep was necessary, though she rarely got more than four or five in one stretch. However, waking up at five in the morning hadn't ever been good, even when she was a youngster of thirty or forty. But awake she was and, as soon as she opened her eyes, she knew something was wrong.

A strong cup of tea, blacker than night before she'd loaded it with cream and sugar, helped to sweep away the fuzzies from her brain before she went to her personal meditation room. At the east altar was a huge moonstone globe atop a simple black pedestal. It was four inches in diameter and as flawless as any moonstone had ever been. She waved her hand near the base and a small LED light switched on under the globe making it glow from within. The light pulsed from dim to bright fifteen times a minute and its soothing, hypnotic effect helped the old woman focus her mind.

"Computer, dim lights to ten percent, please." Now the orb commanded her mind and vision to the exclusion of everything else. Within seconds, she was 'inside' the pearly florescence with thousands of possible future events swirling all around her. Time stood aside when she was in this state so she didn't know how long it took before she 'saw' the future that had awakened her. There wasn't any way to misinterpret this vision; it was as clear as a video and as frightening as any horror vid.

Over the years, she'd learned to never leave her moonstone world abruptly; the mental consequences were always unpleasant. But occasionally her emotional reaction overpowered her sensibleness and she was propelled back into the mundane world without the usual rituals. This was such a time. She had to pause and hold on to the back of her chair as she got to her feet. A few centering breaths was all she could afford before she staggered out the door and down the hall to her office.

She didn't waste time going through normal channels to get a message to the president. She had Lisandra's private PerCom address. When the woman answered, Lady McGuire spoke only eight syllables: "Shangri-La is under attack."

She saw the security chief move before giving a nod indicating she'd received the coded massage. Maggie's screen went blank a half a second later but she now had alerted the one person whom she knew was the president's best protection against the eminent attack she'd foreseen. Many months earlier, she'd arranged some phrases that could be passed to her grand daughter and initiate specific actions without question. At the time, she'd hoped she would never have to say any of the coded phrases, but she nevertheless had put them in place. They were obscure enough that the possibility of any of them being communicated by accident was infinitely small.

If she'd said, "Tom Thumb isn't big enough," it meant the president was the sole target of an attack. But the phrase she'd spoken this day meant the entire area around the president was in danger. Each coded phrase was seven or eight syllables long and totally without logical connection to any real life situation that could be imagined. If Lisandra received the message from any source whatsoever, she was to act on it immediately. It was the best Lady McGuire could come up with to protect the person she had foreseen being the only one who could preserve the Craft into the next century.

Few people viewed history as Lady McGuire did. She knew that most of the time people accredited with 'making history' were pretty much just along for the ride. Their greatness didn't have to do with any sudden changes made alone by that person; it was because they were perfectly suited to be the vehicle for the changes that would be channeled *through* them. Change *always* happened everywhere in the universe; the role that most 'great' people played was to be the one who was the catalyst for that change manifesting as it did. Starr Draper was the person who would 'cause' an important change in Paganism to express itself in a positive way.

The Lady sat back in her chair and knew she'd done the best she could. But she couldn't help worrying if it had been enough. In spite of her many years, Lady McGuire remained a worrisome person. Although she had faith that the gods would form the future as they willed, the Lady always felt that she was supposed to do certain things and behave in certain ways to facilitate that future to comply with so-called Fate. It was egotistical and she knew it. But she had justified her worry-wart demeanor to friends by telling them that it was probably *her* fate to be that way. Of course it wasn't true; it was just a way to deflect doing something about a personality flaw. But she wished she had the courage to change herself so that she didn't feel so, so... *worried*!

----- <> -----

Lisa spoke into her PerCom to the rest of her team while quickly moving toward the president's private quarters. "... and put *everyone* not directly assigned to this building on a flesh and blood cordon on the ground two hundred meters out. Also, Tanner? Get the squadron leaders at both McChord and Whidbey Island flight bases to put an umbrella over this entire area." She was almost to the president's private quarters.

"Brannon, get the Bullet crew ready."

"You can't launch the Bullet in this weather; it's suicidal!"

"I don't intend to unless it's necessary. But I want that option. Tell them to get it ready... NOW!"

She had reached the door of the president's quarters when she finally addressed an irritating sound that had started seconds after activating her inner ear PerCom. "And Jones? Lose the damn gum!"

Lisa wouldn't normally barge in on the president. She was aware that the doctor had been summoned only two hours ago and not left. Lisa had a pretty good idea what sort of 'treatment' the president was receiving. But privacy was not the issue; this was about the president's security which was Lisa's responsibility. The president could fire her later. She charged into the rooms a half second after overriding the locks and was moving towards the bedroom door when she called out. "Madame President, this is Agent Morgan. Code purple, code purple!"

She was through the bedroom door just as the president and Dr. Watson were sitting up in bed. It was obvious neither of them had on a stitch of clothing, so Lisa grabbed the president's bathrobe and threw the doctor the pair of pants lying on the rug at the foot of the bed. She turned back to the doorway and spoke into her PerCom.

"I've got POTUS and the doctor. Addis and Rodgers, meet us at level three, B-1; we're moving there right now." Lisa saw both the president and the doctor come into the living room space. She held up her hand to keep them from moving toward the door yet. She touched her ear and spoke. "Ferris, get Mr. D'Amico and Wineheart down to B-1 as soon as you can. Sung, is the hallway secured?"

She listened a second and then turned back to the president. "We're moving you to a secure bunker. If need be, Madam President, there's a tram and tunnel to both the Bullet and the air strip from there."

Instead of the robe Lisa had thrown at her, Starr had put on a pair of jeans and a wool lumberjack style shirt. She seemed completely awake and alert to Lisa, which was the only reason the president's next directive was obeyed.

"I want Mr. and Mrs. Akisawa moved to the same bunker, Lisa. No arguments."

"Ferris: put the Akisawa's on your list of occupants for B-1." She listened to her agent's remark about protocol and interrupted him mid-sentence. "Just do it, Ferris."

Lisa opened the door to the hallway and noted the two agents standing there. They gave her the sign that everything was clear. She quickly shuffled the president and Dr. Watson straight across the hallway, a mere six feet, and through a panel in the wall that the president hadn't noticed before. Once through, Lisa joined them and pressed a lighted stud on the space just to the left of the opening. The panel slid shut as the floor began to lower so quickly they all felt weightless for a second.

Lisa turned to both her charges and explained. "This will take us to the B-1 shelter which is designed to protect you against everything short of a very sizable nuclear bomb, Madame President.

You have provisions for thirty people for ninety days there and it has every communication structure in place."

Remembering the flickering lights at dinner earlier, Starr asked, "What about power during this storm?"

Lisa smiled, "Our little secret, Madam President. B-1 is completely autonomous and off any grid. Another two hundred feet below it is a reactor with enough juice to power DC for a century."

Starr smiled but then said with a slight frown, "The poor taxpayer."

For the first time since being barged in on, the doctor spoke up. "I can think of a lot of other uses for the taxpayer's dollar that are much less sensible."

Their rapid descent was slowing and Lisa turned to look at a reading on the wall of the elevator. "We will be traveling sideways in a moment, Madam President. You might want to grab that rail on the wall; the change in motion can catch you off balance." No sooner had she said it than the elevator stopped. There was a momentary pause accompanied by some faint mechanical vibrations under their feet and then they were pressed against the back wall of their container. To Starr, it was slightly disorienting but she thought of the old Star Trek reruns she'd watched as a child and she realized this wasn't a new concept, just one she'd never experienced before.

She looked over at her security chief with a smirk. "Why haven't they developed a way to just 'beam' us there, Scotty?" Lisa's returning grin proved that this time, she'd caught the president's reference.

❧ 43 ❧

Cassandra was soaked to the bone and exhausted. Her trip to the Olympic Peninsula had taken more time and energy than she'd thought it would. Lack of sleep and guarding her cargo of the mag-spheres had already drained her and now she had to make her way overland after literally reaching the end of the road. She estimated she was almost five miles from the western Camp David in the valley to the south-east of Jupiter Mountain in the Olympic range. Somehow she would have to make it there, dragging the spheres all the way. The command in her brain wouldn't let her stop, even though she was now sure of how her efforts would play out this night. Her PerCom was acting up and she'd forgotten all about calling her father.

She figured she had only hours left to live but she still put one foot in front of the other, plodding on in the torrents of rain with the lightning and thunder coming and going all around her. She was too weak to overcome the compulsive directives that she'd received from her father; she *had* to go on.

The so-called 'hiker's path' she'd found on her map was hardly more than a deer trail filled with blown down limbs, scrub bushes, and enormous roots. In some cases, long dead trees had fallen across the pathway and never been cleared away. Some even had sprouted new trees from the rotting bark of the fallen giant parent. Cassandra might have enjoyed the scenery in the sunlight if she didn't have to drag the two instruments of her and the president's destruction along. But now, in the middle of the night and soaked to the bone, she couldn't even begin to think such a thought. She just had to take one more step... and then another... and another.

----- <> -----

"What do you mean? We've lost the signal?"

"We think it was a lightning strike, Agent Morgan. And not only are the motion sensors out, but we now have less than half of the video feeds working. Our PerCom connections are spotty at best. The only good news is that our old fashion underground cable system is heavily shielded and working fine."

Lisa absorbed the information from Agent Tanner and calculated strategies. She wasn't surprised that most of their electronics weren't working. The storm was wild and didn't care about the puny human devices her people used. She'd already done what she could by placing half her team out in the elements. But she knew there weren't enough of them to provide good coverage. A cadre of thirty people that couldn't depend on their communication wasn't adequate coverage. She could reinforce them with more of the agents inside but that would mean fewer assets in the event her outer forces were breached. It was a chess game of sorts.

The worst part was she didn't know in what form the threat would come. She didn't have any doubt that her great grandma's warning was real. But how the entire compound could be threatened meant only a couple of things. A bomb would be the most likely but that left the method of delivery in question and therein lay the problem. Three scenarios presented themselves to her: It could come by air, either a missile or dropped. It could be already present, hidden and waiting to be triggered. Or it could be transported by land somehow.

The latter was the least likely, of course. The only land route to CD-2 was through six miles of thick forest. There weren't even any real trails. Access to the compound for supplies and people was by air only so she didn't think a land assault likely. The president was always covered against air attack and Lisa's alert to scramble flights from both McChord Air Base and Whidbey Island Flight Station only added to what she knew was already in place overhead. Now, with POTUS in a sealed bunker a hundred and forty feet underground, there was little anyone could do but wait.

Of all the things an agent had to do, putting his or her life on the line, acting as servants much of the time, keeping secrets and being poster children for 'the silent service,' the hardest part was waiting. Waiting, and almost never knowing what you were waiting for. Waiting and trying to keep sharp and alert: it took its toll. No matter how disciplined and well trained, no matter how caffeinated, the waiting sapped you. Rotating a person's responsibilities and changing posts helped but, sooner or later, everyone lost their concentration.

For the first time since Lady McGuire's alert, Lisa sat down. Gods but it felt good. She had hoped to get a few hours of sleep finally after rising at 4:30 that morning… DC time. She knew she wouldn't allow a member of her team to be on duty in her condition but she didn't have any options. She was sequestered in this bunker, a prisoner to the threat just as much as the president was. She had sixty-five agents to command and she had elected to be one of the three who would be the last defense against whatever might be the nature of the threat they all hoped to out-wait. She let her head drop for a moment. Just a moment. Just…

"Agent Morgan."

Lisa's head shot up and she was reaching for her sidearm before she realized it had been Doctor Watson speaking. She'd dozed; it was unthinkable! She glanced at the wall display and saw that she'd probably hadn't been asleep more than a few seconds. Still, to allow herself to fall asleep was totally unprofessional and she was more than embarrassed. She looked over at the president and saw that she was talking quietly with her Chief of Staff at the far end of the room. The Akisawa's were almost back asleep, leaning against one another on one of the couches. And the rest of the people seemed occupied. Even the other two agents were at work stations, keeping in touch with topside personnel as best they could. Although she wouldn't personally forget the lapse, she hoped the doctor had been the only person who'd witnessed it.

She stood and tried to look alert. "Yes, doctor, what can I do for you?"

He almost grinned but was able to put it away before speaking. "I was hoping you'd show me where my station is. I know they have a fully equipped sickbay here but I didn't want to go poking around and maybe get lost."

"Of course, sir; follow me." She led him down a short hallway and into another room about fifty feet away. The doctor quickly surveyed the space and then went to a cabinet against one wall to check its contents. He turned back to Lisa and said, "I was wondering if you wanted a stimulant, Agent Morgan. You've been active for what, about twenty-four hours? Nobody can sustain that workload and operate at their peak. I'm sure your duty to the president's safety would make it prudent to take something to boost your alertness, am I right?"

Great Mother, she thought, he was a diplomat and a gentleman. He was obviously sensitive to her embarrassment a moment ago. He'd just made his 'suggestion' almost a medical order and she was grateful for his consideration. She gave a small smile and said, "Thank you, doctor. You are quite right, of course." She realized his request to be shown where 'his station' was had been a calculated way to privately give her some medical help. Her estimation of the man went a little higher and she couldn't help but wonder how the new relationship between him and the president would play out.

He handed her two small tablets and a glass of water and she let her eyes watch him around the glass as he moved about, familiarizing himself with the facility. His body was well toned, she noted. And, of course, his face made most vid stars look bland by comparison. She thought the president was a lucky woman and, personally, she was happy about the turn of events concerning her libido. She remembered Lady McGuire's comment a few months back: "A happy president is a better president. It's too bad Starr Draper is such a nun." Lisa wasn't quite sure now whether her great, great grandma had meant 'nun' or 'none,' but it didn't matter now, did it?

----- <> -----

Her PerCom was useless because of the storm that she was now convinced would never let up. She was in the middle of the storm *and* the middle of nowhere so her PerCom no longer could function as a GPS. But Cass thought she was less than a half mile away from her target; it had to be just over the next ridge. She'd hauled her two spheres through a jungle of tangled vegetation and managed to get through by shear will power. Sometime back in the last hour she'd gotten her second wind and now she was trudging toward her fate like a tank, letting nothing stop or slow her down.

Part of her mind seemed to be detached from everything. It was as if she were taking a vid of herself, soaked to the bone with ripped clothing and scratches on every inch of muddied skin, trudging through one of the wildest areas in the country. She 'filmed' it with her mind, adding commentary like some corny news anchor.

"Forward, ever forward she marches. Like some Spartan soldier oblivious to obstacles and dangers, she pulls her deadly cargo ever closer to her target, driven by a noble cause..."

Cassandra laughed at herself. What drivel, 'noble cause.' Who said it was noble?

That's right, it was her father. He'd told her he wanted the presidency, that Draper was a pretender and had no real abilities either as a witch or a politician. That's what he'd said. What good was it to have a Wiccan in charge if she couldn't even do simple magic? And she had already signed several laws that were completely indifferent to Wiccan ideals. She was a failure, a pretender! She deserved to die.

Lightning continued to burn her eyes and make the going difficult. Either it was blindingly bright or darker than the bottom of a well with the flash's after-image obscuring everything. She could hardly see the ground under her feet at times.

❧ 44 ❧

President Draper should have felt some kind of frustration being cooped up in an underground bunker but she was strangely relaxed and feeling happy. Strangely? Maybe not. She looked across the room at the doctor and remembered the magical thrill of their lovemaking earlier. It had transformed her and she wondered silently why she hadn't made the move earlier. She realized she was smiling a lot, even when Lisa had rushed them off to this subterranean sanctuary. Lisa had charged in only moments after the president had fallen into a blissful sleep for the first time in, what, *years*?

He must have sensed her looking at him because he turned and caught her gaze. She saw the smoldering fire in his eyes and a slight smile curl his lips. Then he looked down and his smile widened. He gave a little shake of his head as if he too were remembering their encounter and felt just as amazed. He gave her another quick look and then turned back to whatever it was he was doing. Though this communication lasted hardly more than a moment, Starr knew they had made a bond of some kind. Where it might go was anybody's guess but she was determined to find out. Was it just hormones and nerve endings talking or was there something more?

She spotted Lisa and moved over to speak to her quietly. "Is there some place I can go to meditate, Lisa?"

The agent simply nodded her head and said, "Certainly, Madam President. Please follow me." She turned to the door and led the president across the hallway and down twenty feet. "This is your suite." She pointed to a numeric pad next to the door. "The current pass code is 76887." Lisa smirked. "That spells POTUS. But you can change it if you like."

"No, that's fine." Starr entered the code and heard a faint click. She turned the knob and the door opened easily enough though she saw it was much thicker than she expected. She looked back questioningly at Lisa.

"It's a blast door, Madam President. This whole section, as I said earlier, is made to withstand just about any sort of attack, but these quarters are reinforced even more."

"Protective redundancy, right?"

"Exactly. If you require anything, just talk to the computer, Madam President. I'll be just down the hall there," she pointed to a doorway with 'SECURITY' written in big letters on it, "keeping tabs on what's going on topside, if that will be all?"

"That's fine, Lisa, thank you. Wake me if necessary but I'm going to spend a little time to talk with a friend of mine first." She entered her rooms and gently closed the door.

The president of the United States had responsibilities for the lives of millions of Americans and considerable influence in nearly everything else on the planet. Such a duty could never be subjugated to personal considerations but it was impossible for anyone to completely eliminate their private life or keep their office free of its pressures. Very few presidents had entered the White House without some family members coming with them. But, having no husband or children, Starr was a rarity in that respect. It allowed her to spend nearly her whole day working. But the adage about all work and no play was more than true and she was willing to admit her error of not going out and having some fun once in a while.

Since winning the election, she'd worked an average of seventeen or eighteen hours a day, every day. Her indulgence with 'Dr. Hunk' earlier was a powerful bit of healing energy for her. It had not only relaxed her in ways she didn't even know she needed relaxing, it allowed her to see the world and her role in it in a completely different way. The experience was a lesson for her that part of her responsibility to her country was to treat herself correctly... which *included* having fun and making time for some pleasures in her life.

She also realized that she hadn't 'talked with the Goddess' since before her day as priestess for the national summer solstice celebration at the Circle Plaza. Anyone who thought religion didn't have an important role in national policy failed to understand the reason everyone needed a spiritual focus: it let you know that you were connected to *everything* in ways you simply couldn't comprehend.

If she were in the White House at this time, she would have a personal altar to the Goddess in her private quarters. At this western camp, if she weren't in its high priced basement, she could at least go to a window and see outside. Or, if the weather wasn't so terrible, she would take a walk in the woods. These would all be ways to feel her connection with Nature and help her in her worship and meditations. But none of that was available at the moment. So Starr went and started a bath. There was a selection of goodies she could add to the water sitting close to the spacious tub, but she didn't use them. Instead, she went to the other end of her underground apartment, got some regular sea salt from her kitchenette, and went back to her bathroom.

She poured some of the salt directly from the little jar into the steaming waters and quietly spoke. "I consecrate these waters with the purifying powers of salt. Water and salt, join together and become one as it is in my body and in all life. Let this bath be my altar so I may be blessed by its healing powers and my spirit transformed to be in greater harmony with the gods. So mote it be."

She lit a single candle she'd found and then told the computer to turn off the lights. Then she stripped and stepped down into the soothing waters. There were controls to activate jets in the tub that would swirl and pulse the water around her but Starr didn't want them on at the moment. She just wanted to quiet her mind and body. She slipped lower until the water was moving lightly against her chin. Within moments she felt a calm come over her and her consciousness slowly expanded into the cosmos. It spread like a gossamer light everywhere until Starr felt the loving touch of what she called the Goddess. She didn't know if she was speaking aloud or only in her mind, but she knew the words were unimportant since this was a communication between her soul to what made her soul, from her 'self' to the source of all selves.

"I pray for strength and wisdom, Great Mother. I am grateful for your gifts, even when I am too blind to see them. Let me be an instrument of peace and harmony in true worship to you." Starr put one hand under the sole of her foot and the other on the crown of her head and spoke the end of her prayer, *"Everything between my hands I pledge to you, Great Mother."*

Having said her prayer, the president closed her eyes and slowed her breathing. Soon she was asleep and dreaming. She dreamed she was in a village of small huts built mostly of mud and stones, walking with a deep basket strapped to her back. A strong odor of fish came from the basket and the baskets of several other girls walking with her. These were the chopped up bodies of the salmon that died after spawning earlier in the month. Soon they came to a large patch of ground where men and women were working the soil with sticks fitted with deer antlers. Starr dropped her basket at the end of one row and went to help the others make the ground ready for planting. She didn't know how long she'd worked when the village chief presented himself before them all. He too carried a basket but this one was filled with kernels of corn. She knew that these seeds were from the best of the best that had been harvested the summer before.

The man bent low before the furrows of land and poked a hole in the ground. He wiggled his stick and widened the hole to the size of his fist and as deep as his whole hand. Then he reached into the tall basket Starr had carried and took out a piece of salmon. Holding it high and facing the sun, he said a prayer, asking for gentle rain and warming sun from the Sky Father. Then he dropped the pungent meat into the hole he'd made. Reaching into the basket he'd carried, the fellow scooped up a few of the yellow seeds and held them out to the field before him. He spoke a beautiful prayer of thanks to the Earth Mother for the bounty of the past year and asked that She accept the bleached yellow seeds back into her belly as his offering. He then dropped three seeds into the hole with the fish at the bottom.

Starr was close enough to hear the man's final prayer as he bent down to reverently cover the hole with dirt and pat it solid. He spoke of the joining of the Earth Mother and Sky Father and how the seeds would grow and produce food to feed the children who worshipped Them. Then he stood up, smiling at all of them. He threw his head back, raised his digging stick, and let out a high pitched whoop of joy. Everyone who had been working the field joined in and Starr felt the excitement as they all raced to make holes in the ground, fill them with fish and seeds and cover them over with dirt again. It was a wonderful game with them all, a friendly competition to see who could tally the most plantings before the seeds ran out. It took almost a quarter of the day before the celebration in the field was done but the party then moved back to the village where the older people had been working to make a feast for the workers.

It was a strange dream for her. She awoke when the water had cooled below her own core temperature and Starr toweled off wondering what the vision might have meant. It had seemed like a very long dream though she knew most dreams happened in seconds. As had happened many times before, Starr didn't understand what the dream meant and she let the memory of it fade as she finished dressing. She had learned not to try too hard to make sense of dreams. As with many things, understanding would either come... usually when least expected... or not.

Her ritual bath had done wonders for her energy level and she was ready to tackle whatever the rest of the day offered. It was nearly seven in the morning and Starr wondered if any progress had been made determining the security threat of the night before or whether they would be troglodytes for some time longer. She found fresh clothes in her closet and dressed. Then she walked into the common area to the greetings of the other early risers and the magical aroma of freshly made coffee. Helios was busy on his PerCom and held up a finger when she looked over to him, signaling he wanted to talk to her when he was done. She nodded and went to the table set with coffee and drew a large mug of it for herself.

She was making small talk with Mrs. Akisawa when her Chief of Staff came up. Starr ended her conversation and followed him across the hall to the office area. He closed the door and turned to her with a troubled look. "The Vice President is missing," he said quickly. "The Service believes he vanished late last night and they're going crazy right now."

She hesitated only a second, then spoke to the room, "Computer: ask Agent Morgan to come here at once."

"*Acknowledged.*"

Lisandra knocked moments later and Helios let the woman in. The president asked her what was happening.

"We're still trying to pinpoint when he disappeared, Madam President. Our cameras didn't record him leaving and none of the agents saw him outside of Blair House last night. But we know he wasn't there as of eight this morning, DC time. At this time, I'm afraid that's all I know."

"Doesn't he have a chip implanted in him, the same as I do?"

"He very strongly refused it, Madam President." She diplomatically didn't say anything more but Starr could see what Lisa thought about the matter.

"Well, that can be addressed later. I'm sure the Service is doing its best. Has any of this leaked to the media yet?"

"Thankfully not yet ma'am, but you know as well as I that can't last forever."

Starr had made up her mind what she was going to do. She looked at Helios but her words were for them both. "I have to get back to DC. The Akisawas may stay for the next two weeks and I want them to receive every courtesy." She turned to Lisa and said pointedly, "Make sure Mr. Belvedere understands exactly what that means, will you, Lisa?" The agent gave her a quick nod but kept her face neutral.

"And, though I'm perfectly aware there is possibly something out there that's considered a threat, I'm going topside. Everyone is to go back with me on the Bullet or in Air Force One, understood?"

Lisa frowned but the president spoke up before her security chief could object. "I know Lady McGuire is the source of your information, Agent Morgan. And The Mother knows my respect for your great, great grandmother is, uh... *great*, but I've got a job to do. Now, let's get things moving, shall we?"

"I just wanted to say that the storm isn't over, Madam President. To launch the Bullet wouldn't be advisable in this weather, that's all."

Starr sighed. "Stumps. It would seem the gods aren't going to give me any sunshine while I'm here; I was hoping for another thrill ride. Okay, let's get things ready and then we'll go topside and get everybody aboard Air Force One."

"We can get you aboard via the tunnel system down here, Madam President. And it would be quite a bit safer that way." Lisa couldn't allow the president to call all the shots when it came to her safety; the Secret Service could just 'up-and-grab' her if need be. Actually, Lisa thought, they already had done just that when Hump hoisted the president under his arm and made a mad dash for the goal line in Mexico City. Lisa suppressed a smirk at her memory of that incident. "I strongly suggest you take advantage of the security measures designed to keep the President of the United States safe, Madam President."

Starr knew Lisa was right and simply nodded. "In that case, let's make it happen. I'll talk with Julio and his wife myself. The cover story is that the VP is ill and I've got to return early. Lisa, I want them protected from whatever might be out there but let's try to make this an actual vacation for the Akisawas. Gods know they've earned it.

"Helios, get every shred of intel about T.J. to me as soon as you get it." She shook her head in agitation. "I don't know how you can lose a vice president."

There was a lot of activity for ten minutes and Starr was speaking with the Akisawas when Lisa's second, Agent Humphrey, 'Hump,' let her know they were ready to transport her to Air Force One. She gave Alicia Akisawa a final hug and held up her fingertips to Julio. "I hope you two can forgive me for running back to Washington. I've told them to make your time here a real vacation and anything, and I mean *anything* you want, just ask. You both deserve this; don't think of it as anything other than a well earned vacation, okay?"

They told her they understood and thanked her for about the hundredth time. Starr was then escorted to the tunnel where a squadron of rail cars sat waiting to carry people and gear to the hub under the airstrip where Air Force One was being readied. But it took only one car to transport them; most of the personnel and luggage was topside. When they had all settled in and the car began to move, Starr leaned over and quietly asked Lisa, "Any additional information about my AWOL Vice President?"

"Homeland says the FBI had a file indicating a cabin retreat in the West Virginia woods registered under his deceased father's name and they've sent a FAL-Con III to investigate."

The FAL-Con III was the latest version of the Free Agent Logistical reCON flyers used by all branches of the armed services and intelligence groups of the government. They were autonomous robotic spies with artificial intelligence capabilities. Able to stay on station for weeks, they looked so much like a hawk or falcon, experienced bird watchers couldn't tell the difference at fifty feet. The robots even could land on a tree branch to complete the illusion. Each one cost every taxpayer four dollars a year, which was to say they were damned expensive 'toys.' Starr recalled they could reach speeds up to Mach one if needed but then could 'flap' their way at a stately twenty or so and perform some rather sophisticated acrobatics to mimic their namesakes. Also like their natural counterparts, they weren't any good in severe weather situations. But they could hide in plain sight in trees and even soar above the clouds if desired. Earlier models had already proven their usefulness in combat and the current model had received funding without any hassle in Congress.

"Well, if this turns out that he simply is playing hooky while I'm away, I'll have his hide. But it's more than disturbing that he could vanish like that without the Service noticing."

Though the Vice-president's detail wasn't part of Lisa's responsibilities, she felt embarrassment for her colleagues and started to say something in their defense. But she thought better of it and decided to remain quiet.

Their ride to the hub beneath the airstrip's terminal ended and everyone stepped out and began walking the short distance to the elevator. Lisa and Humphrey crowded in with Helios and the president and they began their accent. When the doors opened, they were greeted by brilliant sunshine pouring through the Zellan windows looking out on the airstrip.

Starr smiled. "It would seem, now that I'm ready to leave, the gods have finally decided to let the sun shine. Humph! I think I'll have a talk with the Goddess about this unfair treatment."

"Apparently it cleared up just a minute ago, Madam President. But at least we'll have a smooth take off." Lisa was glad to see the change in the weather. She never liked flying in bad weather and the lightning had made communications and security into a mess. Perhaps now their systems could begin to function properly. Reports had come to her that many of their sensors were still out and probably would need replacing before security was back to what it should be.

∽ 45 ∾

It wasn't fair, she thought. She'd spent the entire last part of the night and much of the morning hauling the spheres all the way from where she'd abandoned her transportation to the edge of the grounds for the Western Camp David. She'd already resigned herself to the inevitable fate of dying but why did the gods make it so difficult? She was exhausted. And now every foot... every *inch* towards her goal required energy she could hardly summon anymore. Each step was more difficult than the last. It had grown from night into day as she'd made her way across a gully just a hundred meters wide awash with muddy runoff. And now she'd finally come to the crest of a bramble covered ridge and found out she'd gone off course and ended up just north of the airstrip where the president's plane sat, placing her nearly a mile from the complex of buildings that made up the actual camp.

Now, when the last part of her mission would be on somewhat level and clear ground, the skies had suddenly cleared. Why couldn't it have been earlier? But she knew that if the horrible thunder and lightning had continued, this latest setback might have actually stopped her. Maybe the gods were playing nice after all. But the night's ordeal had truly sapped her strength. She was not only tired beyond belief but she'd sprained her left ankle and she ached all over. She'd injured her shoulder in a bad fall making her whole left arm sore and now she barely had any grip left in the hand.

The sun made Air Force One seemingly glow a half mile in front of her. The huge aircraft had its nose pointed towards her and off to her right she could see a portion of the terminal for the airstrip. It all was designed for just one person and one plane. She'd heard the whine of small fighters droning throughout the night even in the terrible storm. She wondered at the power of the presidency that it could command such dangerous flights. But then she thought of how her father would be in that commanding position in just a short time later that day.

Cassandra reached into the containers and flipped switches on both the sphere holders. Now they could be detonated by a mere touch of two buttons on her belt. With no more lightning she was able to arm them without them accidently being set off before reaching their objective. She then took several ragged breaths before setting out to drag herself and her deadly cargo the last mile to that target. She'd have to get within about two-hundred meters before being sure the blast would obliterate everything; the power of the compounds within the spheres was tremendous but only over a relatively small distance. If she could get away before sending the signal, she'd do it. But she didn't have any illusions about her chances for escape. It didn't matter; her father would be Mr. President and the Wiccan faith would be made pure once again. She hoped Eric would understand once he knew the purpose of her actions. It was a small price to pay to the gods, she thought.

It was perhaps surprising that she noticed the small bit of movement out of the corner of her eye. Her exhaustion was so great it took an enormous amount of effort just to move. Her brain wasn't able to process much more than the single command to keep moving. But somehow the movement to her right had drawn her attention and she shifted her eyes toward the small terminal building just as a tall woman in black stepped onto the tarmac.

----- <> -----

Lisa hoped she would be able to sleep on the short trip back to DC; the strain of the last forty-eight hours was really beginning to tell on her. She would turn things over to somebody, maybe Tanner, and then sleep for a week. The stimulant Dr. Watson had given her was beginning to wear off at possibly the worst time. The president was most vulnerable when she made decisions that required extemporaneous plans on the part of the Service. And Lisa didn't feel good about the events that had caused this change in plans. But she thanked the gods that the weather had cleared up. The Olympic

Peninsula was well known for its capricious weather patterns and now that she'd experienced them up close she decided that information had been conservative. The crisp, clear sky also meant they had better vision and that was good because their electronics had suffered badly from the storm that had raged for hours without rest. Air Force One waited just fifty meters away and Lisa checked in with the two agents that had been doing the final on-board check before she gave the word for them to lower the stairs. She pushed open the door to begin the long walk with the president.

She and Hump kept checking the perimeter for threats, trying to look in every direction at once. That wasn't easy and it required a high level of alertness and an extraordinary amount of concentration, both of which Lisa was quickly starting to lose. Usually there would be more than enough agents to give double coverage to every sector around the president but their timing had made it so this wasn't possible at this critical point. Lisandra chastised herself for not being sharp enough to anticipate the lapse but it was too late to change things. The president was much more vulnerable in the waiting area of the small terminal than she would be aboard Air Force One. They had to move. She turned and motioned for the president to come out and they moved quickly toward the plane.

----- <> -----

Cass froze. Just after the woman, a huge guy also dressed in black came out the door and started looking around. They both looked like Secret Service agents. In fact, now that she got a better look, she recognized the tall woman: she was the head agent covering the president.

Which meant that Draper was probably in the small building that served as a terminal for the airfield. Cass' heart began to pound in anticipation. But something was wrong. Why would they be here... now? And why hadn't they spotted her already? She could swear they'd both looked right at her. There..., there, they looked again!

They didn't *see* her. What the...? Cassandra looked down at herself and immediately discovered why. She was completely covered with mud, leaves, and pine needles. Even the containers for the spheres were lumps of mud and branches collected throughout the night. She was nothing more than background vegetation to anyone looking at her from any more than a short distance!

If she moved, of course, they'd probably spot her quickly enough. But then she couldn't get close enough to kill the person who now had finally stepped out on the tarmac after the two Secret Service agents. Draper! Cass instantly felt a fire burn inside of her. Her quarry was in sight and the urgency she'd felt all night was now multiplied many times over. Any concern of dying along with the president was dismissed as her body readied itself for a desperate charge so she could trigger the spheres close enough to kill one person: Starr Draper. Seemingly without conscious thought her legs began to move and Cassandra was being propelled toward her final encounter with Fate. Her brain burned; her lungs and throat let out a primal scream of hate with the single purpose of destruction of life as she ran directly toward the president. She was Kali; she was The Morrigan; she was Shiva! She was the Destroyer of Worlds!

----- <> -----

It all happened in a heartbeat. Starr had taken only a few steps into the open air when they all heard what had to be the scream of a wild animal. Everyone turned to look up the airstrip for its source. The president saw part of the surrounding forest moving at great speed toward her. Without thinking, she raised her hand with one finger pointing at the charging apparition. She screamed her rejection of the wrongness that she felt emanating from it, the evil she felt by its existence. Her mouth formed a single word, but her inner being instinctively formed the power behind it:

"*NOoooo!*"

Even before the sound had died in her throat, a brilliant flash of lightning came out of a perfectly clear sky and struck the very thing she had pointed at. In less than a thousandth of a second, every molecule of its existence had been vaporized. In another hundredth of a second there were two more explosions that made a puny addition to the awesome forces unleashed by Nature. The sound of the event reverberated from the surrounding forest and mountains for several more seconds and the universe stopped. All light and sound was gone.

Stillness... almost a paralysis... seemed to fill the space surrounding Starr and everything she could sense. She felt something run through her, chilling her soul for just a moment. She knew a portion of that soul had been ripped away. Not a big part; just a small little sliver really, but gone it was. She had been part of a person's life being taken away and part of her own life spirit had disappeared along with it. It couldn't be otherwise; it was the way the universe was. But she understood it would be something she'd be required to live with from that point on. She took a deep breath and started to pull herself up from where she'd fallen during the explosion.

Several pairs of hands helped her up and she was quickly escorted into the giant plane. Everything happened without sound but she knew that they were going to take off then instead of waiting for the rest of the people; she felt the powerful engines roar into life even before she was seated. Helios sat across from her giving her worried glances every few seconds. And the doctor, her own 'Dr. Hunk,' was fussing over her with much more than professional attentiveness. Lisa had put Humphrey Addis next to her in the seats across the aisle from the president and was speaking rapidly into her handheld PerCom. But without sound it all seemed like a strange silent holo-vid to Starr. She knew what she was seeing but she had to guess what it all meant.

She saw the doctor come around and he was trying to roll up her sleeve, mouthing something to her. She tried to tell him she couldn't hear but she didn't know if what she'd said made any sense until he looked into her eyes and gave a nod. Even through the confidence he was trying to project, she saw the worry written in his eyes. Maybe she was projecting but she thought it was more than professional concern. As he was reaching down for something she touched his hand, making him look back. She let her feelings for him come through her smile. Whatever else had gone on, she wanted him to know she felt better because he was there. He smiled back and then showed her a small vial he was loading into the hypo spray. She didn't know what it was until he mimed his eyes closing slowly and his head lolling to one side. She nodded her ascent and he touched the mechanism to her arm. Seconds later, she was asleep and dreaming of making love to him all over again.

----- <> -----

By the time they reached the White House, Starr's hearing had partially returned. However, everything still sounded like it was being forced through a long tube. Elliot... Dr. Watson... hadn't left her side for a minute. Instead of retiring to her private sector, she had gone to the Oval Office and begun catching up on what was going on with the search for the Vice President. But so far, nothing new was available except reports that there was nothing new.

After a couple of hours, she went up to her quarters to shower and change clothes again. Then she ordered dinner for two and asked the computer to invite Dr. Watson to join her. She only had to wait a few minutes before there was a knock on her door and his image appeared on the screen next to it. She opened it herself and smiled her welcome.

"Come in, doctor. I've ordered some salmon for us both; I hope you like fish."

"Indeed, Madam President. And since we didn't have any time to try catching some salmon ourselves, I'm glad to get a taste of it here... with you."

They dug in to a delicious dinner and ate in companionable silence for several minutes. Starr knew he was politely waiting for her to initiate conversation but she was somewhat at a loss for words. She smiled to herself; that was something a politician should never experience. He must have noticed because he put down his fork and finally spoke.

"I'm guessing neither one of us knows what to say about the eight-hundred pound gorilla in this room. Am I right Madam President?" He gave her one of his nova smiles but she judged there might have been a hint of desperation behind it.

She stalled answering him by taking an inordinate amount of time chewing her last bite. Then she made him wait a little longer by taking a long drink of water... and then a sip of wine. Finally she couldn't hold off speaking.

"First off Elliot, I've turned off the image and voice recorder. No record of what we say here is being made. It's a conversation between just us, two people having dinner. And I'd like it if you called me Starr. This 'Madam President' stuff just doesn't seem right between us, don't you think?"

He was quiet for almost a whole minute and Starr began to wonder if he'd ever reply when he finally broke his silence. "This is awkward but I think I'm going to stick my neck out, Madam... uh, Starr. I trust neither one of us likes hurting another person."

His words immediately brought to mind the incident at the airfield. She was convinced that what happened was necessary and there was no way she knew of that she could have caused that lightning bolt. Still, Starr knew the First Principle of magic was 'everything is connected.' In her heart, Starr felt she had taken a life. And though she felt justified, she certainly didn't like what had happened. Starr didn't know who the person was or their motivations but the doctor was right; she took no joy in harming anyone.

She nodded in acknowledgment and he continued. "And I also believe that both of us are wondering how the other feels about what happened between us last night."

She nodded in agreement again.

"We are consenting adults and all that but the real question isn't about how our bodies feel, which, by the way, mine is very pleased," he graced her with another brilliant smile with a hint of lust.

"But the real question is how our hearts feel. Well, I'm going to hang mine on my sleeve, as they say. I watched you conduct that solstice rite in Massachusetts at the Circle of the Winds. I was one of the people on that circle. I don't expect you remember; Gods, there was better than five hundred of us. But when you stood there with the Goddess called down on you, I fell in love with you... and I still am."

He shifted uncomfortably and took a sip of wine. "Okay, I've said my piece and now I'll shut up. If you want me to go away and practice medicine in Borneo, I'll do it." He took a big swallow of the wine and added, "But I wouldn't like it."

Starr hadn't expected this. She didn't doubt what he'd said but she took her time digesting it. She searched her own heart and then searched it again. She wanted to say a million things but had no idea where to start. She had to admire him for his candor; it was a very brave thing to do. Could she match him? Somehow, she had to. Honesty here was the only way to go. "I'm afraid I don't remember you from that circle, Elliot. I was so busy trying to keep from screwing up my job as priestess that a lot of that night is kind of a blur.

"But ever since that day in my office when you came rushing in because my heart missed a few beats, I've had a desire for, well, you know. I know the difference between love and lust and, although I wish I could say I love you in a romantic way, all I can truly say at the moment is that I'm in lust with you." He started to speak but she went on. "I'm being brutally honest here, Elliot. I'm sorry if that isn't what you wanted to hear but..."

He interrupted as she paused to take a breath. "Lust is good. In fact." he wiggled his brows, "it was *very* good. But what I said was that I was *in love* with you. We both know there's a big difference between being 'in love' and loving someone in the deeper sense. I'm more than willing to try to find out what we could make out of this if that is what you want, but I believe we should be completely honest to one another. I believe," he paused to find the right words, "I think we should enter this relationship in love and trust or not at all."

She sat back and smiled. In many Pagan traditions, the phrase, 'Enter in with love and trust or not at all,' was the time-honored challenge given at the entrance to the circle for those about to be initiated to that group's tradition. They weren't just dramatic words; they had very deep and personal meaning for every Pagan. And, in the context the doctor had just used them, they indicated he believed any relationship between them needed to be a completely honest and committed one, a relationship that would expose their best and worst to each other without masks or rationalizations. Without real love, love that could transcend the doubts and small pains of 'living with your skin off,' as one priestess had put it years back, such a relationship would quickly disintegrate, both parties flying apart as surely as two magnets that had turned their same charged poles to each other.

The doctor had basically said he was willing to commit at the deepest, most meaningful level to a personal discovery of how they could relate to one another. That he was willing to face the raw truth of what could... or could not... be made by them together. Was Starr able to give such a commitment? It was not something anyone should commit to lightly. She took some time before making a reply. But just before speaking, she placed her hand over his on the table and looked directly at the reflection of the dinner candles in his eyes.

"I have given my oath to serve the gods. I am the president of this wonderful country and have given my word to serve it as well. And I will not go back on either sworn commitment for any reason. My heart burns with joy at your words and I am sorely tempted to jump into your arms and say that I too will accept this challenge without reservations. But I have a country relying on me and I will not put them aside. Do you understand what I'm saying, Elliot?"

He didn't even pause before answering. "I understand that you are a person of unquestionable honor and you do not make any commitment without it being a true bond. I understand you fear I might be relegated to some position that would jeopardize my happiness or yours. And I understand that you wish to spare me the possible pain of finding out that we can't have happiness together in this lifetime. I understood all that before this dinner tonight. So the one question that matters is: do you wish for me to abandon my hopes concerning a future with you or are you willing to see if this can be something much greater than physical pleasure?"

She leaned back in her chair and studied him. Picking up her water glass, she saluted him and said, "You should have been a politician, Elliot. You have a way with words and a quick mind. *And* you have the tenacity of a terrier when you think you're right. Right now I'm wondering if I shouldn't have you in my cabinet instead of my bed."

"You think I'm wasting my time being the president's doctor?"

Starr stood and stretched out both hands to him, saying, "I think we're both wasting time being cautious and over-analytical about this whole thing." She took one of his hands as he came to her. She turned and began walking him toward a door at the end of the dining area. "I have been very cautious about men, Elliot. I know we live in a time where women not only have equal rights but equal prestige in our society. I am lucky in that respect. But there will always be a difference between men and women..."

"Thank the gods."

"Er… yes. The biggest difference isn't the physical one, as I'm sure you know. It's the difference in our thinking. You have stated our predicament very well and, I must say, very honestly. You've made an excellent beginning toward being open to me, of relating to me in love and trust."

"I hoped you would feel that way. I've thought about little else since last night."

"Ah, well… I'll address last night in a moment. But first," she opened the door and walked into a darkened room. She looked back, silently inviting him to step in. When he did, she closed the door, making the room completely dark. "Hold still for a moment, please, Elliot," she said quietly.

He heard her move around him and in a moment he became aware of a soft light behind him. As he turned, the light slowly was becoming brighter, illuminating an altar. On the altar was a beautifully sculpted statue of three goddesses seated with their backs to one another. The statue resided in an ornate wooden container with mirrors on the inside and open on the side that faced into the center of the room. The effect was that you could see all three goddesses from many different angles. The lights shown into the wooden chamber so all three forms were clearly seen.

"That's very beautiful. I've never seen the likes of it before; where did you get it?"

"This is a shrine handed down for several generations through my family. It is Hecate, of course, the triple goddess. She is the goddess I consider to be my patron, simultaneously the Maiden, Mother, and Crone. I come here when I wish to feel her strength and wisdom. Between her and my true self there is no deception. I am her daughter, her priestess, and the shrine's guardian." She lit a small cone of incense and placed it on a brazier. Then she brought a cushion out, placed it in the center of the room and asked him to sit there. He did so as she went to the altar, picked up a wand, and slowly walked the perimeter of the room, casting a magic circle with the dark piece of wood. Then she produced another cushion and sat beside him.

The peacefulness of the room began to seep into him and the shrine seemed to glow with power the longer he stared at it. After a while he lost his awareness of time and felt like he was floating. Then, without knowing he had moved, he found Starr in his arms. She wasn't so much looking *at* him as she was looking *into* him and he felt her gaze as a real force, a physical connection. He didn't know if she was speaking or he simply knew what she was saying with that gaze. But he understood her.

"*Beloved Hecate, know my heart: I wish no harm come to this man that I take as my lover and magical mate. Watch over him and keep him well. Let us know one another in love and trust. If it be right, let us grow in happiness together and be as one for as long as we both shall love.*"

And then they made love there in the circle. Not the fierce, needful lovemaking they had both enjoyed the previous night but a slow, gentle, *sacred* joining before the shrine of the Triple Goddess.

⊰ 46 ⊱

Lisandra had slept only three hours since returning to DC. After writing up her report about the strange attack at the western Camp David and assigning a team to assist the Service people already investigating it, she left word with John Schmidt, the person in charge of the VP's security unit, to keep her informed of any news about the Vice President. Then she found 3F and took time to get him caught up. She assured him that she was perfectly fine and that neither she nor anybody else except the bomber had been injured in the incident. Of course there was some video of what happened; both the terminal and Air Force One had surveillance going and Frank and a team were already attempting to put it all together as part of the investigation. But Lisa had watched it with her own eyes and still couldn't quite believe what had happened.

It haunted her sleep and she'd awakened in a sweat after a particularly vivid replay of the moments from exiting the terminal to rushing the president aboard the plane. She was washing some of the perspiration off when a message from Schmidt asked her to come to the Service's Op-Center.

When she arrived, only John and a com-tech were there. She knew without any doubt that what he had to tell her wouldn't be good. Five minutes later she was hurrying along the hall toward the president's private quarters in the White House. She'd been told that Dr. Watson had joined the president a few hours earlier but had not left yet. Lisa guessed she would once again have to interrupt the president at a very personal moment but simply informing her about the VP on the president's PerCom would not be prudent. Nevertheless, two nights in a row Lisa was going to be the person disrupting the president's pleasure. She wondered if she'd have a job after tonight.

Lisa had to wait over a minute before the president answered her request to speak with her. When the door finally opened, the president looked calm and relaxed; she was even smiling. But her expression was quickly replaced with a more serious one when she saw Lisa's face. Even before the agent could speak, Starr knew it had to be about Hunt.

"Where is he? Has he been injured?"

Lisa's job was always considering horrible possibilities and filled with gruesome scenarios. But the worst part of it was often at moments when she had to be a messenger to the president with bad news. She knew the president was one of the toughest women she'd ever known, in many ways tougher than Lady McGuire. So she didn't sugarcoat the information.

"At 10:48 this evening, Madam President, two Service agents assigned to the search for Vice President Hunt investigated a downed air car in the hills eight miles from his hunting cabin. It is our preliminary conclusion that the vehicle was hit by lightning and crashed there some time earlier today. A full investigation team has been detailed and we as yet are unsure if the body inside is indeed that of the Vice President. It too appears to have been struck by the lightning. However, as you know, he always wore the Yale class ring on his right hand and the body at the crash site has such a ring. I'm afraid that's all we know for sure at the moment, ma'am."

Starr stood rock still, holding onto the door as if for support and looking at her Secret Service agent. She didn't say anything for several seconds.

"Lightning."

"Yes, ma'am. They're fairly sure. There were scorch marks on the skin of the craft and it would appear a good deal of the instrument package has been burned out. Also, the body has been... well, considerably *burned* in a way consistent with being struck by lightning."

"But aircraft of all kinds get struck by lightning and most of the time it doesn't do any damage, right?"

"Yes ma'am."

Starr walked back into her living room area and Lisa followed. "All air cars are made to have so-called 'black boxes,' am I right?"

"Yes, they are. We will be looking to retrieve the one from this crash site if it hasn't already been done."

"I want," said the president, "to know *when* this crash happened, Lisa." She turned and looked directly at her agent. "And I want that information to be kept quiet unless and until I say otherwise. It's not to be in any official report or even transmitted electronically without my permission. Completely 'Need-To-Know.' Understood?"

"Absolutely, Madam President; I understand fully."

Lisa did understand. Both she and the president were wondering the same thing: Did the lightning strike on what almost assuredly was the Vice president's air car and the strike out of a clear sky on the Olympic Peninsula occur at roughly the same time? The weather at the crash site had been reported as equally clear and free of clouds. The likelihood of lightning in either spot was phenomenally low. What were the odds of both strikes happening the same day? What were the odds of them happening even close to the same time?

No matter when both strikes occurred, if the media got hold of the information about the similarity of both events, there would be a perfect storm of conjecture about 'black magic' in the White House for sure. It didn't take a rocket scientist to see how such sensationalist journalism could send a chilling message to every Pagan in the country. Lisa began to wonder if her great, great grandmother had correctly foreseen what Starr Draper would have to deal with when she had manipulated the energies to put the relatively young priestess in the White House.

----- <> -----

Oak trees were practically unheard of in the rain forest of the Olympic Peninsula. However, they are a very hardy species and once they get a taproot down a few inches, they can be an unstoppable intruder in any stand of trees. The adage about little acorns merely says they can grow into mighty trees. But it is also true that the tiny acorn can push aside competing species with hardly any trouble. Any piece of ground near an oak tree is likely to be the breeding ground for a whole grove of oaks in a very short – by oak tree standards – time.

Near the edge of an air strip deep in the Olympic National Park there sat a mound of decaying foliage and other organic nutrients that had been swept off the air strip after an attack on the president that only a few people would ever know about. In the damp humus, the winds that commonly blew up the narrow valley below Mount Jupiter had carried a single acorn from a mighty oak that was a sapling a couple of hundred years ago. Its age wasn't important but where it had sprung from was. This old and mighty oak had found an unlikely home in an area that had seen cultivation by Native Americans for many generations. But the people had died; killed by something they never could see. It was called smallpox by the white skinned people who had come to the lands shared by many tribes of the peaceful waters the white people named after a chief of a big boat. They called it Puget Sound.

The tiny acorn was released by the winter wind and it fell into the mound of dirt that was rich with the blood of a white woman who had become lost in the forest. The Sky Father had torn apart the white woman so that she could help the seed of the oak grow.

----- <> -----

And, at the same time in the woods of West Virginia, another acorn fell and fed on the bones of a man who had also become lost.

✑ 47 ✑

The heavy blanket of snow on the back lawn of the White House was a postcard perfect picture outside Starr's bay window. She and Elliot were hosting a visit from her father and their conversation had lapsed into a contented silence, all three looking out at the peaceful view and thinking their own thoughts.

Starr had indeed commissioned a 'medal' for her father, honoring his 'Dedication to Science.' Most people knew the story of his courageous fight against MPN both in and outside of the lab and believed the presidential 'medal' referred to that inspiring show of bravery. However, very few people knew that the medal could be opened and that there was an inscription on the inside which read: 'For service above and beyond the call of duty in an atmosphere of dangerous and smelly gases, this medal for Methane Tolerance is hereby given by Starr Draper, President of the United States of America, to Dr. Martin Draper – 12/21/2076." Even though it had been a 'joke' medal, it had brought tears to her eyes when she presented it in a private White House ceremony that winter solstice. It was a small medal, only about the size of an old fashioned quarter, but her father wore it on his jacket everywhere he went.

Of course, the celebration that accompanied the official announcement of the lab team's triumph had been a grand affair. It was the first time the orbiting platform had been used to its full capacity and then some. The joke was that it was so weighted "down" that the managers feared it would tip over if everyone gathered to one side. Of course, that wasn't possible, but the media had a great time with a cartoon drawn by a New York artist of the day showing a huge circular disk with a clear dome precariously bending a thin cable (with an old-fashioned cable car running up from below). A woman (a characterization of Starr) was shown with a champagne glass in hand pointing to the high side of the disk, shouting, "Somebody carry me to that side, quickly!"

The party celebrating the beginning of the end for MPN was truly wonderful and Starr had never enjoyed her position as president more than on the night she was able to drape medals on every one of her father's team, "for the salvation of the human race."

It was now late January and her dad had come to help with another important ceremony that would be conducted in less than a week on February second. His daughter was going to be handfasted to Dr. Elliot Watson and he would have the honor of being his future son-in-law's Best Man. Starr had asked Lisa to be her Bride's Maid and Lady McGuire to act as priestess. And, in a brilliant twist, she had requested Eric Stamper to be their priest. Her once ardent opponent had accepted the honor and both he and Maggie had made several face-to-face meetings to 'work out the details' of the ceremony.

Before asking Stamper, though, Starr had asked Lady McGuire what she thought of the idea. The lady's answer rocked the president. "Of course, Madam President. How else could we manage to mend the split in our faith group? *This* is why we said it *had* to be you that won the office." Then, with the most innocent face, the woman produced a plate of cookies and asked, "Would you like *another* chocolate chip cookie, my dear?"

----- <> -----

It had never quite been said, but she was sure Stamper knew of Cassandra's fate. Stamper had been in a coma for a week, beginning the day before the attack. When Cass had been identified as the bomber, Starr believed he'd somehow learned of it nearly as soon as she. A private message from him about how unwarranted the attack was caused Starr to personally speak with him to assure him that she didn't hold him responsible in any way.

From that unhappy conversation, Eric Stamper and Starr Draper had started to become unlikely friends.

There would be tons of guests at the reception but Starr had limited the number of people at the handfasting, other than the six who would stand at the center of the circle, to just thirteen of her favorite people. She, her father, and Elliot had been discussing some of the details of the rite that afternoon during a rare quiet time in Starr's schedule.

Her father finally broke their contemplative mood when he stood and walked over to the bar to mix himself a drink. "Tell me," he said to his daughter, "did they ever find out who the bomber was at Shangri La?" The president had decreed that the 'Western Camp David' was to be given the name that the other Camp David had first been called. Reinstituting the fanciful name had seemed like a sentimental act on the president's part. Most people believed it was because she had fallen in love with the man to whom she was to be handfasted at that western camp. Very few knew that it had been Lady McGuire's wording in her warning to Lisa about the attack that had inspired the change of name. But Starr liked the romantic implication of the rumor about Elliot and her and had never said anything to change the media's mind.

There would always be untold secrets of state. Some would die with the persons who knew them and history would never be the wiser. In the affairs of government, it was an unfortunate necessity in many cases. Other times, it was simply not anybody's business except the people involved and history could go whistle. Starr didn't like lying to her own father, but some pieces of information could only be given to those who absolutely needed it. In the case of her father, he had no real *need* to know. Instead of lying, Starr chose the time-tested method politicians had employed for thousands of years: she gave him a misdirecting answer.

"The remains were charred to a crisp, Dad. Not even nuclear tracing could pull out a DNA sample from that. Whoever it was, they met a terrible fate."

Her father turned back and gave his daughter a very direct look. She wasn't sure but maybe he'd seen through her subterfuge. But then he turned to look out the window and said, "Well, better them than you, eh?" Then he turned again and said, "And the country would have been in a real pickle if both you *and* the VP had been turned into charcoal on the same day. I mean, we'd have that nut job Carmichael as President, right?"

Elliot looked up at his future father-in-law and cleared his throat. "I happen to think Brustyer is a wonderful old gentleman, Doctor." Starr gave Elliot the eye; he knew her father's buttons and had willfully punched one just to see her Dad go off on a rant. Elliot looked back at her with a mock 'who me?' face and grinned.

Sure enough, her father launched into a litany of complaints against the man that had been pushed into the VP seat when the world learned of T. J. Hunt's terrible 'accident.' Starr knew that a good deal of her father's animosity was due to Carmichael being one of the politicians that opposed funding her father's lab in the fight against MPN and he never would forget the fact. Starr didn't have many good feelings for the old politician either but the Constitution was clear about lines of succession concerning the nation's leaders. Seeing her father go on about the new VP, Starr wondered if Elliot hadn't said what he did to distract her father from inquiring further into the events of a few months back.

While her father paced and listed the sins of the new VP in a loud voice, the computer let Starr know Helios was requesting to see her. She had the door opened and he entered wearing a waistcoat and powdered wig he probably had to rent from a costume shop. It was obvious he was trying to keep a straight face but was not doing it very well. He ceremoniously carried a red velvet pillow with a small stack of papers upon it. At a questioning look from Starr, his smile grew stronger and he said, "Madam President, may I present to you the perfect gift for your impending handfasting." Then he set the cushion down and lifted the first page to hand to her with a bow and a flourish.

Starr knew a joke was at hand and began to read out loud. "The president's Special Commission on the current so-called 'dead water' issue is pleased to announce a viable method for..." Her voice trailed off as she read the rest of the opening paragraph. Then she read it again. Her jaw dropped open and she looked back up to her Chief of Staff in wonder.

He was beaming and nodding his head. She let out a whoop and hugged him so hard he thought she would break his ribs. She quickly passed the sheet to her father. He read it and in turn passed it to Elliot. Soon there was laughter and cheering from each one of them. In fact, they were so loud that none of them heard the call from the other side of the doors asking if the president was all right. So they were suddenly thrown open and four agents, guns drawn, came storming in to rescue a president who was dancing around in circles with three men and generally acting like a schoolgirl playing ring-around-the-rosy. A couple of seconds later, Lisa came running in and skidded to a stop just in front of her other agents. Seeing everything was fine, she signaled the others to leave. Then she turned back to watch the president act in a way that she was sure nobody would expect a president to behave.

It took several minutes for them to run out of energy and find a sofa or chair to flop into to catch their breaths. The red cushion had been bumped and the other papers gone flying, so Helios had to shuffle through them to find the other page he wanted to show the president. Finally locating it, he pointed out to the snow outside and said, "Here's another finding that is very interesting. This page talks about it but I'll just summarize it for you." As he passed the paper over to Starr, he continued to speak.

"We all know that for about the last hundred, hundred and fifty years the giant glaciers have been shrinking. We also know that, for reasons unknown, that trend appears to have been slowed and, in some cases, reversed. There's been a lot of controversy about the whole thing and nobody seems to know what's really going on. Dr. Jones, the fellow who has given us a way to stop making dead water, has stated that he believes the glaciers *are* returning to their former dominance in Iceland and elsewhere and that it's because of the dead water!

"It seems the ionic properties of dead water are somehow different and the way water freezes is affected by those properties. According to him, the estimated amount of dead water in the Earth's atmosphere and oceans at this time, assuming we stop creating more, will completely reverse the glacial melting by 2250 or thereabouts. This will drop the world's sea level by approximately ten centimeters, bringing it back to about where it was in the mid twentieth century."

Dr. Watson leaned forward. "That's a good thing, isn't it?"

"Yes and no. Dr. Jones' technology for preventing more dead water doesn't do anything to get rid of the dead water we've already produced. By this time next year, every IC engine on the planet will have the new Jones Pellet replacements. But the effects that the IC converters made on our planet's water will be felt forever unless we find a way to counteract them. According to his figures, almost ten percent of our water is now dead water."

"That's a higher number than I've ever heard before," Starr said. "Has anybody bothered to verify that?"

"It's being looked into as we speak. But even if it's a grossly exaggerated estimate, the problem is the same."

"Hold on there, Helios." Starr's father jumped into the conversation. "How can you say that returning the glaciers to their former size is a problem?"

Helios looked at Starr even though he was answering Dr. Draper's question. "Because, sir, it won't stop there." He waved the rest of the papers he'd brought in. "Dr. Jones claims we'll be in an ice age by 2350. And by the twenty-eighth century, he says, more than half the globe will be a frozen ball of ice."

The room had become silent and everyone was lost in thought as each pair of eyes slowly turned to watch the snow begin to fall again on the White House lawn. It now seemed, thought Starr, that the temperature outside was being matched by the chill Helios' words had sent into her bones.

Well, she thought, *there's always a catch, isn't there? Can't have the flowers without the rain; can't have the rain without a chance of flood. If it floods, the overflow renews the fields and the flowers can grow again. The wheel keeps turning, doesn't it?*

And, from somewhere inside of her, Starr heard the Goddess reply:

Yes, my daughter, it does. And it shall ever be so.

ABOUT THE AUTHOR

Blacksun is the Wiccan ecclesiastical or "spirit name" of Bert Dudley. He lives in Washington State (the "other Washington") with his wife Jean and two very spoiled dogs. He has served as high priest for StarWyrm Coven for over thirty years and has written two non-fiction books about Wiccan ritual and spirituality as well as many articles in various Pagan publications throughout the years.

Blacksun served as a representative for Wicca on the Interfaith Council of Washington for five years and was editor of its newsletter for three of them. He was appointed Director of Religious Affairs and served on the Board of Directors for the Aquarian Tabernacle Church, a 501-C3 recognized church body with affiliates over the entire globe.

This is his first published fictional work. He has two more planned for release soon.

Made in the USA
Monee, IL
26 November 2021